The Spy from Palestine

Jonas Shaw and Charly Lawrence, Volume 3

Steve Haberman

Published by Steve Haberman, 2024.

THE SPY FROM PALESTINE

First edition. April 8, 2024.

Copyright © 2024 Steve Haberman.

ISBN: 979-8224225637

Written by Steve Haberman.

Also by Steve Haberman

Jonas Shaw and Charly Lawrence
Where the Bones Lie
The Spy from Palestine

Standalone
The Killing Ploy
Murder Without Pity
Darkness and Blood
Winston Churchill's Renegade Spy

Watch for more at www.murderthrillermysteries.com.

Once again, to my parents Joe and Ruth Haberman. For their values. And for the inheritance.

THE SPY FROM PALESTINE
By
Steve Haberman

Chapter 1

They had briefly motored along Fleet Street in the City of London when Jonas caught their chauffeur's worried glance in his rear-view mirror.

"Mr. Shaw sir, I fear we have someone following us."

"We do?" Jonas frowned at Charly beside him. Then he peered above his *Financial Times* to their driver, who had slid back the glass panel that separated the rear passenger seats from the front.

"Yes sir." Their driver turned his wizened face slightly towards Jonas to ensure he could be heard over the traffic. "When we passed Essex Street, I thought he might be tailing; now I'm sure."

Jonas stared out the rear limousine window. The congestion at that spring hour, a squawking chaotic mess of cars, trucks, and buses, infuriatingly thick as ever. On the crowded sidewalks, some protesters in black leather jackets shook fists and waved signs: BOYCOTT THE LONDON DAILY NEWS and SHAME ON TYCOON OWNER RUMBOLD, SHAME. "That Bentley behind us?"

The chauffeur glanced up again to his rear-view mirror. "No sir. Three vehicles back. That beige van. It just passed the Golden Horse pub and Barclay's Bank. It's in front of that red double-decker bus now."

"You sure, Nigel?"

"Absolutely sir. It's kept us in sight for several blocks. Ever since Seton Hall."

"Christ!" Jonas tossed his *Times* aside. "You see, Charly? I told you this would happen again. Sooner or later." He withdrew a newspaper from his leather satchel and shook it at her. "You're not just another run-of-the-mill journalist."

"He said for the umpteenth time."

"Yes, dear, for the umpteenth time. You write stuff like this. Article after article in the *London Daily News* calling for a homeland for displaced Jews—"

"All right, all right, Jonas. Enough."

"The war may have been over for two years, dear, but Britain still has Nazi sympathizers. Plenty of them, and you should know that." He stared at her model's face. The high cheek bones. The provocatively arched brows above green eyes. Too pretty for her own good. Tempting for some crazy's acid or a slashing attack. "You have a too casual attitude toward danger."

"Oh I do, do I?"

"Yes, dear, you do. That bullet hole there in our—"

"I said, all right, Jonas. Those dark Irish eyes of yours glaring at me say everything. Point made."

"I hope so. Finally."

She shifted around and gazed out the rear limo window. "The beige van three vehicles back, Nigel?"

"That one, Miss Lawrence. It just passed that solicitor and advocate office."

"Any others?"

"None that I've spotted, sir."

They stopped at a traffic light at Fetter Lane. "You really think they're Nazi sympathizers, Jonas?" she asked.

"It wouldn't surprise me. Not one bit. Those death threats we've gotten out at the Cotswolds. The hate mail delivered to the *Daily News.* The letters to Mr. Rumbold. From Hitler lovers or thugs hired by some in the British establishment. God knows, you've angered some pretty powerful people."

"I hope so. It serves them right. I hate, just hate, those bullies. Just like you, dear."

"Sir, the driver's pulled directly behind us. He's blinking his front headlights. Looks like he wants us to pull over. Should we?"

"Hell no, Nigel. Could be a trap." The traffic light turned green. "Try to lose them somehow."

"In this traffic? Your Rolls-Royce can only do so much, sir. But I'll try."

An ambush on Fleet Street? Jonas wondered. Amid the crowds and traffic? At the very center of British journalistic influence and power? Battles had happened there before. Charly's publisher had picked some pretty nasty fights with the *Daily Telegraph,* the *Daily Mail,* and the *Sun.* He had beat them too with splashy front-page exclusives. Still an actual hit and in broad daylight? He found that somehow hard to believe. And yet that tail, which now drove illegally. Some fanatics must not care if they lived or died.

For a moment, no vehicles came at them from the other two lanes; the driver of the beige van pulled even with them on their right. A newsboy's cap pulled down nearly eye level, he glanced at them. He had a nose that looked broken from some street fight, Jonas noticed, and gave him an indifferent look; to Charly a two-finger salute and a brief smile.

"What on earth?"

"What?" Jonas reached for his Colt 1911 in his shoulder holster.

Charly gripped his arm and shook her head. "No, don't. It's Tommy Corbyn, Mr. Rumbold's chief bodyguard and confidant."

The bodyguard-driver signaled them in the direction of the cars ahead as he pulled in front of them. His gestures and mouthing of words unmistakable to Jonas. Follow him.

"Mr. Rumbold doesn't go anywhere without him these days. Where he is, Mr. Rumbold's usually close by." She leaned forward. "Nigel, that delivery van, follow it."

"Not too close, Nigel. You hear? Two, three cars back until we see what's what."

"Not too close. Yes sir, Mr. Shaw."

They followed discreetly three cars behind. They passed the Daily News' elegant eight-story art deco headquarters on the left. There Mr. Rumbold, Jonas noticed, had doubled security to four near the revolving front door. Next an Irish pub. At the intersection, they turned left and headed north on equally crowded Farringdon Street. More protesters in black jackets shouted and angrily waved their placards.

"This is a sticky wicket, Mr. Shaw. This traffic's heavier than normal. That recent heavy rain isn't helping either."

Jonas clapped him reassuringly on the shoulder through the opening. "I'm sure ex-race car driver you will do just fine, Nigel." He shifted his gaze to the beige van ahead. The publisher's experienced driver appeared to execute a surveillance detection routine, as though he feared someone tailed them both. He wove in and out of a warren of narrow side streets. He stopped momentarily curbside next to a shop that sold buttons and fabric. Then he motored on westward, making his way through the unending noisy traffic, past unending pedestrians, in the German bomb-damaged ancient capital struggling back after the recent war. Eventually they reached the southwest part of Greater London.

"I see, sir," Nigel said, turning south onto Wilfred Steet, "the old British sun is playing hide-and-seek again."

And it was, Jonas noticed, looking out his side window. The fickle weather had turned from sunny to cloudy with heavy showers threatening.

They reached an alley at last, the sounds of the bustling metropolis dropping away as they bumped over cobblestones. Halfway down, Jonas caught a sign, TRADESMAN'S ENTRANCE, on the backside of a grimy brick building. Tradesman's entrance to what? he wondered. Their chauffeur, still following the van, steered down a tarred ramp into a dim underground garage. It was poorly lit by a lone florescent light strip, running along the ceiling's center, that flickered off and on.

Tommy Corbyn executed a U-turn, the van's wheels squealing his impatience over something. He eased the van back into a darkened patch of parking space and hefted his bulk out. "Cheers," he said to them. Two more security men, youthful and limber, hopped out of the van's rear. Each wore a dark suit that didn't hide their muscled shoulders and chests. One of them, looking like a loan shark enforcer, strolled quickly over to the garage's now closed rolling door. He cupped his hands around his eyes and squinted out a peep hole.

"Expecting trouble?" Jonas asked.

"Could be, squire," Tommy Corbyn said. "These days, you never know."

"What are you talking about, Tommy?" Charly asked, concern in her voice. "What's this about?"

"I'm just the pickup man, Miss Lawrence. It's Mr. Rumbold's show."

Jonas picked up a strong smell of car exhaust fumes and oil. Here and there off to his right, a few other cars lay parked at a distance from theirs. Someone must have instructed the drivers to keep away.

"Spot any MI5 bad boys, Axel?" Tommy called out to the bodyguard, who had positioned himself by the closed garage door.

"So far, so good, Tommy."

"Let's hope our luck holds." Tommy Corbyn shifted to Jonas and Charly. "We caught the Security Service this morning being naughty again. Parked right across the street, they were. The cheeky bastards watching Mr. Rumbold's Mayfair townhouse. Bloody fools must think there's only one way in and out of that mansion. Trying to scare us is what we think." He jammed a hand suddenly into his jacket as if for a gun, then relaxed. A cat or rat—Jonas couldn't be sure because of the poor light—had scampered across their path to a rubbish bin. "Who knows you two are still in London?" the bodyguard asked Charly, glancing sideways at her.

"Just our servants and our security. And of course, our chauffeur."

"Discreet is he?"

"Nigel? Absolutely. Does he have to stay?"

"For everyone's safety, yes." He kept his eyes on her. "And those servants and groundskeeper at your manor? Discreet as your Nigel, are they?"

"A hundred percent."

"Every single one close-lipped?"

"Every single one."

"Good. Let's hope they keep their bloody mouths shut."

"Tommy, why all these questions for God's sake? I usually see Mr. Rumbold only at his annual Boxing Day party at his estate and on Remembrance Sunday."

Tommy Corbyn laughed, as though he delighted in conspiracy. "Mr. Rumbold's show, Miss Lawrence. His show all the way."

They reached four oil drums planted near the left brick wall that blocked further passage. Tommy muttered something about Mr. Rumbold talking with Hotel Eden management for better underground parking lighting.

The scruffy Eden? Of all the damn places. Jonas shook his head in disbelief. He had heard rumors the luxurious St. Ermin's had housed some Special Operations Executive staff during the last war. The majestic Grand Central, too, might have served as a debriefing center for returning escaped Brit soldiers. But the dowdy Edwardian Eden for anything clandestine? He must have hurried past countless times on Buckingham Palace Road after leaving Victoria Station and only noticed its tarnished historical plaque and red-coated doorman. Just another traveling salesman's soot-scarred way station near Buckingham Palace that had survived the German air blitz.

"Milo, if you would." Tommy unbuttoned his coat. He tossed it to the other bodyguard, who had approached, a man with a blunt head that could serve as a battering ram. Tommy bent waist level, wrapped his weight-lifter arms in a bear grip part way around an oil drum. With an occasional grunt of effort, he wrestled it over on its rim, banging it carelessly against the adjacent wall. "One down, three to go."

"Need any help?" Jonas asked.

"I'm fine, mate. Helps me work off that Indian Pale Ale beer I drink in what off-hours Mr. Rumbold kindly gives."

"That security?"

"That it is. Each filled to the brim with cement." Tommy Corbyn thumped a meaty fist down hard on the top of one drum, sending a dull echo around the garage. "Never a single breach into Mr. Rumbold's secret sanctum. Kept us as safe as the Buckingham Palace royals." He wiped sweat from his forehead. Then he struggled with three more drums, rolling each over on its rim to the near wall until he had cleared a path. "This way."

Milo tossed Tommy's jacket back to him, then rolled on its rim the first of the four oil drums back into place, blocking once more any passage. Charly glanced at Jonas, shrugging puzzlement over Tommy Corbyn's request. Tommy Corbyn led the way ahead into the gloom.

Chapter 2

They reached a blackened metal door, flush with the dark brick wall, Jonas didn't notice until they were within a foot or two. Tommy Corbyn unlocked it, then led them with no small talk zigzagging through a series of dim, chilly brick passages until they reached a service elevator.

Someone, Jonas noticed, had stripped the lift of most markings, as though craving anonymity. All that remained was an Otis Elevator brass plaque on one wall panel. And still Tommy Corbyn offered no small talk. He only gazed up at the brass arrow that ticked off the floor indicator lights as the elevator slowly rattled its way up. Third floor. Fourth. Fifth. Finally, the sixth floor and a long, desolate, silent corridor until they reached 625, the last room at the end of the faded burgundy carpeted hallway.

Somewhere outside Big Ben struck the hour faintly, but authoritatively. Jonas glanced at his wristwatch. Two in the afternoon. The chimes reassured him for the experience didn't seem quite real. He and Charly might be settling into their Cotswold manor about then, happy to have escaped the noise, dirt, and personal danger in London were it not for this abrupt and odd interruption.

Tommy knocked twice sharply with a ringed knuckle. Jonas suspected someone among Rumbold's retinue had squinted through the peep hole. Immediately the door opened part way as if they were expected. Charly slipped in sideways, then Jonas, feeling a conspirator in a hotel of innocents. Lastly Tommy, who took one last glance up and down the corridor. Then he eased the door shut with one massive hand. With the other, he flicked the four dead bolts firmly into place.

Chapter 3

A bespectacled man in a three-piece dark suit stood near the door. Ignoring them, he studied a thin strip of paper with quotes from a ticker tape machine on a massive walnut desk. "The American stock market is due to open sharply up, Mr. Rumbold. Heavy buying in AT & T. Also in RCA. Should we sell into the rally today? Increase our liquidity?"

Maurice Rumbold shook his fist at him to be quiet. "Blast it all, Harry. One bloody thing at a time," he shouted, his fleshy bull-dog face red with anger before returning to his phone. "Tell that bloody Irish SOB Joe Kennedy I'm not the least bit interested in a loan. Not the least, Adam. You know how those Americans are. You've dealt with that Wall Street crowd before. Give an inch, take a mile. That's how they are. Grasping predators, all of them. No! No! No! Absolutely not! Not even as a last resort. Sod 'em all. Am I clear on that?" He shifted left and nodded greetings at Charly and Jonas next to Harry. "Got company here, Adam. Have to go. Urgent business. I trust you'll pass along my sentiments." He slammed down his phone so hard his five other Bakelite receivers on his desk jumped. "I may be many things, Harry," he said turning to him, "but I'm also a Brit. I refuse to sell out to those Yanks. Especially an Irishman. Harry, we'll need privacy, if you don't mind And yes, sell into that rally."

"As you wish, Mr. Rumbold." The financial advisor fetched his briefcase from behind Rumbold's desk and his bowler hat and umbrella on it. Without a further word, he closed the office door, still studying a strip of ticker tape he had snipped off.

"Charly my dear, how marvelous to see you again. Your writing is exceeded only by your lovely beauty. I see you've brought along your good luck red shoulder bag."

"As always, Mr. Rumbold. Never go anywhere without it."

"Whatever gives you peace of mind, huh? And how was Seton Hall? A standing ovation?"

"You kidding? A talk on women's rights, you get some applause and lots of boos."

"Those primitives, incredible. But you stood your ground, my dear?"

"I stood my ground."

"That's my Charly. And you, sir, you must be *the* Jonas Shaw she talks so much about. Haven't had the pleasure until now."

"Nor have I," Jonas said, surprised at the strength of the man's vigorous pumping handshake.

"My Charly tells me you were a prize fighter once."

"Well, once, yes. In my younger days. For a while. That's right."

"'In my younger days,' listen to him, my dear. Not a day over thirty-five or thereabouts, I wager, and looking fit as a fiddle. About five-nine or so, huh, Mr. Shaw? Capable of taking on even the likes of Tommy boy here, I'd say."

"You're very kind, Mr. Rumbold."

"Tell that to my employees, Mr. Shaw. Some hush-hush work for Winston during the last war, too, my Whitehall sources say. Oh, I know, I know. The Official Secrets Act. Can't go into details. No offense taken. So, lad, how's life at your albatross—Charly's words, lad, not mine, so don't take offense. Still use just four rooms in that forty-room Italianate palace of yours?"

"That's all we need. A state bedroom. One room for her office; another for mine. And our library. All easy to maintain."

"Still, a shame, son, letting that historic mansion go to waste. Especially that ballroom. The candlelight dinner parties that were once held there. The dignitaries from all over. Marvelous affairs, absolutely marvelous. With dancing to an orchestra until the wee hours. What glamor. But your life to live, not mine. When Winston presented it for services rendered—seven hundred acres in the Cotswolds, is it?"

"Seven hundred seventy-five, I'm afraid."

"Who's counting, huh? Seven hundred seventy-five then. He didn't tell how to use it now, did he? Still working on that book about Winnie?"

"Muddling along. I'm not cut out to be a writer really. The words don't come easily to me. Like they do to Charly here. But she insists I have a story to tell."

"You do, honey. Guarding one of the world's most powerful men will make a great book. You just have to cut down on your adjectives."

Jonas shrugged. "I happen to like my adjectives. *And* my adverbs."

"Just don't like them too much, lad."

"Well, we'll see."

"And our Charly, still love her, do you, lad?"

"Of course," Jonas answered, taken aback by Rumbold's odd question. "More so now than ever."

"I hope so. She'll need it for what I have in mind. Know much about Palestine, either of you? Besides the usual. The camels, palm trees, the dunes."

A red phone rang. Tommy Corbyn snatched up the receiver as Rumbold, a momentary trace of panic on his fleshy face, gestured for silence. "I'm sorry, but he's out," his confidant said, then mouthed *Your banker* to Rumbold. "No, I'm sorry. He didn't leave word where he'd be. Gone for the day, I'm afraid. Out with the flu because of the weather. By all means. I'll let him know you called, Mr. Graves."

"Blasted City creditor. Not a moment's peace. The swine. So Palestine." Rumbold raised a bramble bush of a brow at Jonas to continue.

"Only what we've caught at some West End cinema." Forty-three seconds or so of small talk from him, Jonas thought. Must be a record.

"Ah yes, the news. Terrible. Just terrible what's going on these days. Some mornings I can't bear reading even my own papers Tommy boy brings in. Brother-in-law, member of the 11th Armored Division, not the most squeamish of lads, understand, helped liberate Bergen-Belsen back in '45. A nightmare for the rest of his days, the way young Freddie tells it. Thirteen thousand or so dead."

"Thirteen thousand left *unburied*, Mr. Rumbold."

"Right you are, Tommy boy. Thirteen thousand left to rot in the sun by Nazi scum. All bulldozed into pits by us Brits. Another 60,000 or so walking skeletons wishing they were. Not a one-off slaughter either, mind. Other camps like it, too. All over. Germany, Austria, Poland. The Hun and his rotten ilk needed to prove how bestial they were."

"They've done that in spades," Charly said, setting her shoulder bag on a nearby table. "I heard Martha Gellhorn was too upset seeing that camp to talk to anyone for days. Including Hemingway."

"Wouldn't surprise me. The bloody swine Germans. Sod 'em. So Palestine. The SS *Arch Angel,* ring a bell, either of you? Charly? Jonas? The *Arch Angel?*"

Charly frowned and glanced at Jonas; Jonas shook his head.

"Some protector, that name. Nothing more really than a refurbished oversized rust bucket of a river boat. But the last hope for many a desperate soul. Under Panamanian registry. It set sail a month ago from Port-de-Bouc, southern France. Six hundred-fifty Jews, two hundred war orphaned children included, on board eager to get the hell out of a Europe that didn't want them dead or alive. Destination, Haifa."

"The Palestinian port?" Charly asked. "North of Tel Aviv?"

"Quite right, my dear. Crammed to the gills, *Arch Angel.* Appalling conditions on it. Absolutely appalling. Only three toilet stalls. No toilet paper. No life preservers. Only one lifeboat. Little food and water. Foul air to breathe. A floating catastrophe. Listed like a drunken sailor a good part of the way a Nicosia-based stringer reported. But made it somehow as far as Cyprus. There, misfortune. Capsized from a big wave by all reports.

"Most drowned. Some made it ashore. The survivors, what few there were, clubbed, kicked, hauled off by his Majesty's finest Royal Navy to some internment camp. With lots of barbed wire. Like Bergen-Belsen, you ask me. And we British pride ourselves on our decency. Rubbish. Still they flee. To Palestine, where else, huh? The only place they feel safe. Roughly 250,000 still in Europe, according to my Berlin bureau chief. By paddle steamer. Schooner. By half submerged, leaky hulks. Whatever floats."

"They're that desperate to flee?" Jonas asked.

"Wouldn't you be, Mr. Shaw? I know I bloody hell would."

"Mr. Rumbold." Tommy Corbyn tapped his wristwatch. "Time, sir." He handed across to the newspaper tycoon a glass of water and some pills on a tray.

"Hell's bells. My Harley Street doctor—he's number four, you two, the others have died— warns me, Maurice, too much drink. Too much food. Too much this. Too much that. Take it easy. Or else the heart, the liver. Sod 'em, these medical experts." He cupped the tiny pills in his big pudgy hand, tossed them back with a gulp of water, and grimacing, ground them up with his enormous jaws.

"Blast it all. Almost as bad as the wife's cooking." He handed the glass back. "Next time, Tommy boy, a little Ricard Pastis in it." He winked at Charly and Jonas. "For medicinal purposes, of course. The Warsaw ghetto uprising, ever hear of it? You Mr. Shaw? Charly dear, what about you? Anything?"

"Vaguely," Jonas said. "Forty-four wasn't it?"

"Forty-three, April. A band of mostly young Jews in the Polish capital's ghetto decided they had had enough humiliation. Decided to stick it to the filthy German swine. A thousand or so insurgents—poorly equipped, let me add; a few pistols, some home-made Molotov cocktails, a few machine guns—against the well-equipped German war machine. Artillery. Tanks. Armored vehicles. What have you. Never had a chance, those resisters. They must have known it, but decided to die their way, fighters rather than as Nazi slaves. The battle lasted almost a month, believe it or not. Against all odds, they fought that long. Like lions, every single one. Absolutely heroic, what those people did. Most died, of course. A few survived."

"I read somewhere they were all killed."

The red phone rang again. "Leave it, Tommy boy. *Massacred* is a better word for it, my dear. Children, babies, the old, the pregnant included. Burned alive, a good number of them. The Warsaw sky black with smoke during the day; during evenings, red for nights on end, witnesses said. Some, a few, escaped. Through the filthy rat-infested sewers, if you can believe that.

"A photographer in Greece somewhere, might have been Thessaloniki, took some photos of a few of the lucky ones, who made it out. Their idea. To memorialize their feat. To show the world the fighting Jew existed no matter the odds. Lined up, clutching machine guns and pistols, looking fiercely into the camera. Not a one smiling. Who could blame them? Huh? Made some of the major newspapers...lucky bastards, the scoops they got." Rumbold patted his jacket pockets, then checked the inside ones. "Hell's bells, Tommy boy. Where's my Dunhill?"

"Back at your townhouse, Mr. Rumbold. In your smoking room."

"Mayfair, Tommy boy? There? Can't think straight without that pipe. Sod' em. Anyway, a few weeks ago, you two, a friend of mine from my Oxford days, Johnny Radcliffe, telephoned from Tel Aviv. Could barely hear the old boy over all that bloody awful static. A marvelous writer, Johnny. Made financial reporting, all that nuts-and-bolts balance sheet, annual reports stuff, actually entertaining. But Johnny took too much fancy to Portuguese port wine and was shown the door. Got religious. Discovered Jesus in the Promised Land. Runs a newspaper clipping service over there these days in Tel Aviv. The Middle East Clipping Service. Hardly original that, but there you are. All that wine must have dulled his imagination.

"Johnny monitors many of the majors the world over. *News of the World,* the *Sunday Express,* Italian, American, French, whatever might interest his clients. Keeps him busy, alert. Johnny claims he caught sight of this young woman while 'dining,' his word, not mine, at some café there and snapped her photo. Here, my dear."

Charly looked at the Kodak color photo, and her face caved in with shock. For a minute or so she simply gazed at it, speechless, as though unable to understand what she held. "Good heavens," she said at last, "how old is this poor thing?"

"Hard to tell. Estimated age, Tommy?"

"Around eighteen, nineteen to thirty or so."

Rumbold nodded. "My guess, too. Put a magnifying glass to her face, you two, you see a blush of youth. But still, all those wrinkles."

"Eighteen, nineteen? Incredible."

"My dear, you see family, friends, community leaders murdered, raped, gravestones used as latrines, and the world does nothing, you'd look like that."

"Whatever the poor thing witnessed must have shocked her."

"Johnny won't swear it's her, Charly. But could be. Right color hair, blonde. Right height, about five-feet-five or so. Right stature, bosomy. Might walk with a slight limp, according to reports. From her Warsaw fighting days. Used her left hand to hold her tea cup at that café. The woman in that Greek photo used her left to grip her assault rifle. So, my friends, I agree. Close enough."

"What's her name?"

"Don't know."

"Don't know? Not even a first name, Mr. Rumbold?" Charly passed the color photo across to Jonas.

"Not even a first name, my dear. Not even a middle initial."

"With her blonde hair, she could pass for a German *Fräulein.* Even a Pole."

"Easily so, Mr. Shaw. Which might have saved her life in her escape. Not exactly a crumpet, what with all those wrinkles. Attractive enough still. But hell's bells, after what she witnessed in that inferno, what can you expect, huh? Hedy Lamarr? Lana Turner? Wading through the human filth of Warsaw sewers to escape, my God." Rumbold shook his head sadly. "You Yanks, Mr. Shaw, should have dropped those atomic bombs of yours on Berlin, not Hiroshima and Nagasaki. The sewers, my God. And we complain about the traffic on Fleet Street."

"Mr. Rumbold." Tommy Corbyn tapped his wristwatch.

Maurice Rumbold plucked a pocket watch from his vest pocket and raised an eyebrow at the time. "Right you are, Tommy boy. *Tempus fugit.* My financial backers are waiting. Christian charity, my dear, demands we help our brothers and sisters in need. For the foreseeable future, you are going to disappear."

"I am?"

"You are, to Palestine. A scrape of land two hundred fifty miles long along the coast, give or take. Eighty mere miles or so at its widest in the south. Twenty- three miles more or less in the north. Palestine. The size of your New Jersey, you two."

"As narrow and long as a fingernail clipping."

"Right you are, Tommy boy. The news center for now. And if my Middle East sources are correct, for years to come."

"Palestine?"

"Yes my dear, firebrand you are going there. To Palestine."

"Mr. Rumbold, with all due respect, sir, that's not my usual beat."

"Oh rubbish. The change from covering Europe will do you good. So will that sun."

"But—"

"But nothing. Hush. Find that possible Warsaw ghetto survivor. Before those Fleet Street jackal competitors get wind of it."

"Palestine," Charly muttered, still looking dismayed by her assignment.

"Bribe. Get travel permits or visas forged. Seduce. Whatever it takes. But find this young woman," Maurice Rumbold continued. "See if she did in fact survive that Warsaw inferno. If so, a profile on her, please, for a front-page exclusive. A series. Ten thousand words minimum. Plus photos. Put a face on these poor people. Their tragedy. With your large readership, it might make the world take note...if they have a conscience which I sometimes very much doubt. That's the only way those buggers in Whitehall will take action. Help them get their own country. Also put us well ahead of those press jackals."

"How long will I be away?"

"As long as it takes, my dear."

"Mr. Rumbold, what about my work here? Why can't this Johnny Radcliffe handle it?"

"Johnny has the gout, that's why. Tommy boy's giving me the look. I know, I know, Tommy boy. With my appetite, I'm headed in that direction, but at least I'm enjoying the ride."

"Mr. Rumbold, I just can't drop my assignments."

"You can, and you will, my dear."

"Including my articles on women's rights? Drop those interviews? Just like that?"

"Just like that. *You can, and you will*. When you return, you can indulge your hobby horse again."

Charly's face reddened. "Mr. Rumbold, with all respect, sir, it's hardly that."

"Understood. I would be derelict if I didn't mention my chief military correspondent predicts war in Palestine. Henry's a Sandhurst graduate and knows his stuff. Egypt, Syria, Iraq, who else, Tommy boy?"

"Saudi Arabia, Mr. Rumbold. Lebanon, too, from shortwave reports."

"Right you are. Saudi Arabia, Lebanon. Transjordan...their Arab Legion, commanded, by the way, by our very own British officers. The swine. Prancing around, King Abdullah's soldiers, in their red-and-white-checkered keffiyehs. Despicable shits. All against a few hundred thousand Jews. And against what pitiful air force they can muster. A few Piper Cubs and other planes from several sources, held together with string and glue. A gang up, you ask me. Bloody cowards, those Arabs. Swines, all of them. Only good thing about them is their food."

"War's the least of my concerns. I did cover the last European conflict for you. Your roving correspondent, remember?"

"I most certainly do. With only a toothbrush, typewriter, and passport. You sent us first-rate dispatches. Every one of them."

"Tel Aviv is a needle-in-the-haystack problem looking for her."

"Oh nonsense. Be an optimist. Tommy boy, the population of Tel Aviv."

"Roughly 230,000."

"There, you see. A small town." He picked up a thick, ordinary-appearing envelope from his desk and thrust it at her. His decision was final. "Here, my dear. Johnny's address. Lives in the northern part of that town. Close to the Yarkon River. Near Dizengoff Street, a major road. For a landmark, a store across from where he lives. Sells marvelous Persian rugs from what I hear. Shouldn't be hard to find. All you'll need is here," he stressed tapping the packet. "Thomas Cook brochures of Palestine. Traveler's checks. Contact names, if needed, British police included. Plus the address of your Tel Aviv man-about-town. Porter is his name. Oliver Porter. A splendid chap. Would trust him with my life or my wife. He'll pick you up at Lydda Airport. Find this young Jewess. Put a face on her people, their tragedy. Tommy boy, gloves."

Charly dropped the thick envelope into her shoulder bag. "What if she's not in Tel Aviv, but in one of those farms?"

"You mean a kibbutz? Doubt it," Rumbold said, his attention more on tugging on the second of his black calfskins than her concern. "She's not the kind"—he momentarily eyed her— "who knows how to raise poultry, cattle, or whatever those Jews do on their socialist collectives." Then back to his glove. "She's a city girl. From my sources, likely grew up in Warsaw. Enjoys that culture stuff. Art, music, whatever. So more than likely Tel Aviv. If not, we'll cross that bridge at that time. Tommy boy, coat. Should you need to reach me, I shall be, ah, somewhat incommunicado, my dear. Due to, shall we say, pressing business issues at hand.

"But"—he slipped one arm through a coat sleeve—"I shall trust your seasoned judgment." He fixed them both with his battered, watery brown eyes. "David versus Goliath all over again, you two. Much bigger this time. Oswald Mosley and his thugs. But of course, you already know that. Some big-name anti-Semites in the British establishment, too. Died-in-the-wool Jew haters. Responsible for that atrocious policy paper back in '39. The White Paper. Calling for restricting Jewish immigration to Palestine and land purchases. The nerve. All while *Herr* Hitler murdered their kind left and right. This, despite Lord Balfour's effort."

"Lord Balfour? I don't think I know the name, Mr. Rumbold."

"You should, lad. Lord Arthur Balfour, son. Foreign secretary in Lloyd George's government. Promised, and here I quote, 'a national home for the Jewish people,' closed quote. Which he meant in Palestine. One of the Just. I wish I could say the same for Bernard Montgomery."

Rumbold slipped his other arm through the remaining sleeve, while Tommy flipped up the coat's collar. "Our own Allied commander of ground forces during the D Day invasion of France. Maybe bigoted. His subordinate for sure. That Evelyn Barker fellow. General officer commanding our forces in Palestine before he left. Vile chap. Full of libelous venom. Those oil-rich Saudis, of course. What can you expect, huh? Courting Ernest Bevin and that silky public school boy Arabist crowd over at the Foreign Office. Underneath all that elitist polish at the F. O., duplicity, you ask me. What do the Jews have? A few weapons and a dream to reclaim their biblical homeland. Their own homeland, I ask you, is that a crime? David versus Goliath, like I said. Keep that in mind while you're over there, my dear. For the rest, sod' em all."

Jonas caught Charly glance at him and her shrug. She had her marching order. She raised her right hand in a mock salute at Maurice Rumbold as he turned to leave. "Sod'em all, Mr. Rumbold."

Chapter 4

Everything made sense now, Jonas realized, as they bumped their way down in the musty elevator to the garage and their chauffeur. The surveillance detection route Rumbold's driver had taken to see if anyone followed. Rumbold meeting at his Eden hideaway and not at his very public Fleet street headquarters. Maurice Rumbold, war veteran and victor of many newspaper wars, wasn't easily frightened. But despite his bluster, he was. Of hounding creditors? Not likely. If worse came to worse, Charly had once revealed, he would sell his glossy magazines to keep his flagship paper afloat.

More likely, the mogul feared MI5 for the Security Service would report to certain high-level anti-Semites in the British Establishment. They would try to hound Maurice Rumbold into stopping his editorials and articles championing a Jewish homeland. Rumbold wouldn't budge. Neither would certain powerful ministers, and that left Jonas with a feeling of a vague danger over Charly and himself.

Axel, left hand primed inches from his shoulder holster, peered out and checked the alley ahead for trouble. Then he trotted to the end of the narrow passage and glanced up and down the intersecting street. Still satisfied no one watched, he waved them forward. As they cleared Eden's underground parking, Axel, in a sentimental gesture of support that surprised Jonas, crossed his fingers high in a show of good luck. Jonas could still hear phones ringing in besieged Rumbold's hideaway office. And also the warrior's defiant "Sod 'em all" rumbling up from the depths of his robust, barroom bruiser's physique.

Chapter 5

The following gray April morning, Jonas and Charly flung dust sheets over what little furniture they owned in their Cotswold mansion.

After lunch, they gave notice with two months' pay to housekeeping, some teary eyed, and explained they'd be away for a while. Should Charly's work extend beyond that period, their London bank would pay extra into their accounts.

They kept their eight-man security force, white-haired retirees from the London Met; some fanatic might go beyond mailing death threats and set fire to their sprawling estate. Or have better luck next time aiming a sniper rifle.

That next morning, Jonas held a meeting with the chief of security in the huge kitchen. Noah Smythe understood its importance, Jonas could tell, since the death threats had tripled. Sitting across from him, Noah sipped only occasionally his Early Gray tea and not one nibble from a biscuit. Not even when his prized retriever bounded in, skidding across the vast checkered marble floor to him, did he break his attention. He absently patted the dog's light golden coat, while he remained focused on the man sitting across from him.

Had Noah's protection boys, Jonas asked, noticed any vehicle parked near the main entrance gate? A car, van, or truck? Even an innocent-looking horse and cart, or bikes, anything at all?

Had any bodyguard seen any loitering near the north gate? Anyone asking for directions? Searching for a lost border collie or any other dog? Selling gardening tools?

What about when Maude had driven into the village for her weekly purchases? Did she report anyone following her out of the Village Shop and Post Office? Anyone casually ask the manor's address?

Noah assured Jonas his team had not spotted a single threat. Not even a suspicion of one. But at the dreadful hour of two the next morning, hours before leaving for Croydon Airport, their telephone jangled. As Jonas fumbled for it in the dark, he accidentally awoke Charly, naked beside him.

"He's what, dead?" He clicked on the bedside light and momentarily put a hand over the receiver. "It's Noah. He says Trevor died in an accident, and he's at the scene. You sure it's him, Noah?" Then back to Charly. "It happened about half an hour ago near the Queen Elizabeth Inn." Their second in command was on his Brough Superior motorbike when a car at the intersection broadsided him before speeding away. Trevor slewed across the country road and under a delivery lorry, nearly getting decapitated.

Never an incident before on that country lane from his parents to the estate for his night shift. Something stunk, Jonas said as he yanked the man's manila folder from his office wall safe. Noah had felt the same way, he added as he re-entered their bedroom.

Why? she asked, throwing on her bathrobe.

Because, he answered flipping through the pages until he found five sheets of paper, of these, he continued. And he waved them at her with the organization's pedigreed name in gold script at the top. They were Trevor Bailey's entry and disclaimer of liability forms for five cross-country motorbike races in unforgiving, mountainous Scotland. In each, he had placed first.

Because he also placed first twice in a daredevil motorbike race through the treacherous wastes of Morocco.

Because Churchill's chief bodyguard, Detective Inspector Walter H. Thompson himself, had vouched for Trevor's professional competence and physical fitness.

Because a wealthy industrialist had thought so highly of Trevor's expertise, he had given him that rare, pricey motorcycle.

Because no rain had fallen that evening to cause dangerous driving.

Because the well-lit Queen Elizabeth Inn provided excellent visibility for the security-conscious man.

Because Trevor's death fit an alarming pattern: the hate mail, the bomb threats, the sniper's rifle shot that had just missed Charly's head in their Rolls-Royce days before.

Recalling Maurice Rumbold's warning, *"my chief military correspondent predicts war in Palestine,"* he placed two calls. One to his solicitor's Knightsbridge home. With profuse apologies, he said he knew the hour. But their counselor must drive from London out to their estate. He and Charly had to update their wills, leaving more to their help, before they left on a dangerous Middle East assignment.

He placed a second call to Noah Smythe for an emergency meeting. They huddled again in the kitchen when the watch commander returned to the manor, looking tired and sad, but still alert. He assured Jonas they had stockpiled enough Stens, Brens, and even a few well-oiled Lee Enfield rifles to withstand a German invasion.

At the end of their hour-long meeting, Jonas clasped Noah Smythe's hand. He said he and Charly appreciated the sacrifices he and his men made.

He made his way down the creaky stairs to the musty basement. Fumbling in the dark just past the last step, he found the cord and yanked. An overhead light flicked on. Past the barrels of wine and whiskey and rows of furniture covered in dust clothes, he spotted the lump. It lay under a protective tarp. Just where Noah had unloaded them months ago after Charly's first death threat. A small stockpile of surplus WWII British weapons and ammo the senior watch commander had bought from an armory to protect her.

He slipped into his jacket pockets several boxes of cartridges. For one hour, he whipped out his Colt 1911 for straight-ahead shots, for shots at an angle. He practiced until satisfied he still was quick. He'd need that as well as the semi-automatic revolver's fire power and the angels on their side too. They were headed into violence.

Chapter 6

Early next morning, Nigel steered their Rolls-Royce out the drive for the two-hour trip to Croydon Airport, south of London. They passed hamlets of honey-colored stone homes with thatched roofs, a solitary pub, a couple enjoying a stroll after the unseasonably harsh winter. Jonas nudged Charly to enjoy the painterly charm, the intense greens and yellows of the countryside. She just nodded absently while staying engrossed in her Baedeker guide to Palestine.

Soon they neared a crossroad on the ancient, narrow Roman road. A girl in chic equestrian clothes trotted past on her handsome Shetland, waving. He and Nigel waved back. But Charly, still all work, shoved her guide into her red shoulder bag. She turned to a pile of European and British newspapers beside her and circled some Middle East article in red.

The gorgeous, peaceful English country gave off such flowery fragrance, Jonas noticed, yawning. Such sweet, sweet intoxicating Cotswold wildflower fragrance...

He shook himself awake. Crap. He had dozed off. The Shetland on its path ahead had reared up. It had sensed something threatening and nearly thrown its petite girl rider into a patch of snow. And then he noticed.

A pea-green four-seater Jaguar had slipped in front of them. It headed south at a leisurely pace. The driver ignored Nigel's honking to speed up. The car itself washed, but the windows dirty? As if a screen? Jonas's mind raced...the recent attempt on Charly's life. Trevor's odd death. Now this? A lone passenger in back, masked, leaned out his side car window. He fired.

Jonas flinched. "Get down!" A slug slammed into the windshield cracking it. But its bullet-proofing held.

"What?" Charly jerked her head up from reading.

Jonas pushed her down into his lap and squeezed off two shots. "Go, go, go."

The Shetland again reared up, neighing alarm. Its rider screamed, but hung on and spurred it hard. They galloped away from the danger toward grassy hills.

Nigel powered the Rolls ahead. Its reinforced front bumper rammed the rear of the Jag. A sharp metallic clang rang out. A frightened falcon fluttered out of a hedge into the sky. Nigel shouted profanities at the driver as he battered the Jaguar again and again. The Jag screeched sideways off the road like discarded scrap. It rolled several times, then toppled onto its left side into a deep, muddy ditch. An explosion inside blasted off the driver's door. It spun end over end along with shreds of a bloody arm and top half of a head high into the air. A window popped out from the intense heat. With a whump, flames shot out. Another explosion. Boom. Jonas couldn't spot anyone scramble to safety.

A black Rover now raced alongside on the verge. Nigel, gritting effort, swung his heavy machine right, jamming the Rover. Sparks flew from its side. Strips of chrome and a front headlight clumped off as the Rover skidded off the road. It crashed headlong through a fence, splintering its wood into deadly projectiles whirling everywhere. Beyond, a flock of sheep in a pasture scattered. The car bounced down an embankment, smashed into a giant elm, and exploded in a thunderous fiery ball. Tree limbs crackled and whooshed into flames. A man in a seaman's cap screamed something inaudible. He pounded frantically on the left rear passenger door. He tried scrambling out. Another boom sounded. He slumped back, dropping his rifle into some leaves, yelling in pain, engulfed.

The heat melted the tires to liquid. It had got, Jonas felt, too hot to rescue anyone. They sat in their Rolls watching secondary explosions erupt from the Rover. One, then another, then a third. Boom. Boom. B-o-o-o-m. He felt his stomach turn and pressed a button that rolled up his window. Charly and Nigel did the same for theirs. The smell of burning flesh and rubber tires melting had gotten to them. The Rover's trunk lid exploded. Black, ugly smoke spewed out. Maybe from more ammo stored, Jonas thought. Maybe from grenades. He didn't really care. They, whoever they were, appeared armed to the teeth with an arsenal on wheels and out to kill.

Nigel glanced worried over his shoulder through the opened glass partition. "Everyone fine back there? You, Miss Lawrence? You, Mr. Shaw?"

"Yes, yes, I'm fine," Charly said, over more explosions going off. "Believe me, I've experienced worse, Nigel."

"She's fine, then I'm fine." Jonas reloaded his Colt. "Great work, Nigel. We've got us a plane to catch, remember?" He wanted to break every bone in their bodies. But, whoever the bastards worked for, they had all died. Still, for the rest of the trip to Croydon Airport, he gripped his reloaded pistol by his side, ready for any others.

Chapter 7

At Croydon's Booking Hall, Nigel did a quick walkaround of the Rolls for damage before hurrying inside. He'd make, Jonas knew, one phone call to the police to report the attempted assassinations. Two to Mr. Rumbold's offices, one to his official Fleet Street headquarters, another to his hideaway near Victoria Station. He'd reassure him his hardened war reporter, Charly, was okay. So was he and Jonas. He'd also warn the secretaries to double up security. The fourth call would warn their manor to cancel all security leave and to beef up the patrols.

Jonas strolled around, hands in his pockets, inspecting the Rolls. The radiator grille was badly dented. Good. The front stainless steel license plate had been knocked askew. Great. The right-side view mirror was broken beyond repair. Better than hoped for. A long streak of silver paint scratched off on the driver's side. Super. But all in all Churchill's ritzy gift, strengthened at his urging, wasn't banged up enough to get rid of. Dammit!

"Sure you're okay?" he asked as they made their way out to a huge beast of a plane on the dewy tarmac.

"Honestly, Jonas, you and Nigel. I'm not some dainty rich girl. You should know that by now. News from mother. She said hello in her last phone call."

"Your mother, Dame Mink Coat Lawrence? Taking time out, sailing the family yacht to say hello to lowly retired detective me? She's thawing out. At last."

"Jonas dear, don't be so harsh with her. She says you're the only FDR New Deal Democrat she's ever liked."

"She only knows me through your letters. Wait till she meets one of the unwashed in person. She'll faint. When she comes to, she'll disinherit you."

Their plane suddenly sputtered to life; white smoke billowed from one of its four powerful engines. The aircraft dwarfed the mechanics near it, Jonas noticed, and one laughed the "old bird" was junk except some rich Londoner had bought it for a song. He stopped abruptly, recalling turbulence flying into Berlin's Tempelhof the previous year to meet Charly. Charly shouted over the clattering roar he must trust Mr. Rumbold's experienced ex-Second World War pilots. She added if he had faced down the New York Mafia, he could handle their flight. "Now move it, dear," and she gently pushed him abroad, reminding him to take his sleeping pills.

He awoke many hours later, when she nudged him. He had slept through a refueling stop—did she say "Malta?" he wondered still groggy—they were now landing at Lydda Airport, and did she say it was Sunday? He stretched, thankful they'd soon be out of the narrow, cramped fuselage, and glanced out his porthole. A robed man herded a pack of camels across the tarmac ahead. Welcome to Palestine, old boy, he thought.

In the Arrivals/Departure Hall, past Passport Control, a jolly-looking, double-chinned man waved greetings. How Oliver Porter had met the publishing mogul, he didn't explain as he insisted on taking their luggage. Only that they had fought together during the First World War. Nor did he explain what his business imported and exported as he slouched into the driver's seat of his Opel. He chatted too much for Jonas's taste, about the construction in Tel Aviv; about archeological digs to Tunisia...he and his wife found Roman-era Carthage fascinating; about how he enjoyed the sunny Middle East after enduring London and Berlin winters. He seemed to throw up a screen to avoid questions. But as Jonas undid some buttons to his shirt, he assumed the muggy heat made him too critical of their chatty Palestinian contact.

Far off, hills on their right simmered in a heat haze as they neared the outskirts of the city. In the near distance, Jonas spotted beyond an orange orchard black smoke, looking more threatening against the blue sky, drift eastward. Oliver Porter muttered "Oh dear, oh dear" to himself at what he saw, then braked abruptly. Ahead near a checkpoint, a long convoy of trucks with farm produce and cars heading north stalled. A huge canvas umbrella protected three British soldiers within a sandbagged enclosure from the heat. Jonas noticed all wore the 6th Airborne Division patches. A fourth, looking like their commander, stood outside the protective barrier, smoking. He loosened his chin strap, removed his khaki pith helmet, and wiped his neck and forehead again and again with a kerchief. Then he lazily gestured forward with a flick of his finger the next vehicle.

"I'm afraid Maurice sent you two into one very nasty cauldron." Oliver Porter tapped a headline, "More Palestinian Violence," from a newspaper pulled from his white linen suit pocket. "It gets bloodier by the day."

Jonas glanced over his shoulder. Charly scribbled away in her notebook, not shaken by the comment. "Why just the other day," Oliver Porter continued, "the Brits removed several land mines here." Charly flipped to another page, a foreign correspondent to the core, seemingly unfazed.

After waiting a time in the heat, Oliver Porter inched his Opel up to the roadblock and peered out his car window. The commander, the cigarette still dangling from his lips, stared sullenly at them before he checked their papers. "Again?" Oliver Porter asked.

"Third time this week, mate." The soldier studied a passport. "Some fool Jews took a camel track to resupply a kibbutz. They must have thought that safer. Ha, fat chance that. A gang of Arabs ambushed the bloody lot of them. Three trucks filled with food blown up. No survivors." He indicated a row of ten covered bodies in the field opposite the checkpoint before motioning they could leave.

When at last they entered Tel Aviv, Jonas realized the reality clashed with his imagination...camel caravans loping through wasteland, huge tents sheltering a sheik and sprawling family and retinue from a brutal sun, scrawny palms around an oasis in the middle of endless dunes rolling off to the far horizon.

But this? In the middle of nowhere, in one of the most unforgiving of deserts on the planet? Beating staggering odds, the parched land, enemies everywhere, this? And on a Sunday? The hustle and optimism of a small American East Coast city not that far from the bleak Dead Sea? Sometimes he muttered a few words—"Can you believe this?" Mostly he just stared at the Levantine modern wonder. The rows of parked cars. The swarms of pedestrians. The crowded sidewalk cafés with aproned waiters rushing table to table. The new style of architecture with its simple, clean lines. The trio of European-looking businessmen, suited and briefcases in hand, hurrying to some appointment. Charly, too, watched speechless as Oliver Porter, his good nature tested, honked through one traffic jam after another to their hotel. The Jericho, at last.

Chapter 8

"Attention! Attention!"

Oliver Porter jumped, his pillowy stomach pressing against his Opel's steering wheel. Hearing the sharp, metallic voice felt like a knife to the heart. Suddenly he found himself sweating. What he had feared day and night was about to happen, and he couldn't do anything about it except brace for arrest. Despite Father Karl's hours of security briefings, he must have slipped up. British intelligence had found him out. At last. British police would drag him from his car, cuff and interrogate him to death at their Kirya headquarters, and there would go Father Karl's sacred, off-the-books operation.

"Attention! Attention! Anyone found outdoors after curfew will be arrested. Attention! Attention!..."

The sharp, metallic voice passed by him. From the street, a chorus of boos, swearing in Hebrew and English exploded, and several big rocks clunked off the British armored car's gray plating. Tel Aviv's response to yet another clampdown. Who can blame those poor sods after what they had been through? he thought. But Father Karl's operation remained undiscovered.

The war-battered Daimler with its mounted speaker puttered left onto Dizengoff Street and trundled north to warn beach goers, and he felt his heart settle back into its normal rhythm. Next time, he might not be so lucky. After a time, he drove around a block while he fiddled with the dial of his shortwave radio. The reception was again strong. The announcers' voices, clear.

He turned the volume low to avoid attention. Radio Damascus and marching military songs. The Voice of Istanbul and some politician's shouting speech. A station in Alexandria giving the weather. Voice of America..."Unconfirmed reports have stated fugitive Nazi Doctor Ariber..." Radio Syri— What? Aribert Heim? Oliver Porter pulled abruptly to the curb, earning an angry blast from the bus driver behind.

He switched back to VOA in disbelief as his Opel idled. My God! The Butcher of Mauthausen death camp possibly here? In the Middle East? The man responsible for so many murders? "...and may have taken refuge with the government of Egypt's King Farouk. In other news of the..."

He clicked off the radio. Aribert Heim, one of the most sought-after evil men of the Third Reich on the run, maybe here, so close to Palestine. Incredible. Maybe headed toward the Holy Land for some reason? He must add that intelligence to the transmission to Father Karl that night. Even if he stayed on air seconds longer, risking discovery by the British. Even if that violated Old Sauerkraut Karl's golden security rule.

He purchased some pita bread at a bakery, glancing now and again in his rear-view mirror. Still safe. Still no British surveillance on him. He motored on to a café near the seaside where he bought two bottles of Galilee wine the owner had saved for him. Still no military radio-detection-finding vans spotted. He could safely head home at last to his Neve Tzedek apartment. Hopefully, no problem this evening transmitting to Father Karl.

For weeks, after agreeing on security procedures when he returned to Palestine, he had done his recce as his mentor had instructed. From his rooftop apartment, he'd watched the British radio-detection military vans with binoculars. Daily, he worked out their routines. The streets covered. The tea breaks observed so regularly he could set his watch to them. Their equipment. The numbers of patrols. Storing everything in his head. Nothing incriminating if British police or soldiers barged into his apartment. Taking the utmost precautions as Father Karl had insisted again and again. Karl, his voice dripping with loathing about the suspect treachery, about the whole nauseating matter, had stressed too much was at stake. No leaks, or it was all over, and there was flight with the scoundrel still unpunished.

Sometimes, the RDF vehicles roamed randomly through the narrow streets of his neighborhood. They might start at midnight or early morning as if wanting to catch the unwary off guard, in the very act of subverting British rule. Other times, they ran on schedule, predictable like a muezzin's call to prayer. They seemed to hope their war relic creaking along, antenna twitching for any Jewish underground broadcast of intelligence, would unnerve neighbors.

He doubted the skill of those who would track him down, no matter how professional. Father Karl was even more professional. He was Oxford University brilliant and had served at the highest levels in both wars, not just the last. A professional among professionals, that was Karl for you. A seasoned doyen, who had worked both sides of the street, intelligence and counterintelligence. He had studied Abwehr military intelligence so much, some had whispered, only half-jokingly and always in fear, the bald austere Prussian look-alike with his monocle, must have German blood. He appreciated the super-secure one-time pad's value for sending secrets through the ether. All the tricks of deception really, even making some up, clever Karl did, and even improving some of the latest electronic equipment. A spy's spy for sure.

He reached Shabazi Street at last. A Jewish underground faction, he had recently heard, used the home at Number 65 to make explosives. But he was concerned only with high-level treachery and drove past with not even a curious glance left until he reached his apartment. He parked his Opel in a bit of shade, hefted himself out, and paused to catch his breath. That heat, always that blasted heat.

He jerked out a kerchief from his rear pocket, patted away the sweat from his head, then huffed up the steps to his second-story apartment. Once inside, he chided himself again for the weight packed on. Too many Lebanese dates from that Carmel Market. Next month he'd definitely quit his addiction. Definitely.

He turned the three deadbolts to his front door, heard the comforting metallic clicks, and eased open a window to air out the day's heat. Peeking out from the heavy curtain, he saw the sky darkening. The best time to transmit during the twenty-four-hour cycle. He approached the wooden stairs to his bedroom. Under the fourth stair tread, he eased out the concealed drawer and withdrew his equipment, marveling again at how light all that metal felt. All that wired, soldered electronic wonder held in one hand! Even if war surplus, incredible what that American company Philco had achieved.

He quickly encrypted his message. Next looped the fifteen feet of copper wire antenna along the wooden beams, then set up everything else before scooting his chair to his desk. He pushed aside his unpaid bills to ensure space for his right arm, planted his feet firmly flat on the carpet, and glanced at his watch. It was now fully night.

He slipped on his headphones and switched on the little transmitter. It hummed and flickered to life. He felt once again that thrill from his Berlin days working under unflappable Karl. That I-can-outsmart-your-surveillance rush, while he watched the second hand on his wristwatch. Tick. Tick. Tick. Even if he had missed a sighting, the chances of the British military vectoring him were slim. Tick. Tick. Tick. 22:18 hours. Now! Several quick taps of the Morse telegraph key followed, short-coded transmission bursts, as Father Karl had demanded. *K: Possible A. Heim sighting, Cairo.* He paused momentarily on the Morse key to let that news sink in. Then, finally, the last part of his report: *Two Amer contacts made.*

The wily old fox would be thrilled with both bits of news.

Chapter 9

That May night was as cloudy as his meteorologist friend Otto that morning had predicted. Not a single star showed. Not even a glimmer of a moon. In the funnel of his Ford's beams, only occasional headlights from a rare vehicle passed as he sped south on the coastal road past the ancient trading port of Jaffa. Perfect cover for any plan, his Haifa German Colony *Kamerad* had assured winking at him. As if Otto relished anything underhanded against the Zionists. Say what you would about Otto and his drinking, he at least respected him. Never once mocking and calling him *Stefan*. Too bad he couldn't say that about that slimy Ops Officer Angus. *Stefan*, *Stefan*, the nerve of that Angus. Always enjoying annoying him with that despite all that prized intel on the Soviets he furnished!

He turned off the road onto a narrow dirt path. Most of Tel Aviv and its surroundings slept. If anyone could sleep peacefully, he thought. In Palestine these days, with all the bombings, kidnappings, and shootings, you couldn't take anything for granted.

The tires crackled over the stones from the car's weight. He grimaced at the noise. He eased his foot off the pedal and rolled quietly to the end of the south wing of the abandoned textile factory, headlights off. He tapped, tapped on another pedal. His car came to a gentle stop at last, his well-tended brakes not sounding one dangerous squeak. He sat completely still, hands gripping the steering wheel, ready to escape if needed, and waited.

He waited for someone to accidentally reveal himself by lighting a cigarette before cupping it.

He waited for a nervous cough or a careless bump against abandoned tiles and shingles, against the piles of discarded silicate bricks, or other debris that would betray his position.

Somewhere toward the east a horse snorted, and a dog howled. Somewhere above in the absolute darkness, a lone seagull cried out as it circled. Across the two-lane coastal road to the west, the Mediterranean cascaded again and again against the long, ancient shoreline. But he detected no human threat.

He eased himself out, but left the driver's car door ajar, key in the ignition. You had to keep one step ahead of the Jew. He had learned that long ago. You never knew when you might need to flee quickly. The survivor in him gazed around again at the heaps of junk, squinting for any threat. That assortment of tumble-down buildings still appeared deserted. Nearly, anyway.

He made his way back to the entrance near the coastal road, reminding himself to change his license plates before returning to Tel Aviv. Frost had insisted they meet in that abandoned industrial wasteland. Fine. No problem. Security was security. For them both. But rendezvousing in the dark with his Ops Officer always made him queasy. Some gang of Jews could ambush and bundle him away to some painful fate. Toss him half dead to desert jackals.

He pulled on the shed's damp handle. The heavy metal door creaked open, grating against the rough cement floor. When would they learn to oil the damned hinges? The creaking sounded like a public call to the Jewish underground, "Here he is for all to see; come get him." Next time, if he and Frost met there, he'd bring his own lubricant.

A match flared, hissing in the darkness several feet off to his left. "Well, Stefan, there you are, old boy. Right on time. As usual. Splendid. Come in, come in." Frost's smiling face loomed out of the dark into the wavering candlelight that flickered from a draft somewhere. It gave his military taut underside a ghoulish expression, despite his very English florid complexion.

Frost as Palestinian host still asserting his dominance, still needling by calling him *Stefan*. "Angus, good to see you. As always." He made his way over to a metal folding chair on the other side of the table. He unfastened the top button of his shirt, then fanned himself with his hand. "Some night."

"Some night is right. It's hot as hell."

"This Palestinian spring, Angus. Hotter than usual, I heard, with this summer-like weather. Just when you think it can't get any hotter, it does. I've never gotten used to this place. The flies and mosquitoes from the swamps. Terrible. Next time bring a fan, okay? And some quinine in case I catch malaria."

"It's a deal, Stefan. In return for more intelligence on the Soviets."

"It's three in the morning. I don't think you called me here to tell jokes."

"You're right, Stefan. Stefan, as your operations officer I feel compelled to deliver some rather bad news."

"Oh?" Stefan took a long drink of water from his canteen, then resumed fanning himself with his hand. "Well? What is it?"

"I have a brother-in-law in the Foreign Office. A mid-level London mandarin there, and Roderick hears and reads things at the F. O. I have been given to understand we are most definitely pulling out of Palestine."

"It is absolutely certain then?"

"Absolutely. Some 6th Airborne Division wallah has also confirmed. We conquer so we may give the gift of our civilization. Unfortunately, the natives don't always appreciate our generosity. It's *all* over in fact."

"What do you mean?"

"Just that, the British Empire, old boy. The whole kit and caboodle, as the new power-to-be, *those* uppity Yanks like to say."

"I still don't understand what you're saying, Angus."

"I mean, old boy, we're finished. Rule Britannia, that's what. We no longer rule the waves. Not here. Not in India, our crown jewel. Elsewhere. Too much money spent. Too many assassinations and bombings. Little appreciation for our service. Here in fact, thousands of embarkation cards for our soldiers are being printed as I speak."

"I had hoped Clement Attlee's government might decide otherwise."

"I'm afraid not. Roderick says His Majesty's government has made up its mind. Garrisoning 120,000 soldiers has gotten to be too much. That's nearly one-tenth His Majesty's entire empire army. It's costing us a pretty penny, Stefan. Between 30-40 million pounds a year. It's not sustainable. Here, a copy of recent secret cabinet minutes. Roderick managed to smuggle it out. I got it in yesterday's post."

As Angus rose to hand it across, Stefan noticed something metallic glint from Frost's right hip in the candlelight. Probably a British Webley revolver. He wished he could carry a gun, any gun. Even a pocket pistol, a Beretta. But it'd not look right. It'd arouse suspicions. "When?"

"Still to be determined, according to Roderick."

Stefan glanced at the document briefly—"SECRET"..."CABINET"... "disastrous"..."out of our control"..."concluded his review"—grasped the gist and returned it. "What about me? Where will I go? Those British and American war crimes investigators—"

"Settle down, Stefan."

"That's easy for you to say, Angus."

"We will do what we can to protect you."

"I hope so. After all the intel on Soviet aims I've given."

"We fully appreciate your intelligence on their intentions in Europe. But understand there will be war once we pull out. Of that, I am absolutely certain. Egypt, Syria, Transjordan, Iraq, other Arab states will invade Palestine and slaughter every single Jew. I'm like you; I loathe the lot of them. A slaughter of that damned race would not bother me one iota. A thorough comb-out would finish Hitler's work. Once and for all. Sadly, there are those who feel otherwise. There will be an international outcry over the killings once fighting breaks out.

And an international spotlight with lots of reporters, United Nations observers—"

"That is something I can't afford."

"Nor can we. We are working on a plan to get you out. I shall keep you informed, of course."

"I hope so, Angus."

"There is something else. My sources have informed me an American reporter and her lover have just arrived in Tel Aviv."

Stefan took another sip from his canteen. "So?"

"So you should be worried."

"Worried? About this reporter? A woman correspondent at that?"

"Definitely."

"She isn't the only journalist in Tel Aviv, Angus."

"Not like this one, Stefan. Listen very carefully. The reporter is Charly Lawrence. She goes by *Charlotte Lawrence* in her byline."

"Charlotte Lawrence? Charlotte Lawrence, Charlotte Lawrence. Sorry, I haven't come across the name. And you know how I read the newspapers religiously. To see if anything about me has cropped up. Every day I do."

"Then you haven't read enough at that café of yours, my friend. She's a prize-winning journalist. A regular for the *London Daily News*. A large circulation paper with a large international readership. Her lover boy is Jonas Shaw. My sources in MI6 say he worked for that drunkard Churchill arse during the last war. Doing what, we don't know. But obviously something important."

"And your point is?"

"They are worldly, Stefan. Not easily fooled. *And* not easily intimidated."

"Both dangerous? Them? Really?"

"Yes, really, Stefan. So don't smirk. She's hardened from covering the last war. As for this Shaw fellow, he investigated criminals in New York City, despite the American Mafia threatening him. They couldn't scare or buy him off. He also killed, so we've heard, a top Swiss Nazi. As if that's bad enough, they know important, powerful people in London. More so than other journalists. Churchill and that Jew-loving London press baron Maurice Rumbold for sure. Maybe others, as well. And maybe also back in Washington D. C. Why they are here is anyone's guess. But it's best you watch yourself."

Stefan laughed. "Watch myself? Angus, do you know who you're talking to? I've been watching myself for years."

"Don't get cocky, Stefan. All it takes is one slip-up. Just one, and you're in the soup."

Stefan laughed again. "*Me?* Angus, one slip-up, and *we* and many others higher up, my good fellow, will be in the soup."

Chapter 10

That same early morning, Jonas prowled the Jericho's dusty lobby, unable to sleep because of the blistering heat. Against Charly's nagging, from time to time he scratched a rash that had broken out on his right arm. That would only worsen the irritation, she had insisted. The inflammation might even spread to his face, she had teased in vain, and mar his rugged good looks.

The hotel looked like a faded Hollywood starlet, he decided, who had seen better days. Probably in the 1920s when Christian pilgrims had docked at Jaffe and trekked there on their dusty way to Jerusalem. Or when a German emperor and his retinue had visited years later. Certainly, when a Greek shipping tycoon from Constantinople had started it in the early twentieth century.

But now its red-and-black pattern Persian rug in the cavernous entrance hall looked frayed. The vast terrazzo floor beneath appeared dulled from lack of polish. Dust powdered the frames of the wall photos of kings, actors, and diplomats who had chanced sleeping there in the volatile Levant. World wars and bloody clan feuds showed in the bullet holes in the two thick temple-like columns at the foyer's chipped stone steps. But at least it had, as Charly had noted, character and a faded elegance of another time.

On their second night, with no sleeping pills left, they lay in bed listening to Palestine bleed.

Staccato small arms fire crackled off and on in the smoky darkness beyond.

Now and again artillery shells thundered dully in the distance. Their hotel room's windowpanes rattled. The sconce lights in their bathroom flickered off and on. Charly's desk shuddered, her pen rolled off onto the carpet, and several pages of notes fluttered down near a potted jade plant.

Now and then a woman screamed in some street, a child wailed. Nightmarish sirens shrieked and howled, whether police or ambulance, he couldn't tell.

A frightened elderly man hobbled on crutches up and down their corridor yelling, "Watch out, Arab patrols. What out, Jewish patrols."

Jonas crouched toward one of their room's windows and peered eastward, curious. Two streetlamps at either end of the road below dimly lit the scene, and from time to time he commented to Charly on the fighting. She warned him about stray bullets. He said he had survived New York shootouts, told her not to worry, and peeked out again.

Charly complained her back ached from making love and remained in bed. Her shoulders against the headboard, her feet drawn up, she furiously wrote in a notebook that rested against her naked thighs.

A Jeep screeched to a halt at the Workers Theater across the street. A helmeted fighter, the darkness hiding the face, hopped in. As they sped off, the foot soldier fired some kind of gun expertly, as if done hundreds of times, at some unseen target. Further down, a bomb blew out the windows to the Palestine National Bank. Hundreds of glass shards showered onto the sidewalk. An alarm inside clanged incessantly.

In seconds, it was over, whatever it was. Jonas slumped down, resting his back against the wall, the adrenaline draining away. Who had been involved? What had he just seen? A bank robbery? A wanton terrorist attack? Some kind of intelligence-gathering operation? The attack was as murky as the night, as Palestine itself.

And this was only their second evening in the Middle East? What would all the others bring? He fluffed his pillow and closed his eyes, trying to get some sleep.

Chapter 11

Hours later at dawn, arms shiny with sweat, he could feel the heat already building as he lay in his underwear in bed. Muttering curses about the blasted hell of Palestine, he took a cold shower, but he couldn't dry off the humidity. He tossed aside the towel, aggravated over the discomfort. Yawning from little sleep, he called Reception. Their room faced the street from where much of the fighting had erupted the previous night. Could they get a quiet change and soon? And with a fan this time, please! As he hung up, he thought he heard a soft click on his line and frowned at the receiver.

"What's wrong?"

Jonas put a finger to his lips, quiet. He pressed the black phone hard against his ear. He cupped his free hand against his right ear to block out street noise. Did he hear something faint and metallic and menacing on the line?

A raw, impatient blast from a horn sounded from outside their hotel. Charly dumped her Rolleiflex camera into her shoulder bag and grabbed her canteen of water. "Come on, let's go, Jonas. That must be our taxi."

Jonas stared at the telephone receiver, concerned. He gazed around their little hotel room, now suddenly suspect. To the courtesy notepad on the desk near the window; it might leave traces of any message scribbled. To the courtesy fountain pen, with the Jericho's rams' horns logo; it could be rigged to pick up conversations. Then back to the phone, whose receiver he still held in his trembling hand, fearing the faint clicking he might have detected.

"Jonas, honey, come on," she said, the adrenalin rush to land a story in her urging. "Worry about whatever you heard on our way to Johnny Radcliffe's apartment."

Their driver sounded another raw, impatient blast, and Charly was insisting. "All right, I heard you."

In their taxi, he thought about the unsettling background noise on the phone. With it came memories of his dangerous New York City detective days and being on the run from Nazis during the last war. The sinking feeling lasted all the way through the modern-day Tel Aviv bustle to the north of the city.

Maurice Rumbold's directions to Johnny Radcliff's address, they discovered, proved useless. The journalist's address, near Dizengoff Street, wasn't even close to the filthy, smelly Yarkon River. But by then their taxi had sped off in a minor dust storm, leaving them alone, hot, sweaty, and feeling abandoned.

A sudden gust of hot wind blew some sand into his eyes. Jonas spit out some grit along with a curse, "Blasted land." He rubbed his eyes clean and wiped sweat from his brow with his forearm. Then he stopped a passing street vendor, whose donkey sagged with its heavy load of goods for sale. He showed the Arab the scrap of paper with the address, damp with his sweat, and shrugged. The old man, the Middle East summers burned into his wizened face, pointed south and held up five fingers. Five blocks? A five-minute walk? Five Palestinian Mandate coins for his help? Neither Charly or he could decide. But that was par for the course, he decided, in this strange British protectorate. They sent off in what they hoped was the correct direction, Jonas glancing up, squinting resentfully at the mercilessly hot Palestinian sun.

Several blocks on, he spotted a street of modest, white-walled dwellings, and as Maurice Rumbold had described, a ramshackle cinderblock store that sold Persian rugs. Across from it, a three-story, flat-roofed huddle of apartments. Johnny Radcliffe's address. Arab shelling had blown off the corner of a small, rounded, open balcony of a second floor living quarters. To the side of the white- walled Bauhaus building, a Vespa lay parked next to a Jeep with *Press* painted in white on the dusty hood. Probably Radcliffe's. But Charly had let out a cry of pain and stumbled.

She hopped to Radcliffe's glass-fronted entrance, explaining she had twisted her ankle. She pushed aside a crate of oranges, eased down on one of several sandbags, and said she'd shortly join him.

From Radcliffe's airy cool stairwell, he heard crackling faint lyrics from the direction of his apartment above.

> "This road leads to Rainbowville
> Going my way
> Up ahead is Blue Bird Hill
> Going my way
> Going my way
> Going my way
> My way
> My way
> My way"

The stylus of an ancient gramophone must have stuck in a record's vinyl groove.

Radcliffe's front door lay suspiciously open, he noticed. But then he spotted bottles of Iberian wine in a nearby cardboard box. Just great, he thought. A boozer as the lone source for finding any Warsaw ghetto survivor. Thank you, Mr. Rumbold. Thank you very much.

> "My way
> My way"

"Mr. Radcliffe," he called out as he wandered inside closer to that annoying, scratchy, stuck record. "Mr. Radcliffe." He wasn't in the naturally lit living room. Not in the bright bedroom or kitchen either. Passing by the bathroom, he noticed puddles of water on the tiled floor and bubbles of soap suds foaming in the shower drain. He peered into the adjoining dim study, and there he was as feared, Mr. Johnny Radcliffe in his bathrobe in a drinker's pose. He lay slumped over, his forehead resting squarely near the edge of his cluttered desk. His sun-bleached blond hair, still glistening wet from bathing. His right hand near his old reliable to see him through whatever demons beset him, a big fat bottle of red Portuguese wine. Thank you, Mr. Rumbold. Thank you very much.

"My—" Jonas lifted the tone arm off the record on the gramophone on a nearby bookshelf; the apartment fell into silence except for the joyful cries of children playing outside and crows. He glanced around for a container of English tea. But in the dusty shambles of the semi-dark study, bundles of newspapers on the floor, boxes stuffed with clippings on shelves, rolled-up paper maps in one corner, he spotted nothing to sober up the drunk. He examined the drink encased in a wicker wrap, sniffed it, and drew back. He'd stick with his Johnnie Walker. "Too much Quinta Lisbon, Mr. Radcliffe? Hey, Mr. Radcliffe." He gently shook the shoulder of the drunk. "Mr. Radcliff, Maurice Rumbold—" The reporter keeled over onto the art deco rug with a soft thump, sounding louder in the quiet, and remained in a fetal position. Johnny Radcliffe wasn't drunk, he realized. Johnny Radcliffe was dead.

Chapter 12

Jonas briefly glanced away; the sight of a dead human never easy. A single shell casing lay off to the right on the rug. From a British Webley revolver maybe. He brushed away some flies as he crouched next to the body. He saw no need to check for any pulse. Johnny Radcliffe probably never had a chance. Maybe after stepping from the shower and dressing, he had heard a noise, turned, and then...

A single bullet had blasted through his back, leaving a good-sized bloody mess roughly one inch across. The fading heart still pumped out a trickle of bright red blood from the opening that pooled. A few specks of blood had spattered on the back of his head, and they appeared fresh. Oddly, the back of Radcliffe's cantilevered chair showed no entry from that ballistic. The killer, after murdering him, must have propped the dead Radcliffe upright as a sadistic joke only he understood. Or maybe to admire his work before he heard him climbing the stairs, panicked, and fled?

"Jonas, you found—? Oh my—"

Jonas swung around, aiming his semi-automatic at the doorway. Charly stood at the threshold, her green eyes wide with fear.

"No, don't," she shouted.

"Christ," he said. "Don't *ever* sneak up on me like that again."

"What on—?"

"Radcliffe is dead." He shoved his Colt back into his shoulder holster and pushed himself to his feet. "Come on. We're getting out of here. The killer might be close by." He grabbed her roughly by the arm and pulled her quickly toward the apartment's front door.

"But what about—?"

"Come on, dammit." Charly still shocked, unable to grasp fully. "It happened moments ago," he added as they took the stairs down two at a time, their flight echoing in the stairwell. But he didn't care if any neighbor heard. Get out, go, he heard his warning self demand. "Just before we arrived."

"A robbery?"

"I doubt it. His apartment looked lived in, but not ransacked."

"What then?"

"I don't know. But it might have cost him his life."

"We'll have to call the police."

"Yes, definitely. Their station at Mount Scopus."

"I've got to call Mr. Rumbold, too. Explain about his friend. Maybe he knows an attorney here if we need one. Maybe that Oliver Porter can help?"

"We'll see. But we don't call"—they reached the second floor—"from the Jericho."

She stopped and glanced at him. "Not from there?"

"No, absolutely not. It's not secure. Come on."

"You sure?"

"Hell yeah, dear. Someone tapped the phone in our room. Maybe all of them at that hotel."

"Oh my God. Any idea who?"

"No, none. Come on, Charly, let's move."

"Where do we go then?"

"I don't know. Maybe another hotel. We'll see." They reached the ground floor of the apartment building, breathless. It was thankfully empty, he saw, and outside pedestrians either didn't notice or care about their flight. They were in the war zone of Tel Aviv in the larger battleground of Palestine. Jews against Arabs. Arabs against Jews. Sometimes Jews against Jews and Arabs against Arabs. You survived by not noticing. The Vespa, seen earlier parked near the Jeep, now sputtering off toward the end of the block. "I spotted soap suds in the shower drain. Radcliffe must have finished showering and put on his robe when his killer knocked him off. The guy didn't use a peashooter, that's for sure."

"Why do you say that?"

"The bullet wound was massive, Charly. Almost fist-size. Vengeful." Jonas glanced over his shoulder; no one followed. He pushed her into an alley, stinking of raw sewage, crowded with feral cats. "Like what I saw in New York. To settle some score. Or to silence a witness. The killer usually used something high caliber. Christ, the smell here. Let's go."

They hurried south along Dizengoff Street, blending in with other pedestrians, past cafés and bakeries, toward the center of Tel Aviv. Charly suggested a taxi. Jonas said absolutely not. Investigating Radcliffe's murder, the Palestinian police might interview cabbies in the area, and one might mention them. Young Americans. Fear on their well-fed faces. Looking as if they were fleeing. Further on, sure, a taxi, he added. But definitely not there.

The investigation could spiral out of control, he continued as they walked quickly. Maybe ensnare them like he had seen happen to innocents. And that's what they were, innocents in a land edging daily toward war. He had no desire to see them rot in a filthy dangerous foreign prison, maybe stripped of their rights, while they struggled to prove they weren't involved.

Chapter 13

He waved down a taxi, and it drove them back to the Jericho. Charly hurriedly tossed their clothes into their suitcases, while he checked out. As he collected their passports at Reception, he spotted through a crack in the back-office door, carelessly left open, his fear confirmed: a swarthy man, hands clamped over earphones to hear better, hunched over a notepad writing quickly. Before him, a boxy tape recorder attached to the telephone switchboard recorded some guest's conversation. Within reach, seven folders. For seven guests? Among them him and Charly? Jonas felt a sudden chill of fear.

Outside, he flagged down another taxi. As he flung their luggage and Charly's typewriter into the back seat, he asked for a hotel recommendation. The cabbie's puzzled, suspicious look—But why are you leaving one?— on his dark face begged for an explanation. An army of bedbugs, traffic at all hours, thin walls, loose toilet, and Jonas added a few other horrors they had experienced in their world travels.

Their driver put his cab in gear and nodded understanding; a booming city like Tel Aviv had its share of rat holes. Some builders were just low-life *ganefs*. "I take you to the Berliner," he added. "Excellent hotel. It's been around since the 1920s. Many dignitaries stay there. The owner is nice man from Germany."

The hotel lay several minutes away, near Allenby Street and Rothschild Boulevard in the south-central part of the city. As they neared the accommodation now in view, Jonas wondered if he had tipped too much for it. For at first glance the Berliner didn't appear excellent at all. Sandbags piled up to the top of the ground floor's arched windows gave it a medieval besieged- fortress air. But as they drew closer, he noticed the four stories above featured white balconies curved gracefully out from the white façade, and its Moorish roof protected guests from the scorching heat.

He pushed on the ornate wrought iron entrance gate, saw it was locked, and pulled a brass chain. The cowbell under the archway jangled loudly, scaring off pigeons perched on the cast iron crown. Moments later, a tall man in conservative gray skipped nimbly down the stone steps, as though almost floating on air. "Excuse me, you're staying here?" Jonas asked. "Maybe you can give an opinion of the hotel?"

"Well, yes, you could say I'm staying here," he said, laughing. "I am Hans Peters," he continued, smiling as he swung open the gate for them. "The proprietor, and I must say it is excellent. The absolute best in fact in all of Tel Aviv. I was just running an errand, but I do have a moment." He held up a bundle tied with string. "Some guests rush off and forget something from time to time—Parisian underthings. Italian silk ties. Custom-made British shoes. If they don't claim them, we donate to the German hospice in Jerusalem. Can I help you with something?"

They needed a quiet room, Jonas stressed, for at least two weeks. Hans Peters said a couple had checked out that morning, flying back to Alexandria. The Berliner offered Western features: daily maid service, fresh towels, a twenty-four-hour front desk, and tours. Plus a breakfast of Middle East dishes, a waiter with a tray piled with food and a bucket of champagne, added as he flitted past.

"And that, too." Hans Peters lifted his wrapped bundle to indicate his errand. "Sorry I can't chat longer. I must be off. The Jews and Arabs have declared a *very* temporary truce. I must take advantage of it, while I can. We're upgrading our elevators to handle heavier luggage. I'll leave you in the capable hands of my head porter. Abdul has been here longer than any of us, me included. We joke he's the power behind the throne." He clapped his hands twice. "Abdul, take our lovely guests' luggage up for them. And explain security."

Rushing up to them, Abdul, in baggy pantaloons and white waistcoat, straightened his fez cap over his black kinky hair. With a friendly nod, he gripped both suitcases in one hand. In the other he held a metal ring heavy with keys as he mounted the carpeted stairs. Running a hotel in a war zone wasn't easy, he said, climbing more steps. There was one key to open the downstairs gate that led from the side street up to the hotel. A second to open another gate that led into the hotel's lobby. Finally, their room key.

"Yoo-hoo, Monsieur Abdul."

A look of distaste passed over Abdul's dark, youthful features. Then quickly he brightened as a stout woman in a fur coat, despite the heat, bustled toward him. Behind her trailed a preposterously handsome gentleman, appearing years younger. Behind him, a porter strained as he tugged with both hands a cart nearly toppling over with steamer trunks.

"Lucien and I can't find Hans, and we're leaving. Will you be a dear and give that lovely man our address and phone number. He must visit us at our Loire chateau when in France. It's the least we can do to repay him for his most splendid hospitality."

"Consider it done, Madame Bouvier." Abdul pocketed the card. As the couple proceeded down the hall, he dropped his smile and set both valises beside Room 425. "She still thinks we believe Lucien's her son," he said accepting Jonas's tip. "Thank you, sir. You are most kind. Most generous."

"Can Miss Lawrence call London from our room?"

"Easily, Mr. Shaw. In the strictest of privacy. The British company that put in the King David Hotel's system did ours. The French foreign minister, Empress Dorthena, others staying here have never complained." He picked up a pair of leather shoes a guest had left out for polishing and hurried away to another task.

Charly stood just inside their room. "With that blond hair and blue eyes, Mr. Peters looked like some Viking god, when he came tripping down to greet us."

"He's the hotel owner—he bought it from a family who fled back to Cairo. His slicked-up look is part of his stock-in-trade."

"You sound jealous."

Jonas shrugged. "Oh, maybe a little."

She gave him an affectionate peck on his cheek. "Well, don't be. And there's more to come."

He nudged her as he gazed around. "What do you think?" Their room was more than they had expected. It smelled faintly of lavender like the corridor. Opposite them, next to a billowy curtained window, a ceramic bowl jumbled with fresh grapes and oranges rested on a teak wood desk. Next to it, a bouquet of roses in a vase. Propped against it lay a welcoming note from management.

Arrayed around the beige walls hung black-and-white photos of pre-war Berlin. A stage-lit Brandenburg Gate on one wall. Next to it, a moody boulevard Jonas thought looked like Unter den Linden, a high full moon in the background. On the opposite wall, a Potsdamer Platz scene with fashionably dressed pedestrians. A sad nostalgia, he thought, hung heavily in the air. An irredeemable loss for Hans Peters, who tried to hold onto some memories.

"Mr. Rumbold gets into his office at ten our time. We'll have to wait until then."

The hotel owner, Jonas discovered, could make them comfortable only so far. For that early May morning offered still another day of Mediterranean humidity and heat. Jonas stripped down to his underwear and lay stretched out in their canopied four-poster bed. He started on the third chapter of *Arch of Triumph,* but after sweat had dripped onto a page he gave up. The steady hum of the ceiling fan also grated on him. He tossed the Erich Remarque novel aside and fanned himself with an issue of the *Palestine Post.* Charly, too, had discarded most of her clothes. She sat in her bra and panties at her paper-cluttered desk typing, but he felt too hot and sweaty to get aroused.

The Venetian blinds banged again and again against the windows from a hot breeze that rattled the slats. Jonas yanked them up to stop the racket, winced from a blast of sunlight, and let the blinds drop into place once more. "Jesus, and I thought New York and Paris summers were bad. Abdul said the temperature this morning hit 96 degrees."

"What'd you expect, dear? It's the desert."

"You never told me it'd be *this* hot."

"You never asked. Besides, how would I know? This is my first trip, too. In case you forgot."

"No, dear, I haven't forgotten. Bloody hell place, this Palestine. Always sweating. Christ!"

"Bloody hell? Jonas, you're putting on British airs again."

"Oh listen to—" He caught his temper. It was the goddamn heat, he realized. That and the humidity. "Look, truce?" he said.

She took the newspaper from his hand and started fanning him. "I'm sorry, darling. I really am. You're right about this weather. Truce."

He pushed himself up and caressed her hair. "I'd almost forgotten how lovely you are. Now, now, don't look at me that way. I said 'almost.'" But then he noticed an envelope slipped partly under their hotel room door in a ray of dusty sunlight. Someone, fearing discovery, had quickly left it and fled. He sprang to the door and yanked it open. The corridor was empty. But he caught a man in sandals hurriedly clop down the flight of stairs off to his left. "Hey you!" Yet he had no desire to chase him in his underwear.

"What is it, Jonas?"

"I haven't the foggiest." The front of the envelope was a dirty nondescript white. Nothing revealing showed on the back. When he pinched out the content, he saw it was only two sentences. They were typed, not written, to keep the sender's identify hidden. On an American or a British typewriter? Impossible to tell, he decided. But the machine was evidently quite old. Desert dirt from some gummy keys had clotted the *a's,* the capital *A,* the *w,* and the *0.* Yet the message was still clear: "Café Tel. 16:30. Today, Tuesday. Just the two of you. Asher."

Chapter 14

"Some guy named Asher wants to meet us at a café today. The Café Tel. Here." He handed the message to Charly and checked his wristwatch. Only a few hours away. The meeting sounded urgent, but why and with whom? Word they looked for a Warsaw ghetto survivor must have spread from the crowded cafés, the packed bazaars, or the many kiosks. "Someone's sniffing around for us for some reason. I don't like it."

"Why, trouble?"

"Could be. This Asher used military time for this 4:30 p. m. rendezvous. He's probably connected to an underground cell. It could get hairy. You want to go?"

She smacked him playfully on his shoulder with the anonymous letter. "Of course I want to, silly."

"Just checking, that's all."

"I'm a reporter, Jonas. What am I supposed to do? Hide under some bed while you go out to who knows what? There might be a story there. A big one. I feel perfectly safe with you, dear."

He felt again the weight protecting her, a beautiful problem. Her courage amazed him more. But sometimes her recklessness infuriated him. He pointed his Colt away from her on their bed toward their window. He released the magazine, checked it, it did contain eight rounds. He pushed it firmly back into the base of his 1911. Don't jam, he thought, slipping it back into his shoulder holster, regretting he hadn't brought his ankle one.

That was that. But what the hell was this Café Tel and what was its address? He caught Hans Peters as he greeted arriving guests with flowers at the bottom of the steps to the narrow street.

"The Café Tel, Mr. Shaw? Well, yes. I've heard of it. It's in the south of Tel Aviv. What is your reason for going there, if I may ask?"

"On business."

"On business, there? If it were me, I would definitely go elsewhere."

"You would?"

"Absolutely, without a second thought. The clientele is not, how can I put it, the kind we would welcome here. No respectable hotel would. It's a rough and dangerous crowd. A stabbing and several shootings in the last week alone. Rumors too of arms and human smuggling from Syria and Lebanon. Also of hashish dealers. Tel Aviv has a number of better ones to choose from. It's almost like being back in Paris, Berlin, or Vienna, there are so many. You could try the Café Lorenz. Or the Café Tarshish for that matter. If you play chess, there's the Ditza. There are also several on King George V Street."

"Don't forget the Café Ravel," Abdul said, struggling past with heavy valises under each arm.

"I would be more than happy to write down their addresses, if you wish."

"I'm afraid, Mr. Peters, my client insists on that café."

"I question your client's judgment. But very well, your decision. I shall call a taxi. Please be very careful."

Hans Peters clasped Jonas's hand and held it a moment longer, smiling good will. He bowed slightly to Charly, a bit of Old-World courtesy in the bloody Middle East. He wished them a safe outing at the Café Tel. He reminded them the Berliner had a trip to Petra and a banquet of Druze cuisine coming up. He and his staff were available twenty-four hours a day to help, whatever their needs. Sundays included, he hollered as he watched them stroll toward the cabbie on the narrow side street.

Passing by Reception, he glanced at their signatures in the registration book.

That Athens shipping tycoon, that Milanese banker, that Geneva diplomat, and the others had never complained about the Berliner. Not once! Most had marveled at the Middle East dishes served, the hotel tours to religious and archeological sites, the cafés recommended. A few had seemed suspect, he had to admit. That gentleman from Beirut especially. Judging by his bodyguards, perhaps a gun runner to the highest bidder, Jew or Arab. He had caused sleepless nights and loss of appetite, that itch like in the old...well, best not to think about that, he decided. Best to keep his thoughts to the present.

And the last two? Just another challenge. Just like all the others. He was good at what he did. Better than most, actually. "Abdul," he called out. "Our guests in Room 425, the Shaws. See they get whatever they need during their stay."

Chapter 15

Their driver, his undershirt darkened from sweat, leaned against his bone shaker of a cab, reading a newspaper. A large map of Central Europe showed on the front page. Above it a huge headline in Hebrew, all in capitals. Jonas could still tell the lead article concerned more death camps discovered in Poland. The taxi itself was so dusty he thought it held half the Negev Desert, but the interior of taped-up Naugahyde seats looked clean enough.

Their driver stuffed the paper into a pant pocket and plucked a toothpick from his mouth. "Where you want to go? I make for you a special."

"Here, to this address."

Their cabbie looked at the scrape of hotel stationery with the café's address, then at him, eyes wide, incredulous. "You want for me to take you there? In south Tel Aviv? Not the best part of town. Even in daylight like this. Look, mister, I have family to think of. I drop you a block away, and you go on your own."

They were running late. Jonas didn't feel like arguing. "Fine. Drop us off, and we'll walk."

Their cabbie set off south on Rothschild Boulevard. "You American people?" he asked over his shoulder. "I like America," he continued, as though Jonas's accent had already convinced him. "Good people. Someday, God willing, I visit family in Brooklyn."

Their gabby driver, Jonas discovered, was one of those who spilled his life story in minutes. Like other Tel Aviv immigrants he had chatted with, he discovered it wasn't a pretty history. Their driver had grown up in Munich. His parents, fearing Hitler, had paid passage for him on a ship that sailed out of Genoa. He hadn't heard a word from them since. Glancing in his rear-view mirror, he said he feared the worst. His only recollection of his hometown was all its newspapers showed caricatures of Jews with big noses. "Some memory, huh? The only one I know like that is your Mr. Big Schnozzola himself."

"Ah yes, Jimmy Durante," Jonas said. "A family favorite. What an act. And he's Catholic."

"Roman Catholic," Charly added. "With a capital *R* and capital *C*."

"When I flee to Tel Aviv in 1937," their driver continued, "46,000 lives here. Today, a miracle. Over three times that. Maybe four times, who knows; it grows so quickly. Building, building, always building everywhere. And everyone hurries, hurries. Like in Berlin, you know? And the traffic, my God." He blasted his horn and shook his fist at the driver who had cut in front. "*Dummkopf!*" he shouted out his cab window. Then back to them. "The traffic here, terrible. Almost as bad as Potsdamer Platz before that *schmuck* Hitler destroyed Berlin."

A bulldozer lurched in front of them and trudged along on the tree-lined avenue. That brought another angry blast of the horn from the driver. "Hey, *schmo,* move it!" Drivers behind also hooted out impatience in long blasts.

"Do some other kind of work." Jonas glanced at Charly. With her reporter's talent for details, she jotted down the local color in her notebook, the cafés, the art galleries, the shoppers, the newspaper kiosks.

"I am." The bulldozer driver swung off the street onto a massive construction site, but not before the cabbie let loose with another shouting curse. "You *putz!*" Then to Jonas. "An architect is what I study for. They've invented a new style here. Bauhaus. All up and down this Rothschild Boulevard." He twisted around to them. "Hear of it? Beautiful. Is good for surviving our hot summers."

A motorcyclist shot ahead, weaving in and out carefree to some destination. Rothschild Boulevard and the shade from its fictus trees, Jonas thought. The optimism of the city's founders showed in the broad thoroughfare. Laid out when there was nothing nearby except orange groves, sand dunes, and more sand dunes. He patted his forehead with his handkerchief; the day was heating up. "Here! Here! Stop here," he said, catching himself daydreaming, nearly missing the street sign, their driver, too engrossed chatting to notice.

"My card. You want tour of ancient Roman port city Caesarea, Mr. American? Much history there. Amphitheater. Aqueduct. Hippodrome. Much, much more. Let me know. You ask for Elie at this café, the Nitza. I make for you a special good price."

"I'll keep that in mind, Elie." A hot breeze, heavy with the smell of exotic spices, hit them as they got out. Jonas undid the top button to his cotton shirt to cool off. Off to their left, a fruit stand displayed apples and oranges in crates. Huge slices of watermelon, wrapped in cellophane, were also set out. Nothing threatening there, he decided. Next door at a barber shop, a grandmother held open a gunny sack, while a teenage girl in pigtails and shorts shoveled in dirt. Nothing threatening there either. Just another sandbag filled for the coming war.

A half block from their rendezvous, he stopped abruptly. Their last chance to turn back. Someone might be setting them up. To kill. To kidnap. For whatever reason, they might wait for them in the smoky noisy dimness beyond. He checked his Colt 1911; it was fully loaded. He looked sideways at Charly. She had money and class and sexiness written all over her face. A tempting target for whatever reason. "If I say we get out, we get out. No questions asked. Okay?"

Charly nodded. "No questions asked."

He grabbed her by the arm as she shifted toward the café, unsure if she fully understood the possible danger. "Wait. I know how you love to get a story, Charly. Regardless of the risk. But not here. Here is different. Here, no questions asked."

"You say we go, we go."

His pulse quickened. He moved ahead of her to the Café Tel, left hand inches from his shoulder holster.

Chapter 16

From the doorway of a family grocery, Oliver Porter watched the American couple enter the Café Tel. The traffic along Boulevard Rothchild and farther south was bloody awful that Tuesday afternoon. He'd been lucky to follow them from their hotel. Luckier to find parking close by and track them on foot through the narrow back streets clotted with civilians and soldiers.

He didn't mind sniffing around. A family-and-work friend was a family-and-work friend. Quietly checking from his Palestinian outpost a shocking Whitehall whisper Father Karl had overheard. About monstrous treachery. About monstrous crimes. Once an agent, always an agent, Karl had said. Even if retired. As if working all those years in secret in Athens, Nairobi, and Berlin made them blood brothers for life. Thick as thieves. Or as spies, he thought, briefly smiling.

Still...so what if Karl's Croydon Airport source had spotted that famous reporter Charly Lawrence and Jonas Shaw on that Tel Aviv passenger manifest? Maybe her flying in gave truth to a filthy rat among others in the Holy Land. Maybe for another reason. So far for the time spent, he could only report them changing hotels for whatever purpose. If dear old Karl wanted any intel for his off-the-books dossier, fine. No problem. But friendship didn't pay the bills, and he had a pile of them running his import/export business. He could spend just so much time rumor chasing, however sickening that tale.

An old beggar, reeking of cheap souk tobacco, shuffled up to him. Several tawdry trinkets jangled from his wrinkled neck. Some authentic wood from Christ's tomb at the Church of the Holy Sepulchre? Good price.

Oliver Porter flicked him away with some choice Hebrew. The stink of the beggar remained in the midday heat. The Tel, one of the worst Tel Aviv cafés around. Dirty. Bad food. Overpriced. Dangerous with arms smugglers and drug dealers. He wouldn't go in himself. Not even with an armed escort. No matter what that German colonist had said about their beer and loose women. But that American couple had. It must be for something important. He snapped open the *Palestine Post* and pretended to read, while he waited for them.

Chapter 17

At the café's threshold, Jonas noticed the conversation suddenly stopped. All the patrons shifted to them, intruders into their territory. Charly slipped a hand into his and moved a step closer. A bearded Palestinian, sitting alone in a nearby corner, swatted away flies as he eyed them suspiciously. Then he returned to smoking a hubbly bubbly pipe. The conversations of others resumed, a babble of German, French, snatches of Italian, Hebrew, some Yiddish. On a narrow stage to their right, a gramophone played a staticky tango. A miasma of cigarette and cigar smoke swirled and eddied from a lone ceiling fan that creaked as it slowly revolved in the heat.

Even back in New York, he thought, he hadn't felt that threatened. Except for that Mafia shootout in Bedford-Stuyvesant. He gestured to a small table against the wall farther back. "Over there, okay?" It offered a clear view of everyone. "And remember what I said. I say we get out, we get out." A waiter, in a white knee-length apron like he had seen Berlin servers wear, approached. "May I suggest the house specialty, our Arabic coffee?"

Jonas shrugged; coffee was coffee.

"Arabic coffee's fine," Charly said.

On a nearby table, Jonas spotted the headline of a left-behind *Herald Tribune,* European edition. A Saudi Arabian king promised to wipe any Jewish country in Palestine off the map. In the secondary headline below, an Iraqi general boasted to fill the Mediterranean end-to-end with Jewish blood. Fuckin' cowards, he thought. He wondered if he should try to pull Charly out of Palestine, yet knew the damn reckless woman would refuse. She was too much like him. She feared yet loved danger.

Their waiter returned. He settled their brightly ornate, handle-less cups in front of them as well as a plate of dates and sweet cakes. Jonas took a sip, scrunched up his face in distaste, and put his cup loudly down in the little saucer. "Christ!"

Two men at a table ahead jerked their unshaved heads around in their direction. They stared for several seconds before returning to their hushed conversation.

"What?" Charly said.

"That stuff I just drank. The stuff that's supposed to be coffee. Terrible, unless you like carbolic acid."

"Great neighborhood."

"The best." He chewed several dates, their sweetness lessening the coffee's bitterness. "You get the feeling we're being watched?"

Charly wiped some crumbs off her mouth and nodded slightly. "Do I ever. Definitely. From the moment we walked in."

Especially at you, he thought.

"We got American written all over us," she added.

Jonas glanced at his wristwatch, 4:39, then looked around as if checking for the toilette. "I don't like it, Charly. Not one bit. I didn't think it'd be this bad. You're right, we stick out like a sore thumb. We wait just a few more minutes. This Asher guy doesn't show, we head over to the Café Roma for some pastries. Mr. Peters recommended it." They watched a couple near the stage. The woman kicked up a leg to the Argentine music, while he nervously drummed his fingers on the tabletop. 4:52. He lit up a Camel, took a puff, passed it to Charly, who put it to her mouth. "I think it's time we—"

"You are the one who seeks?"

Charly jumped, dropping her cigarette to the floor. A tall man, his arms and legs thin as stilts and looking extremely pale, had approached to their right and from behind. Jonas also jumped, fearing ambush. He reached for his gun as he shifted in that direction, then paused. Despite the dim lighting, he could see the red-veined eyes of a world-tired old young man who stood over them. European appearing, he looked like he worried a lot. From his pasty appearance, he seemed to spend too much time indoors, and slept little. Maybe with his own gun under his pillow, if he could afford a pistol.

"What?" Charly glanced up at him.

"The one who seeks, you are her? Please, may I?" Without waiting for a response, he scraped back a wicker chair and settled in across from them.

"Seeks who?"

"The woman who fled. Leah."

"From Poland?" Jonas asked. Still no apology for being late or why.

"From Warsaw, yes. Her."

So that was her first name, Leah. The youth's breath, Jonas noticed, smelled of onions and hummus. "We're looking for this woman."

Charly pushed across the color photo Maurice Rumbold had given. She thumped it with a finger. "This woman. And you are?"

Jonas kept his eyes on the man's hands, worried he could be armed. "Asher."

"Asher what?" Charly asked.

"Just Asher." The patrons seemed too engrossed in their affairs to notice him. Still he glanced quickly around, looking nervous over some possible trouble. Then he offered a slight nod of recognition toward the photograph. "We go."

"Wait. Go where?"

Asher leaned into them, the first time of any intimacy. "There has been a change of plans. It is not safe here," he whispered.

Jonas now noticed beads of sweat on the youth's furrowed forehead. Sweaty patches under the arms of his short-sleeve khaki shirt, too. Signs of fear. "You expect us just to get up and follow you out?"

But Asher didn't appear interested in what Jonas thought. He shifted toward the café's side door off to their left that led to a narrow street. He had a feral animal's edginess over something.

"She's not here?"

"Here?" Asher glanced at Charly. "No. Here is not safe."

"What do you mean?"

"Not here, please. The British...it is not far, this place, and I explain." He rose abruptly and headed toward the side doorway.

Jonas with Charly at his side followed into the white humid heat of the Palestinian afternoon.

Chapter 18

They had walked only a block when Jonas heard whistles, sirens, and shouts behind them. British soldiers, some with German Shepherds, others with mine detectors, had jumped out of Jeeps and armored personnel carriers and burst into the Café Tel. "Who are they looking for Asher? You? Leah? Someone else?" But the man who called himself Asher said nothing, only took long, purposeful strides.

"Asher, what are they looking for?"

They passed a British soldier searching through an elderly woman's purse. Asher still ignored Jonas. He now seemed in a hurry to get to his destination. Every so often, he looked back to see if anyone followed. As he did so, part of his jacket flapped open. A gun showed, Jonas noticed, shoved into his waistband. Maybe an old British Webley revolver.

"How much Hebrew you know?" he whispered to Charly, who hurried beside him.

"Besides *gesundheit*, I know—"

"That's Yiddish, isn't it?"

"Just one word then, *shalom*. About as much as you, dear."

But Jonas doubted Asher or his friends were interested in peace. A black-veiled woman, head averted, hurried past, scolding her brood of dirty children to follow.

Further on, an Arab in his headdress glanced up at them, then quickly returned to his potter's wheel. Jonas picked up the spicy smells of cumin and cardamom before a hot breeze wafted the scents away; someone must be cooking.

"You must keep up with me. You have a camera, Charly Lawrence?"

"Of course. I'm a reporter."

"I insist no photos. None. Not even one. You understand?" He threw her a warning glance. "If you take, you might harm our safety, and I cannot guarantee what will happen to you and your Mr. Shaw."

"Okay, no photos. How much further?"

"It is not far."

"You keep saying that."

Asher ignored her comment. He just kept taking his long, purposeful strides deeper into south Tel Aviv. This wasn't like the northern part with handsome modern homes and well-laid-out streets, Jonas noticed. This area was poor, littered with warehouses, auto repair shops, junk yards, and hole-in-the-wall sewing and upholstery stores. There were few shade trees to protect from the merciless sun. A bouncy melody from a mandolin floated out some open window as counterpoint to the desolation. Jonas slipped on his dark glasses; Charly, too, and also handed him a tube of skin protection lotion.

They entered single file a narrow alleyway, hemmed in by walls, the masonry cracked, almost two stories high. Charly walked behind Asher, and Jonas behind her. She appeared calm, but he knew she must be like him, worried. Further back, he spotted two men, both slightly built like Asher, who had materialized at the far end of the dim passage's gloom. Both wore yarmulkas. "Do not worry," he heard Asher say. "They are ours." Ours? But he knew better than to ask their organization; in the secretive ways of Palestine, he was learning, their escort most likely wouldn't answer.

"Hot today," Asher said over his shoulder.

"One hundred degrees Fahrenheit, I heard," Jonas said to be civil. "Another scorcher."

"You want water?"

Jonas held up his canteen. The metal had grown warm from the heat, he noticed. "We brought our own."

They proceeded through a labyrinth of more passages with debris, left, right, left once more into a shantytown of corrugated huts packed together. Pigeons, frightened from their hurried approach, exploded toward the rectangle of blue sky high above. Off to his left, a Doberman strained at a chain, its ears pricked up as they passed. Here and there, the cobbled path buckled, and scraggly weeds protruded through wide cracks. Jonas understood why Asher hadn't blindfolded him and Charly for their secret meeting. Asher and his gang had purposely disoriented them, going in circles in a part of the city few foreigners dared visit.

At last, they reached an open doorway halfway down a block of three-and-four-story apartments with balconies. Jonas glanced up, didn't spot any street name anywhere or a number above the entrance of peeling masonry. On the second story and above, laundry, flapping in the hot breeze, hung out from windows, some with broken panes, to dry. Asher trotted back to the two men, said something in Hebrew, something about Mizrachi Bet Street or was it Mizrachi Bet Avenue? He wasn't sure. It meant nothing to him, but then Asher returned. "You are armed, Mr. Shaw?"

It was a rhetorical question, Jonas knew as he handed over his Colt with a reluctant sigh. Everyone in Palestine, it seemed, was.

The two guards stationed themselves in front of the entrance. "We'll give it back later," Asher said over his shoulder as he led the way up the stairs, their hurried steps sounding rough on the raw cement.

The third floor, empty except for the buzz of flies swarming over a pile of trash and a wild cat. A baby stroller next to the nearest doorway the only sign anyone lived in any of the rooms. Asher proceeded to the third door down from the stairs, knocked twice. The door eased open cautiously, just enough for him to mutter a name, "Leah," then something more through the crack in—Hebrew? Yiddish? Polish?—Jonas wasn't sure.

"Quickly, inside. And remove your dark glasses." He pushed Charly roughly by her back, then Jonas, surprised by his strength, into the little apartment.

Chapter 19

And there she was. She stood at the far end of the room ahead in a floral blouse, baggy pants, her physical features as Johnny Radcliffe had described. Her blonde hair a tangled mess, as if she hadn't combed it in days. Every detail as described except for the eyes. The journalist's newspaper photo hadn't captured their burning intensity. Jonas doubted nothing could; the photographer or artist would have had to share her hell in the slaughter pit of the Warshaw ghetto to achieve that.

In a room behind her, an uneven line of students watched an instructor. Christ, Jonas thought. Some looked not over fifteen; others, well over sixty. In front of them, a middle-aged woman jammed a palm under her male partner's fleshy chin, while she jabbed a stick-as-a-knife into his ample stomach. The man staggered back, complained his Sarah had done the palm strike too hard. The self-defense instructor said hardening up was for his own good. "A punch to the throat. An eye gouge. A kick to the groin. Whatever helps fight the British or Arab terrorists, Samuel."

Asher eased himself down onto the cement floor and sat cross-legged, gazing up at her. He looked like an acolyte, Jonas thought, deferring to Leah. Having escaped that Warsaw ghetto massacre and making her way to Palestine must have given her an almost mythic presence, even among tough Palestinian Jewish fighters. Maybe on her way, the two had met at a displaced persons camp on Cyprus Island.

"What I should do for you?" Leah asked, as blunt as the direct, unflinching gaze of her eyes on them.

Cigarette butts around her mud-caked leather sandals littered the cement floor, Jonas noticed. On a sleeping bag nearby lay a box of cigarettes with a Turkish brand on the front. Next to that, a canteen, a Bible, and an unopened tin with BRITISH ARMY RATION PACK printed on the top lid. Otherwise, the square room, built of concrete blocks, was anonymous. One of many in one of many run-down buildings in south Tel Aviv.

Charly said she was a reporter for the *London Daily News,* one of the largest circulation newspapers in Britain. "Here are some articles I've written." She reached into her shoulder bag for several back issues of the newspaper and held them out for Leah to examine.

Leah glanced at them coldly, briefly, then exhaled another funnel of smoke toward the ceiling. "So?"

"Well, maybe another time." Charly started to stuff them back into her shoulder bag.

"No, wait!" Leah said, barking out her order. "Give them to Asher. He reads English better than me."

"Some of the articles cover the Italian resistance in the last war. A few others about reporting from Berlin afterwards. That was last year." She introduced Jonas and said he had done very important work for Winston Churchill during the last war. The *London Daily News* publisher had asked to seek her out in Tel Aviv, get her story about fighting in the Warsaw ghetto. That might increase support for a Jewish state.

For all that, Leah still looked unmoved. She lit another foul-smelling cigarette and tossed the match indifferently aside. Then resting the elbow of her smoking hand in her left palm, she coolly appraised them through a haze of smoke. "Who is, please, this Mr. Rumbold you speak of?"

"A wealthy Londoner and newspaper publisher. He wants to help Palestinian Jews start their own country."

"Wants to help?" She grunted contempt, as though she had heard that too many times. "Asher, another nice person wants to help. An Englishman. Where have we heard that before?"

Asher laughed. "How kind of him. We've had so many in our long history."

"This rich Englishman wants news of us to print? There hasn't been enough already? Auschwitz, Dachau, Treblinka, Sobibor aren't enough news for this nice Englishman? Words, that's all you journalists have. Words." Another shake of the head; more contempt. "This,"—she said, brandishing a German Luger from her back—"this is the only language people understand. Certainly, Germans, many British. And most Arabs."

Her English was surprisingly good, Jonas realized, relieved she hadn't used Hebrew. So was Asher's. A survival language maybe picked up from the Brit forces in Palestine to understand and outwit them. That Warsaw ghetto battle had toughened her well beyond her years, he also noticed. Eighteen or nineteen or whatever, going on thirty-five or so. And it wasn't going well either. "Do you have any questions for us? Anything to set your mind at ease about who we are?"

"Wants to help?" Leah repeated. "Really, Mr. Shaw. We Jews have been waiting for help for hundreds of years. Even before Hitler slaughtered millions of us, we waited. We waited in Odessa, you know that? In Vilnius, too. We even waited in so-called enlightened capitals. Paris. Vienna. Berlin. And what did we get for all our waiting and waiting? Russian pogroms with thousands murdered and government edicts from democracies like your Britain and your France telling us we could not do medicine, we could not do the law, we could not do this and that. After hundreds of years, Mr. Shaw, we have learned not to wait any longer for so-called help. A thousand years of history tells us this waiting is not so good for our health, you know? We have learned to rely on ourselves. Only ourselves, that is what we have learned. So please, take your help back to this nice Mr. Rumbold man." She tossed her half-smoked cigarette down to the muddy floor in contempt. "Tell him we don't need any more kind offers of help from him or from anyone."

She winced, Jonas noticed, and paused to massage her right thigh. Maybe Mr. Rumbold was right. Maybe she did limp from a war wound.

"Wait, please. Listen to us. This time is different," Charly said.

"Oh, this time is different," Leah said, her tone mocking. "My, my, my. Such news, Asher." She stuck another cigarette between her chapped lips, appearing more concerned about patting her pants for a match than Charly's response. "You are millions too late with your help, Miss Charly Lawrence."

"But what about the living?"

"What about them?"

"Your story might help give them sanctuary. Here in Palestine. Their own country."

"It might give them hope," Jonas added.

Asher suddenly uncurled his legs. As if attuned to some danger, he sprang to his feet.

"What is it, Asher?" Leah asked.

But Asher didn't answer. Cat-quick, he was at one of the heavily draped ribbon slit windows before Jonas realized what had happened. Leah paused lighting up again, the lit match an inch from her cigarette, and fixed on him; Charly seemed puzzled at Asher's change of behavior. He no longer appeared sure of himself. A look Jonas had seen too often crossed Asher's face, a look of someone alert to some terror. He peeked out, then was at the door, ear pressed to it, listening. "We're fine," he finally said to Leah. She finished lighting up and tossed her match carelessly aside. "Yes," Asher said, continuing the conversation, "here in Palestine, no longer at the mercy of others." He whispered something into Leah's ear while she stared, still unmoved, at them.

"Asher is impressed with your articles, Miss Charly Lawrence. He says you're very brave and fair-minded. He also says we can't offer coffee, tea, or sweetcakes. But we would be rude if we didn't show some hospitality. I give you something for coming here. You want my story? Fine, a little bit of it anyway. An important part. The Warsaw ghetto uprising part."

Chapter 20

"I was one of several hundred fighters there in the ghetto. Many of us have no use for rabbis, writers, philosophers. For these *thinkers*. We believe we have as much right to live as anyone else. And—here is the difference from those *brilliant thinkers*—we would die fighting for that belief rather than go pray and then go quietly to our graves, to our slaughter.

"Like you Americans, Miss Lawrence, Mr. Shaw, and your own revolution. You know? Your American one. Fighting for your own country. Except for one big difference"—she gestured with her cigarette at them—"we know what will happen if we let ourselves be arrested." She drew a finger slowly, dramatically, across her throat. "That. Just like everyone else, that. Including our babies and our old. That.

"So we fight. Six hundred, seven hundred of us beginning soldiers. Who knows how many against the criminal Nazi gangs? But thousands of them. With a few pistols and rifles smuggled into the ghetto, we fight. With our own weapons we make, we fight. Sometimes hand-to-hand, we fight. From bunker to bunker. With almost no water. Little food. Eating mostly dry, hard bread. For almost one month, that. Only us. For nearly one month. Abandoned by everyone else. Words of support, yes. But almost no arms. Having only us. Against the great SS commander Jürgen Stroop. Against his tanks. Against his artillery. Against the mighty German army. For one month, we fighting Jews, we fight.

"Of course, they win in the end. We understand that at the beginning, what our fate might be. Death. But we take our fate into our own hands. Not let them. Afterwards, they deport thousands of survivors for the killing. I escape because two good Catholic Poles hide me. I was lucky."

"Wait." Charly rested her pen on her notebook. "Why lucky?"

"Yes, Miss Lawrence, lucky. Look at me. Blonde hair. Blue eyes. A nice Polish, Catholic peasant girl, you know? And I go to a nice public Warsaw school, not religious one, so speak with no accent. Like a Pole. Who would suspect?"

"Did these friends know you weren't?"

"Of course. Both the priest and the nun know. They know I came from good family. I sneak through ghetto cellars. Creep across roofs. I find manhole that good priest and nun know. Next through sewers—I never know until then how many Warsaw has, miles of them. Climb over ghetto wall. I hide in a bunker, under gravestones in Jewish cemetery on Okopowa Street I had heard about. Can hold only four people. But I also heard nine hid there. Nine! Like fish in a can they are. They had moved on, and it was only me. From there, I escape Warsaw. But I am caught and sent to Majdanek death camp."

"M-a-j-d-a-n-i-k?" Charly asked.

Leah nodded. "M-a-j-d-a-n-*e*-k. With an *e*. A death camp for thousands."

"Outside the city of Lubin. Lubin, Poland," Asher said.

"I escape Majdanek death camp and make contact with Jewish partisans in the forest. Cross Tatra Mountains to Budapest and Palestine Bureau helps with false papers to come here."

"And fight some more."

Leah picked some tobacco from her tongue. "Asher is right. I would like to live like other Jews here. Buy land from Arabs, plant seeds, cultivate, and build. Have normal life. But for now, fight some more."

Charly paused in her notetaking. "Even against the British?"

"Especially them. Despite their arms embargo. Why not?"

"Against the mighty British Empire?" Jonas raised a brow at Charly. Was that possible to fight them?

"Of course," Leah answered as if their underdog status didn't faze her at all.

"Do you hate them?" Charly asked. "The British, I mean."

"I read Shakespeare. Also some Dickens. Asher, too. Especially the battles. I don't understand a lot. But I learn the Englishman is not so perfect. But hate the British people? Do we hate the British, Asher?"

Asher glanced from peeking out the window over to her. "Depends."

"Many in British intelligence we call the Good Englishman. This Good Englishman understands the value of our intelligence against the Germans and Italian military we gave in the last war. But we hate the British Foreign Office—especially their Colonial Office—for their policies against us. We call them the Bad Englishman. We want their soldiers gone. Out of Palestine. All of them. Back home. Forever. So we can have our own. Everyone has a home, Miss Lawrence. Why can't we?"

"We have nowhere else to go," Asher added.

Charly looked up from her notetaking again. "Not even back to Europe?"

"Back to Europe? You think that is such a nice place for us? Where the Nazis and their helpers, the Poles, the French, the Dutch, and others murdered our families and friends? Where our fathers, our mothers were hung by meat hooks in slaughterhouses? You want us should go back there? To what, I ask you?" Leah curled her lips in contempt at the idea and tossed Asher her box of matches.

Asher took one of her Turkish cigarettes from the box that lay on top of her sleeping bag and slipped it into his mouth. "Europe is nothing but a coffin." He lit up and exhaled. "Poles, Germans, and others, they are all unhappy their hero Hitler didn't kill all of us. They want to finish the job. Murder even concentration camp survivors."

"Asher is right. We have nowhere else to go. Your noble America puts quotas on us entering, Miss Lawrence, Mr. Shaw. We are filth to them. The British put quotas on us, too. They blockade us from immigrating here. A country isn't given to a people willingly. We will have to fight for our right to exist in our ancestral home. Against the British colonial power. Against Arab guerrillas. Soon against Arab armies. Even against the few Germans who help the British. To determine our own fate." She tossed down onto the filthy floor still another cigarette. "There, my story. You have it. Now go print it."

Even against the few Germans who help the British? Did Leah understand what she had just said? Jonas glanced over to Charly, but she was furiously taking notes. She must have heard every single shocking word Leah had uttered.

Charly flipped to still another page. "Could we have a follow-up interview?"

Jonas smiled at her. Good for you, Charly. You did catch it. Maybe we'll get an explanation for Leah's German comment.

"I must think about that, Miss Lawrence. Asher will contact you."

She didn't say how or when, but Jonas didn't doubt the worldly woman would. He noticed she tossed down onto the floor still another Turkish cigarette. Her tenth one smoked and Asher's eighth. His impression of her matched his first. She appeared frightened or uneasy about something. They both did. About something.

Chapter 21

Tuesday in that same grim industrial south at that same time.

An alarm clock frightened awake a youth who, when with certain others, called himself Daniel. Ignoring the clanging, he lay in his lumpy bunk bed staring at the cobwebbed ceiling, sweating fear. Jewish intelligence had found him out. They would drag him, hooded, to a blood-stained interrogation cell in some Mount Carmel cave. They would club the truth out of him, whom he worked for, what secrets he had passed, how long he had betrayed them. And afterward, dump his body in some isolated Mediterranean coast cove in a pile of bat shit.

But they couldn't possibly have discovered his true role, he thought as he silenced the clanging. He was good at what he did. Hadn't the One From Beyond said he spoke Hebrew like it was his mother tongue? With his dark features, couldn't he pass for a persecuted Jew, who had fled to Palestine from Tunisia or Yemen or Iraq or Morocco? And as a native Palestinian, couldn't he, if Jewish security stopped him, easily rattle off whatever they asked about Tel Aviv? The butcher shops that sold the best spices. The location of that telephone exchange on Koresh Street. That travel agency near Jabotinsky Street. The vegetable stands with the tastiest melons and oranges. The Café Levant on Allenby Street where writers and poets gathered. Or the Café Fez on HaYarkon Street where dock workers gathered. He knew the city for what it was, his home.

But those gangster Jews weren't his people. They never would be. His imam preached they were all rich and ran America's banks, newspapers, and the movies. Brothers Akeem and Jabir said the same. Why their militias had so few bullets for target practice in the coming war still puzzled him. Probably to make his own Arab brothers think they were poorly equipped. Like some of their soldiers whining they didn't get paid or had no bus fare to their training camps or stole chickens and sheep to eat. All lies to trick.

Funny, though they had met several times, he couldn't recall the One From Beyond's name. He was so nervous meeting him the first time, he must have blanked it out. And too embarrassed to ask from then on. The One From Beyond had praised him about the open drawer memory test. Only seconds to get everything right. But he had! Still, Daniel found something cold about him. The One From Beyond, however, understood the Jew devil, even though he wasn't Palestinian. Or from anywhere near Palestine or Egypt or Syria. But he was an old man. Maybe thirty-five. Maybe forty or fifty. Probably experienced dealing with those criminals.

He caught himself fingering imaginary prayer beads and stopped. One slip, he reminded himself, would reveal he wasn't Jewish. Then not even his kind face, his pleasant smile, and gentle manners would save him.

He yanked some rope attached to a ladder and pulled it over to him. He swung his legs over onto the first rung and climbed down slowly to the dirty linoleum floor. Omar's bunk bed was still empty. His barely touched plate of hummus and beans and pita on his thin blanket. An empty, crumpled packet of Dubek cigarettes beside it. Next to it, a wrinkled towel. A sweat-stained shirt in a hanger dangled from the upper railing of his own bunk bed.

The previous evening, Omar had staggered to the Government Hospital in Jaffa with stomach pains. Thanks be to Allah, that old card shark must still be there, the other bunk beds remained empty, and he had the tiny immigrant worker's hostel room to himself. No need to worry mumbling secrets in Arabic in his sleep then. Still, the walls of the two-story shack were thin. Some neighbor might overhear him and sell him to the evil Zionist infidels.

He padded barefoot over to his shorts, which were slung over the sole wooden chair in the room. He felt the khaki material; it was dry enough. He slipped one foot, then the other through, zipped up, finished dressing.

He didn't have much to report to the One From Beyond. Only a rumor backgammon players had mentioned while he mopped the floor in that Jaffa card room. A boatload of 5,000 or so Jewish immigrants might arrive at some date off the Palestinian coast. Maybe north of Haifa. At the Jewish fighters' intelligence briefing at the Jerusalem Café later that day, he might pick up more. Then pass it on to the One From Beyond. With Allah's blessing, those British would sink it.

Chapter 22

"Any messages for me, Charly Lawrence? L-a-w-r-e-n-c-e. Anything at all?"

"We're in room 425." Jonas pushed aside on the Reception's ledge a vase of white orchids with an overpowering scent.

The veiled front desk clerk quit cooling herself with a hand fan as she read her Koran. She pointed toward *425* in gold in the wooden pigeon-hole message box behind her. It was empty. "We would be most happy to notify you if any arrive."

Letters displaying postmarked stamps of the United States; Argentina; Italy, maybe for refugees, he thought; Germany, for refugees definitely, showed in the many slots. "Please do. It's important. Whatever comes in."

"Very important," Charly added.

"I've made a note for the next shift. "

"And for Abdul. He's very reliable."

"And for Abdul, of course, madame. Any messages or mail for Room 425 to be delivered quickly."

"The police still haven't returned your phone calls?" Jonas whispered to Charly as they climbed the stairs. "Strange."

"They've had time to report something, anything, about Johnny Radcliffe's murder. Yet all I get is silence."

"Middle East inefficiency. The heat. Maybe tomorrow they'll call." Sweat running off his face, he checked his worn wallet as they reached the second floor and raised an eyebrow surprised. Only a few Palestinian pound notes left? Again? They'd have to cash more traveler's checks at the Ottoman Bank. He saw the look in her green eyes. Too concerned about money. Despite the wealth service to Churchill had brought. The poor boy still and always from that dingy five-story New York walk-up.

Charly searched in her shoulder bag for their room key. "You've had time to think it over on the ride back. And your verdict is?"

"The same."

"Because of those bodyguards?"

"Because of everything. Them. The precautions taken sneaking us to that Leah. Asher insisting no photos. Leah needing a hideout. How she and Asher acted. The tenseness on everyone's faces from the slightest sound outside. I know fear, Charly. Believe me. I saw lots of it back in New York. Leah and Asher are on the run. Maybe they all are."

"From whom?"

"From the British. From some rival political faction or militia. Who knows? But definitely on the run."

Housekeeping had placed a fresh bouquet of roses on the teak wood desk that overlooked the street. They had whipped off day-old sheets, smoothed out fresh ones. And put fresh towels and fresh bars of citrus soap in the little wicker basket in the bathroom. A fresh hotel room. "Hans Peters and his team are spoiling us rotten," she said, "with this royal treatment. Wish he could do something about this weather."

Jonas splashed cool water from the bathroom tap on his sweaty face and neck several times. "I feel like I'm on fire," he called out. He placed a towel soaked with cold tap water around her shoulders. "Better?"

She placed her fingertips on his and gazed up at him. "As long as you do it."

He flopped down onto their king-size bed, kicked off his shoes, and sighed.

"Tired?"

He reached for a hardback on the night table. "Those years in the ring have caught up with me. My feet are killing me. So's my back."

"Going hatless in this terrible heat didn't help, babe. I told you to wear one, but as usual, Mr. Tough Guy, you wouldn't listen. You look very dashing in a fedora, you know. Hint, hint. All those *New York Times* articles about you? And that high society columnist, a hint of danger with it on, as she put it. Hint, hint, hint. Jonas, are you listening? Jonas!"

"What?!"

"Will you put down that book and look at me."

"Okay, dear, done. Now what is it?"

"Can I be frank with you?"

Jonas laughed. "You're going to be frank no matter what I say. You know that."

Charly laughed, too. "That's true."

"Which is one reason why I love you. Let me guess. I should enjoy our wealth more? Quit complaining about that Churchill gift, that Rolls, as too showy? Get over my distaste of a steamer trunk as a sign of money and buy one?"

"No, dear, something else this time."

"How refreshing. Go on, get it over with. Be frank."

"You don't have to keep on proving you're tough. What you did during the war, spying in France for Churchill, it was just as dangerous as fighting on the front line."

"You don't quit, do you?"

"They don't call me The Bulldog for nothing."

"Ain't that the truth."

"That Churchill citation in that private ceremony still hasn't sunk in? 'For services rendered beyond the call of duty.' Ring a bell, just a little?"

"Vaguely." Jonas picked up his book. "Enough frankness for now. Some other time, dear."

"I've done my good deed for the year. No more lecturing. Promise."

"You promise, ha!"

"Last night, I dreamed I slept in a bathtub of ice. How's that for a change of subject?"

"Alone?"

"No, babe. With you. It's true, I did. What are you reading?"

"Something Mr. Peters recommended in the hotel library. *The History of Roman Palestine.*"

"Well, look at you. I remember when I had to drag you to museums. In its original Latin?"

"Very funny. It's really very interesting."

"I'll stick with Mr. Scott Fitzgerald."

He glanced up from the page. "Read the chapter on the siege of the ancient fortress of Masada." He held up the book, tapping on a map for her to see. "Here, that big red dot. Masada. On the eastern edge of the Judean Desert. Near the Dead Sea. A few hundred Jews against thousands of Roman soldiers under the generalship of Lucius Flavius Silva. Pages 150-200, if interested. Kind of like what's going on today. One moment. Hold it. Charly, stop! Don't!" He tossed the hardback aside, jumped out of bed, and grabbed the phone from her.

"What on earth are you doing, Jonas?"

He gestured to be quiet. He cupped one hand to his ear to block out any noise. Pressing the receiver close to his other ear, he listened for several seconds. At the same time, he peeked out their window. Across the street, many apartments were shuttered against the sun. On the third floor on the balcony of one apartment, a woman watered her roses, while a man in an undershirt cleaned his rifle. The other balconies were empty.

Then he studied the narrow little side street below, end to end. Only a couple on the other side cuddling on a bench, blocking out the impending war. The woman on the balcony now cleaned her own rifle, he noticed as he handed the phone back to her. "I don't think this line's tapped." Or anyone's watching. But he kept that to himself. He didn't want to unduly alarm her.

She placed a long-distance call to Maurice Rumbold's very public office on London's Fleet Street. When at last an hour later they got connected, his secretary twice hung up, and Charly loudly suspected the woman, loyal to a fault, feared she might be a Trojan Horse for a growing list of Threadneedle bank creditors. The third time, after an hour again waiting for the connection, Charly shouted over the protective assistant's shrieks she was on assignment for Mr. Rumbold. Yes, that's right, Charly Lawrence in Tel Aviv. Yes, *that* Charly Lawrence, and *that* Tel Aviv. The one in Palestine where all the trouble was she no doubt had seen on the cinema newsreels. You know, the car bombs and sniper fire between Jew and Arab, and turning to Jonas mouthed, *where there is going to be one fucking massacre of hundreds of thousands of Europe's castoffs and native Palestinian Jews,* and then calmed down and merely told her she absolutely had to reach Mr. Rumbold. But the secretary, Charly feared, might ring off still again, so she shouted, "Don't you dare hang up again, Hilda. You understand me? This is an emergency. Mr. Rumbold. Now!"

"Hello, hello, Mr. Rumbold. Can you hear me okay?"

"Yes, yes, fine, my dear. Very clearly."

"Same here, Mr. Rumbold. Loud and clear. It's almost as if you're in the hotel room with me. Mr. Rumbold, I'm afraid I've got bad news."

"One moment."

Without warning, he put his phone down and attended to some business she must have interrupted. "It's fine with me," she muttered. "You're paying for the call." A man with an Italian accent asked him to turn around to face the mirror and to stand up perfectly straight. Rumbold's Savile Row tailor must be measuring him in his very public Fleet Street office for his umpteenth suit.

"Now then, bad news, you say? A spot of street vendor food poisoning? You absolutely must watch what you eat there. Especially their lamb shish kebab."

"No sir, it's about Johnny Radcliffe. He's dead."

"Dead? Johnny Radcliffe? Good heavens! Tommy boy, Johnny Radcliffe's dead. From drink, my dear?"

"No sir. He was murdered. The Palestinian police are investigating."

"Murdered? Him? Johnny Radcliffe? Couldn't hurt a fly, that boy. Never had an enemy in his entire life. Not a one."

"He made at least one in Palestine."

"Apparently so. Spare me the details of his passing, my dear. I just had lunch at the club. Tommy boy, send flowers and a note of condolence to whomever. Carnations or whatever will do. They're on sale. From that flower stand girl downstairs. That spirited little smidgen who calls herself Cosette. Yes, that one. Sorry for the interruption. Johnny had his good points. I assume you've talked to the police?"

"I have, and they're tight-lipped...at least so far."

"Tight-lipped? Over him, Johnny? Strange."

"That's what Jonas said. Strange. They haven't even questioned us."

"Not even once," Jonas said.

"Not even once, Mr. Rumbold."

"It stinks like a Texas outhouse."

"Jonas says the death stinks like a Texas outhouse."

"All Johnny did was clip articles. Maybe the old boy did more than that and enjoy his drink. I want the bulldog in you, my dear, to keep on them."

"I already have, sir. Three times. At the Criminal Investigation Department headquarters in Jerusalem."

"And?"

"And nothing, I'm afraid. At least so far. Like I said. The CID seems to be holding back. Why, I don't know. Jonas suspects Johnny Radcliffe was onto something."

"And I still do."

"He says he still believes that. I'll keep trying. Maybe I'll have better luck at their branches in Tel Aviv and Jaffa."

"Use your famous Charly Lawrence womanly charm, my dear. It's worked wonders before."

"I'll do my best, Mr. Rumbold. Whatever it takes."

"That's my girl."

"There's something else. Jonas and I located that Warsaw ghetto survivor."

"Can you speak up? You faded out, I'm afraid."

"I said, Jonas and I located that Warsaw ghetto survivor. How's that?"

"Better. Splendid work, my dear. Splendid! Absolutely splendid! I knew when I put my number one reporter on the scent, you'd come through. How is she?"

"As well as you'd expect, considering."

"Considering yes, I can imagine."

"She appears much, much older than what she may actually be. She also acts years older, too. It's hard to believe she ever had a childhood."

"In that part of Europe with its unhinged cruelty, maybe she didn't."

Jonas momentarily put aside *The History of Roman Palestine*. "She may be in her twenties, but looks in her thirties. And acts it, too."

"Jonas says she looks and acts like someone in her thirties. I'll be filing my story on our meeting shortly. It'll have lots of quotes from her."

"I expect nothing less from you."

"But no photos, unfortunately."

"No?"

"For security reasons her bodyguard forbid it."

"Understood. Keeping track of your per diem expenses?"

"Absolutely. As always. You know me, Mr. Rumbold."

"With receipts?"

"As usual. Of course."

"Not writing a novel on the side, I hope."

"Shame on you for thinking that, Mr. Rumbold. I'm devoting one hundred percent of my time to reporting."

"Hells bells, Johnny Radcliffe dead. There's a page one story there. Those Palestinian Jews outnumbered two-to-one, according to short wave reports and my sources. You see, David versus Goliath. Sod 'em all, my dear."

"Sod'em all, Mr. Rumbold." But he had already hung up.

Chapter 23

"Well, that was rude of him. Hanging up abruptly like that. Thank you very much, Mr. Rumbold. Maybe I *will* write a novel. Maybe even a play. A murder mystery. To open in the West End. And continue indefinitely. The longest running play in Theatreland, Jonas. About a tyrannical, inconsiderate old boss who gets bumped off." Charly stared at the phone a moment longer as if she and her boss were face-to-face before she slammed down the receiver. "Fucking bastard!"

Jonas, still sprawled out on their bed, legs crossed at the ankles, put aside the hardback, chuckling. "I could hear every single word he said. Clear as a bell. And you counting to ten and still exploding."

"'That's my girl,' honestly, Jonas. Maybe I'll expose his secret hideaway to his creditors. *All* of them."

"Charming as ever, huh?"

"As ever. And sending flowers to a murdered friend. But only those on sale."

"He's all heart."

"You can laugh. You don't have to work for him."

"True. Point scored."

"'That's my girl,' the nerve of him saying that. I'm thirty-two. I've risked my little ass covering umpteen battles for him. Won several prizes. I've tolerated his late pay checks, gotten interviews with the likes of Churchill, Roosevelt, and Mussolini before any other woman reporter, and he says *that?*"

"Calm down. He's a mogul."

"Oh, so that gives him the right? I should have stayed in London and deprived the old buzzard of that D-Day landing exclusive."

"I'm sure he patronizes everyone. Male reporters included."

"Pity them. You know what's amazing?"

"What?"

"His wife has stayed with him. Despite his affairs."

"Because of the status and their kids. You gripe about him. But you know what? You're lucky to have that crusty skinflint for a boss."

"Oh, I know, I know. He just gets on my nerves sometimes. But you're right. I'd want him on my side in any fight. And he did hire me when no one else on Fleet Street would except as a lowly stringer."

"What the hell did that Leah mean with that German-British comment?" Jonas pushed around some clothes in his suitcase on their hotel bed. "You seen my Onoto Magna pen anywhere?"

"Check the dining room. You might have left it there when you did those French crosswords." Charly paused typing up her interview notes and flipped through several notebook pages. "I got it, what she said. Somewhere here anyway. Word for word. Found it. 'Even against the few Germans who help the British.'"

"That's one hell of a comment. She knows something."

"Yeah, whatever it is." Charly settled her cigarette in the ashtray and glanced over her shoulder. "What she said hit me like a sledgehammer. I tried to keep taking notes; I just hope she didn't see my hand tremble, alert her we might be on to something, and clam up. But, you know, I thought, What is this? Bitter enemies in two world wars."

"Especially that last one."

"Especially that one. And now they're in an alliance? The Brits and the Germans? Here in Palestine?"

"Some are anyway. I'm going down to check for my pen. If Clementine Churchill learns I lost her gift..."

"Yeah, I know. Good luck."

The dining room. The smell of the last dinner of spicey roast chicken served still faintly in the warm air, he noticed as he reached the top of the carpeted stairs. Of all the dumb places to leave that expensive pen. With so many guests eating there. Way to go, Jonas. You're getting forgetful in middle age. Better lay off the Johnnie Walker. Someone might have stolen it. How the dickens explain any theft... Well, I'll be. There it was, at the bottom step, glinting like a diamond from an overhead chandelier. Right where it must have fallen from his pocket. Shame on you, old sport. He stooped to pick it up and froze. A crash of dishes from the kitchen off to his right, then curses, broke the quiet. An employee had dropped plates on the floor. Someone else yelled at him.

"You stupid, clumsy Arab!"

Jonas stepped back into the shadows, accidentally bumping loudly against the railing. But those inside the kitchen, evidently preoccupied, hadn't heard. "I'm so sorry, kind sir. It was an accident. I beg your forgiveness." The voice, that of Abdul, pleading for understanding from Hans Peters, sounding almost tearful.

"Oh shut up! I should take it out of your wages. Better yet, fire you. That was expensive china dinnerware, Abdul. Expensive, if you know what quality means. Why I agreed to keep you on when I bought this hotel is beyond me. Get out of here. You make me sick just looking at you. No, not that way. The back door. That's all we need, a guest seeing you crying like a little baby."

Jonas heard the sound of a rear kitchen door softly, meekly closing. Then Peters muttered to himself as he swept up the debris. "Goddamn Arabs. They haven't done anything since the pyramids."

Jonas stood still, listening to Hans Peters' rant, stunned, his frown deepening. It was definitely there, a subtle yet disturbing sound. He'd heard it more strikingly the previous year at a POW camp. An American soldier demanding a captured German to wipe his smirk off. The SS officer berating him for his order, his guttural *r*'s rolling off his tongue in contempt, as if his country was never defeated. The same guttural *r*'s coming from Hans Peters' mouth. Something about him, Jonas thought, seemed off key.

He stepped lightly up the stairs, unsettled. Hans Peters, thinking he had privacy, might have revealed another man, brutal and ugly and alarming.

Chapter 24

"I'm telling you, Charly, I know what the hell I heard last night."

"You're imaging it, Jonas. You hate all Germans."

"Oh come on. That's bullshit, and you know it. Look how Willy Jaeger and other Berliners helped us last year."

"Okay, low blow, I'll admit it. But your idea about him is farfetched."

"Hardly."

"It is, dear. Clearly. He lost his temper against Abdul. That's all."

"Lost his temper, that's putting it mildly."

"Well, he did. He said some awful, ugly, ugly things. Granted. But he's under stress. Lots of people are these days. Tel Aviv is one stressful city in a stressful land. It's nothing more than that. War jitters, that's all it is. And this weather doesn't help matters either. Don't make a mountain out of a molehill."

A couple in formal attire swished past in the hotel corridor. "I'm not saying I'm one hundred percent certain," Jonas said, lowering his voice.

Charly glanced at him as they reached the first floor. "Near enough, dear."

"I have a suspicion, that's all."

"Yeah, some suspicion. An ex-Nazi hiding among a people he wanted to destroy? That is farfetched. To say the least. He ran a hotel in Berlin off the Ku'damm. The Nazis expropriated it and housed some Third Reich cultural offices there. All the more reason to hate them. He fled with practically nothing but his shirt on his back. Like many refugees, let me add. Now he runs a hotel here. It's simple."

"Maybe, maybe not."

"Says you."

"That's right, says me."

"Jonas, thousands of people, Hans Peters included, from all over Europe have escaped here. Others have fled from Syria and Egypt and Iraq."

"*And* from Morocco. *And* from Tunisia. From other parts of Africa and the Middle East, too. I understand that. But why here?"

"Why? What kind of question is that? To escape persecution, dear. To start a new life. That's why."

"But why here? Have you ever wondered about that? Did he have a Jewish wife? Jewish relatives or friends? Why not London or Paris or Rome?"

"Maybe he just wanted to get away from all that destruction in Europe. All that horror and tragedy. The millions and millions of lives lost. Like everyone else."

"So he comes here and not the States?"

"Sure, why not here? Maybe he lost loved ones there. Maybe the few survivors are here. Have *you* ever wondered about that? War's traumatizing, dear. I know it. And you, of all people, should know that."

"So he curses someone out just because he's Arab?"

"When you're on edge, it can happen. Yes, absolutely. Especially when you run a hotel in a war zone. Jittery guests dump on him, he dumps on employees, employees kick their dogs. It happens, Jonas. It happens to the best of people."

"To the best of people. My God, save me," he muttered to himself and sighed. Damn woman. Maybe she was right. Every eyewitness to war paid. Sooner or later the bill came due. In night sweats. In drinking. Nightmares. Even uncontrolled rage, he had to admit. And Hans Peters wasn't the only innocent German who had fled to Palestine. Still, discussing his hunch, he realized, was pointless for now. "To be continued," he said. "Where do you want to get a bite to eat?"

Mr. Peters, she said, had suggested a restaurant with rooftop dining. It offered a view of the Mediterranean and the ocean front boardwalk like the one in Atlantic City, and the Yemeni owner cooked up an excellent chickpea falafel.

They reached bustling Allenby Street, near Rothschild Boulevard, and strolled north. Along the way to the restaurant, Charly said, they must absolutely try Hans Peters' other suggestion, the vibrant Carmel Market. It was the largest in Tel Aviv. They could get anything at that *shuk*. Clothes. Spices. Fresh fruit. Vegetables. "We can hone our bargaining skills there," she said, raising her voice to be heard over the rat-a-tat blast from jackhammers across the road. "See who comes out ahead," she continued, nudging him playfully.

Their cabbie was right, he realized. Tel Aviv boomed. He could almost taste the energy, the optimism. But he also saw fear on many Jews' faces as they hurried past. An impending, apocalyptic war. The final destruction of those who still were alive.

He flipped through a complimentary old Hotel Berliner brochure earlier picked up at Reception. It was written in German, Hebrew, and English.

> Number of inhabitants: 1909, 550. 1926, 40,000.
> Number of houses: 1909, 65. 1926,3,050
> Number of factories: 1909, 0. 1926, 170.
> Number of worksho—

"Hey mister, watch out!"

Jonas frowned at an old man ahead gesturing excitedly at him, then understood. But too late to react much, he realized as he dropped the pamphlet, alarmed. A rusty dump of a car bumped over the curb ahead and screeched to a stop. Rear passenger doors flew open. Two men in coats jumped at them, guns drawn. Jonas jammed his left hand toward his shoulder holster. The taller one chopped it before he could grip the Colt's handle. Jonas winced from the pain, still managed to ball his fist to strike, but stopped, horrified. The taller thug, his Smith & Wesson 45 at Charly's head, shouted, "Get in, get in." The voice, gruff, no-nonsense. Pedestrians froze in fear. A woman screamed and fainted. A shocked bicyclist crashed into a nearby bus bench.

The other kidnapper, Jonas saw, had sprinted behind him before he realized. A pimply kid. More color in his face than his buddy, but not by much. He jabbed a Baby Browning pocket pistol into his back. Nervous, he kept wiping his free hand on his khaki pants. But Jonas didn't doubt the youth could kill.

A teenager, dark hair sprawling from beneath her beret, sat in the driver's seat. She flexed her fingers on the steering wheel, looking anxious to flee. She tossed her cigarette out the window, shifted gears.

The pimply kid snatched Jonas's Colt from his shoulder holster and pocketed it. "We blindfold you," he said, pushing him into the back. "Those are our orders."

"Whose orders?"

"Orders. That's all I can say." He jerked Charly's shoulder bag open, rifled through it, discovered her Rolleiflex, tossed it to the taller man in the front seat. "Uri, we can use this for our own press."

In moments, it was done, Jonas realized. Professionally quick. Blindfolded, their world now dark.

"You, down on floorboard," he heard the taller one demand in clumsy English over his shoulder in the front passenger seat. "Now!" Jonas stretched out on top of Charly as the car fled north on Allenby Street. The three—brothers and sister, cousins, neighbors—seemed familiar with each other. Still the tall gunman shouted at the driver, "Fourth gear, fourth gear," as if she had rarely driven a car in her short life.

Through the half-open car window burst the sounds of the metropolis. Impatient drivers hit their horns. Police or an ambulance, Jonas couldn't tell, sped past in the opposite direction. Somewhere off in the distance, an artillery shell or bomb, again he couldn't tell, exploded. The three in the car, teen veterans of Palestinian violence, didn't seem the least shaken.

They turned a corner too quickly, wheels squealing. The tall youth once more shouted at her, slow down, slow down; British police or soldiers might get suspicious.

On and on they drove, hiding themselves in silence. Only the car radio broke the quiet. Some crackly station beat out the news. An underground group had blown up a British radar station that tracked illegal ships of Jews trying to land. The United Nations debated partitioning Palestine into two states. A coffeehouse near the Damascus Gate in Jerusalem's Old City—a burst of whistling, teeth gnashing static broke up the rest. The tall gunman furiously hammered a fist on the dashboard again and again; their radio was useless. Jonas heard his heart beating wildly. Death could come from out of nowhere, it seemed to beat as he placed a comforting hand on Charly's and patted it. It was uncharacteristically sweaty.

They continued driving, now along some shoreline. To his left, he heard the thunderous splashing of Mediterranean waves on some beach and smelled the salty air. After a time, they came to a sudden stop. The two men yanked them out, still blindfolded. A herd of goats, bells clanging around their necks, passed as the driver sped off. In the distance palm trees rustled in the warm, soft air.

Jonas groped for Charly's hand, found and grasped it. She squeezed it, reassured by his presence. They proceeded across a road, Jonas not hearing even the slightest presence of a single car approach. He felt isolated, abandoned to strangers and their purpose, whatever it was.

The rusty creak of a gate sounded. They crossed a gravel path, the heavy scent of bougainvillea and oranges all around them, and he thought they must have entered a garden. Another gate creaked open. They were pushed through and into a building. Down a corridor. Around another one. At first, he worried his anxiety caused him to hallucinate, hearing prayers somewhere. But no, he realized as he picked up rhythmic murmurs, a church or a Benedictine or Franciscan monastery then. Not in Jewish Tel Aviv. Probably somewhere in its outskirts or in Jerusalem or Bethlehem or Haifa. The place of worship loaned out by Christian allies. Safe from the British and their informers.

Their kidnappers led them into a cool chamber, pushed them down into wooden chairs, and ripped off their blindfolds, unconcerned about the discomfort caused. Jonas blinked several times, adjusting his eyes to the light. He smiled at Charly, next to him. She smiled back, trying to put on a brave front. As he was too, he realized.

Chapter 25

Ahead sat three men, hands clasped on a sturdy wooden table, like a judgmental tribunal. Three of them in cheap chairs that creaked whenever they shifted. Grubby. Disheveled. Fatigued. Looking like do-or-die guerrilla fighters. Their life's painful struggles, Jonas noticed, etched on their tanned, desert-lived faces.

A bundle of Sten guns, deadly if they didn't jam, lay stacked in a dim corner. An open crate showed French Hotchkiss machine guns, Italian Beretta pistols, and one old Russian Nagan revolver. On the concrete floor lay a box of ammunition, labelled *Mauser Cartridges. Czechoslovakia.*

A mishmash of weapons for a rag tag paramilitary operation probably against the Brits. The arms stockpile from Europe or the U. S. that overflowed with used World War II weapons, from B-17s to Sherman tanks. Easily gotten by smugglers for the right price and doctored paperwork. Good luck, guys. You'll need plenty of it for whatever you're planning. He just caught from a big, boxy shortwave radio a faint, "This is the BBC," before the pimply kid snapped it off and left.

"*Shalom.* Welcome. I am Abraham," the man to Jonas's left said. Bald. Slight build. Marks of torture in a ridged scarring down the left side of his face. He tore off a scrap of newspaper on the table. He sprinkled some tobacco along the length of paper, rolled it into a cigarette. After striking a match on the sole of his muddy boot, he lit up, and inhaled. Smiling satisfaction to himself, he passed the improvised smoke to his companion in the middle. He had high Slavic cheekbones, wore round rimless spectacles, and looked scholarly. "This is Isaac. And the fine looking young man next to him is Jacob."

Abraham's harshly accented English sounded like hammer blows. He's a refugee, Jonas thought. Probably from some slaughterhouse Central European country. Three Biblical patriarchs. Abraham. Isaac.

Jacob. A drole joke. But feeling his heart pump nervously, he found nothing funny in it. Especially the humorless face of young Jacob, who stroked his few hairs that passed for a goatee as he glared silently at him.

"You won some kind of prize, Miss Lawrence, for"—Abraham flipped back and forth through some pages, his lips pinched in displeasure—"it doesn't say what for, unfortunately. Ah yes, here it is. For reporting on the misery of the poor during the London German Blitz."

They had amassed a dossier on her, Jonas noticed. At least five pages. All in neat Hebrew handwriting, as though she merited importance. Their source, one of them anyway, perhaps that guy at the Jericho with the tape recorder. The file bound with two pieces of cardboard held in place with masking tape. And this clapped-together force and others planned to defeat Arab guerrillas and several seasoned Arab armies?

"And you, Mr. Jonas Shaw, you look, I think, like trouble. Are you?"

"I have my opinions."

Abraham laughed. "I'm sure you do. Strong ones, I bet. You did some kind of work for Mr. Winston Churchill himself during the last war. *Mazel tov*! A great supporter of our cause. What you did, we couldn't discover...our staff is rather limited these days." A small smile of regret flickered and died on his lips. "Care to explain what service you did for the British colonial power?"

"No, not really." His file, too he saw, ran to several neatly written pages in Hebrew in another make-shift dossier. His name also maybe on one of the seven folders spotted at the Jericho.

"Something to do with intelligence? If so, let us hope it was against Hitler. But no matter." Abraham jotted a quick note in the margins in Hebrew, writing right to left. Then he closed Jonas's file and tossed it thoughtlessly next to Charly's. "Rivka Kozibrodska, what do you know of her?"

"Who?"

"Riv-ka Ko-zi-brod-ska, Mr. Shaw. What can you tell us about her."

"We don't know anyone by that name here."

"Mr. Shaw, please. Yesterday, you met with her."

"Yesterday, Charly and I met with a woman. Yes, that's right. Somewhere in south Tel Aviv. But she called herself Leah."

"Her name is Rivka Kozibrodska. From Lodz, Poland. Living in Warsaw until that became impossible. Thanks to the Germans." Abraham showed across the table a cardboard document. A British Identify Card. Name of Holder, Leah Krakowski. Place of Residence, Tel Aviv. Place of business, Tel Aviv. Occupation, seamstress. Race, Jew. Color hair, blonde. Height, five feet, six inches. Color Eyes, blue. Build, normal. Age, 22. And at the bottom, the signature of the issuing army officer. "This is her," he continued, "Rivka Kozibrodska. What did she tell you?"

Leah Krakowski, her *nom de guerre;* but Rivka Kozibrodska, her underground true name. Maybe. "Only about how she fought in," Jonas said, "what you call, the uprising in Warsaw. In the ghetto there. And how she has no faith in Britain, France, my country, really any country helping them here."

Isaac nodded at Abraham. "There, you see? The fighting Jew. Our only salvation." Then to Jonas, "What else?"

"Nothing else, that was it."

"That was it? You expect us to believe that? Do you? You take us for fools?" Jacob cracked his knuckles as he turned to the two older men. "We are wasting time with him. With both of them." He pushed back his wobbly chair, its legs scrapping loudly against the floor from his anger, and stood. Two guns showed from the front of the waistband of his gray khaki pants. Both attached to chains hooked to his pants to secure hard-to-get weapons.

Isaac glanced at him. "Jacob, quiet."

"Are you blind? Can't you see?"

"Jacob, you hear me? Sit down!"

"He won't tell us anything unless we force him to."

"Jacob, do as Abraham says. Sit down! Now!"

"Others might torture," Abraham said. "We don't. You should know that. You want to torture, go off to Haifa or Jerusalem. Join Begin's Irgun or what's left of Stern's hooligans. Otherwise, shut up! Rivka Kozibrodska, Mr. Shaw, what did she say to you? The full story."

"I've bloody well told you the full story. She talked about her fight in the Warsaw ghetto uprising."

"Jonas is telling the truth."

Isaac ignored Charly. "Mr. Shaw, we have to know who enters Palestine these days."

"For our own survival," Abraham added.

Isaac nodded. "Yes, for that, our very survival. Are they pilgrims on their way to Jerusalem? Archeologists wanting to see the Roman ruins in Caesarea? Or maybe some crusader fortress? Or lost souls looking for meaning? Are they here to help? Or here to help destroy us? So, we try to have people everywhere. At the telephone and telegraph exchange. At Jaffa and Haifa ports night and day. At Lydda Airport. We know what's going on in Tel Aviv and in Palestine."

"For us," Abraham said, "intelligence is absolutely vital. So do not lie to us."

"I'm not—"

"Three days ago," Isaac interrupted, "you, Mr. Shaw, and the woman next to you landed at that airport. At Lydda. You were on a privately owned airplane. An Avro Lancastrian. You started from London with one refueling stop, Malta. You were driven into Tel Aviv by a Mr. Oliver Porter, a British citizen. He claims to do something in import/export."

"So he claims," Abraham said.

"So he claims. Importing and exporting farm produce and equipment. You stayed first at the"—Isaac reopened Jonas's file and glanced at it—"at the Jericho Hotel. Yes, there. At the Jericho. Then, for a reason we don't understand, at the Hotel Berliner."

"Yesterday," Abraham said, "you met with Rivka Kozibrodska. If you knew her as Leah, fine. We don't care. But her real name is Rivka Kozibrodska. A Warsaw ghetto uprising survivor. One of the few. That meeting lasted for about an hour. We need to know what she told you. From the very beginning."

"I've already told you everything."

"Rivka mention anything about the Mahane Yehuda Police Station?"

Jonas frowned. "Mahane what? Never heard of it."

"Run by the British. On Jaffa Road, Mr. Shaw. In Jerusalem."

"107 Jaffa Road," Isaac said. "Two stories. Two lions on pillars flanking the entrance. The building hard to miss. Well known. Feared and talked about by Arab and Jew alike."

"No, no, and no, guys. Still means nothing to me."

"What about Acre Prison?" Abraham asked. "She mention that?"

"No."

"Also called Akko Prison," Isaac added. "A-k-k-o, Akko. It's north of Haifa. Anything?"

"Still no. Nothing."

"Anything about being detained by the British police?" Abraham asked

"No." Jonas felt himself sweating. "Nothing whatsoever."

"About overhearing a rumor of any kind at Acre? Or Akko, if you will."

"A rumor? Nothing at all about that."

Isaac leaned forward, elbows on the wooden table, focusing on him. "Nothing whatsoever about *any* rumor?"

"That's what I said. Nothing whatsoever."

"About any American intelligence agency?"

"You mean the OSS?"

"About *any* American intelligence agency, Mr. Shaw."

"The OSS was disbanded in '45."

Isaac glared across to Jonas. "For the third time, Mr. Shaw, did Rivka mention *anything* about *any* American intelligence agency paying any fugitive Nazi or fugitive Nazis? Yes or no."

"No. There, satisfied? Nothing about that OSS or any U. S. intel outfit. Clear enough?"

"What about the British MI6."

"Look, this Rivka woman said nothing about the MI6. About any spy organization. About any police station. About any prison. Nothing at all. I can't be clearer, Isaac."

"Anything about Operation Igloo mentioned?"

"Operation what, Isaac?"

"Igloo. Operation Igloo, Mr. Shaw. A British attempt to block desperate Jewish immigration into Palestine."

"To block death camp survivors, Mr. Shaw," Abraham added, "from starting a new life in Palestine. The blockade began in 1946. Anything at all about that?"

"No. Nothing. Sorry." Jonas crossed one leg over the other. He tapped his fingers on a knee, impatient with the questions, anxious over their ferocity.

"What about Cyprus?" Isaac asked.

"The island?"

"Of course that island."

"Why the hell would she say anything about that bloody little place?"

"Nothing about a British detention center there?"

"No, nothing about that."

"As part of that Operation Igloo?"

"No." Christ, could he use some water and a smoke.

"About watch towers? Barbed wire? The poor sanitation there for detainees?"

"I said no, Isaac. Nothing about Cyprus. Jesus! Come on. What more can I say?" Jonas glanced, curious, at Charly. Oblivious to the questioning, she was flipping through her notebook.

Isaac turned to Abraham. "Maybe we make mistake? Maybe this woman isn't Rivka. Maybe Matteo followed them to the wrong street? Or the wrong building?"

Abraham shook his head vigorously at Isaac. "Impossible. Matteo is a sabra. He was born in Tel Aviv. You know that. He's one of our best. He knows how important that meeting is to us. Was there a young man with you in at that meeting, Mr. Shaw?"

"Yes, matter of fact there was."

"Describe him."

Jonas shrugged. "There's not much to describe really." Then turned to Charly. "Just an ordinary looking guy, wouldn't you say?"

Whatever fear about their kidnapping she had first felt had disappeared. She nodded slightly as she, apparently preoccupied, flipped through another page of notes. "Tall," she said absently, not glancing up. "Like some American basketball player."

"About six feet or so," Jonas said. "Skinny as hell. Blood shot eyes. Early twenties. Pale. Very pale."

Isaac turned to Abraham. "Could be him. Spend all that time indoors, hiding from the British, that happens. You look sickly."

Abraham didn't look that convinced. "His name?"

"Asher."

"Asher what?"

"Just Asher. He escorted us from the Café Tel in the south of Tel Aviv to that meeting."

"Where in south Tel Aviv?"

"I have no idea. I'm just a visitor here. A tourist. Not some native."

"Not even a street name?"

"Not even that, no."

"You mean to say, Mr. Shaw, you walked for several minutes and didn't catch even one single street sign? You expect us to believe that?"

"You can believe what you want. Maybe I should have. But worry about the safety of a loved one can do funny things to the mind."

Abraham laughed. "It must."

"All I can say is they escorted us to some run-down building. In terrible shape. Trash everywhere. The shutters, many of them anyway, nearly falling off. To the third floor there."

"Asher what?" Abraham asked again.

Jonas sighed. "Look, like I said, just Asher."

"Just Asher?" Abraham asked, voice raised, skeptical. "Everyone has a last name, Mr. Jonas Shaw."

"Not him. Not when we met. As I said, he never gave a last name."

"Jonas is right." Charly thumbed through still more notes. "He called himself just Asher."

The man who went by the name of Abraham turned to the other two. "He is telling the truth. They met with her. With Rivka. She must have avoided Jaffa and Haifa ports because of those British. Maybe slipped ashore from Cyprus at some other place not closely watched."

"Or from Gibraltar, Abraham?" Isaac asked. "Then boarded a felucca for here? You were with her in that Majdanek death camp. You know she's clever and tough enough to break through the British blockade."

"And land at some coastal town south of Haifa," Jacob said.

Abraham slammed his fist down on the wooden table. "Enough of this! Enough, you hear? Who knows? Who cares? It makes no difference. She's here. In Palestine. Now. Somewhere here anyway. Beyond reach. For now anyway. With her secret. She revealed nothing what she knows to these two." Abraham shoved their two files into his backpack. "We're done, guys. Let them go."

"Let them go?"

"Yes Jacob, let them go. We're wasting our time holding them. Give Mr. Shaw back his Colt 1911 at the beach."

"But Abraham, you know we're short of weapons."

"Mr. Shaw might need to protect himself."

"We can always buy on the black market," Isaac said.

"From some Brit soldier returning home, who doesn't need his anymore."

"But—"

"But nothing. We're finished here, Jacob. I have a meeting with Ben-Gurion in an hour. Isaac, too with B. G. A war council."

"You don't keep an old warrior like B. G. waiting, Jacob," Isaac warned. "You should know that."

"Hm," Charly mumbled to herself, "it's here somewhere. I know it—Ah, thought so."

Thought so what? Jonas glanced at Charly.

"Here. Here it is." She tapped a scrawl-filled page with a fingernail. "There was something else this Rivka said. She said, quote, 'We will have to fight for our right to exist in our ancestral homeland.' Closed quote. Then she went on to say they'd fight against the British. Against Arab guerillas. Against Arab armies. And so on and so on. Blah, blah, blah. Then and I'm quoting once more, 'Even against the few Germans who help the British.' Closed quote. Jonas and I didn't know what to make of it, but there it is, that's what she said."

Charly was right, Jonas realized. Under the stress of the interrogation, he'd forgotten that quote. Charly had hit a nerve.

Isaac paused polishing his spectacles with the end of his shirt and stared fiercely at her.

So did Jacob, who had stopped drumming his fingers on the wooden table.

Abraham held his hand straight out for her jottings. "Give. Let me see them. Both notebooks. Nothing beyond that? Her quote?" he asked.

British. He couldn't believe it. It was impossible. She couldn't possibly...or was it possible?

"Daniel!"

He jerked his head up, shaken by the loud scolding tone. "What?" Jacob had shifted around and stared, puzzled, at him.

"What are you doing? They're not yours."

Did Jacob notice the fear on his face? "I was just curious."

"Well, don't be. Give those notebooks back to her."

"Sorry, Jacob." Daniel shrugged, resigned, and tossed them back to Charly. Returning them made no difference anyway. The dangerous lines read remained fresh. *Even against the few Germans who help the British*. Could this Rivka possibly know or suspect? Did she pass along what she might have stumbled upon? How could she have come across this? He must notify the One From Beyond as soon as possible. And take other action. Quickly.

Chapter 27

They pushed them out of their car, blindfolds removed, near a deserted section of beach in south Tel Aviv. Jacob flung Jonas's Colt into a pile of rubbish beyond some dunes.

Jonas watched the beat-up car rattle off into the distance. It was the same used to kidnap them, yet different. It was now outfitted with metal panels, and the window glass looked reinforced against bullets. An improvised armored vehicle. "It could have been a lot worse, Charly." He brushed sand off his pistol, then glanced over his shoulder for direction. Off in the distance the ancient port jutted out into the choppy Mediterranean. "Can you believe that back there?" he asked.

"Believe what?"

"That town there, Jaffa. Over 3,000 years old. Ruled once, I read, by Egyptians, Philistines, Greeks. It makes us Americans seem like we just arrived."

"We have, compared to them." Charly pointed to a wooden shack on some dunes, off to their right, that acted as a public toilette and excused herself.

Jonas did the math, while she struggled up the sand to it. Abraham, thirty-five or forty. Isaac, about the same age. Jacob, eighteen to twenty. Maybe that explained everything. The world had touched them and their generations in horrific ways most couldn't fully understand or care about. And he thought how lucky he was to be born far away from what they may have experienced in Europe.

They could catch a taxi or walk back to their hotel, he said when she returned. He decided they'd walk; he needed to work over some things. He shook his head in disbelief as he undid the top buttons to his long-sleeve cotton shirt; even at the sea's edge, the heat felt oppressive despite the breeze.

"You're deep in thought." Charly found her dark glasses in her shoulder bag and slipped them on. "What are you thinking about?"

"What?" He realized she had asked something; he glanced at her.

She slipped her hand into his. "I asked, what are you thinking about?"

"Those men back there who questioned me. Isaac and Abraham. I feel like I went ten rounds in the ring with them."

"Coming from a veteran interrogator like you, that's saying something."

"The way they went after me. Question after question. On and on it went. What were they after?"

Charly shrugged. "Beats me."

"Asking about Cyprus, detention camps, MI6 and the OSS. I kept telling them what we knew. Hell, we don't know anything about that Aribert Heim or any Nazi fugitives for that matter. Yet they kept coming at me as if I withheld something life-or-death important. What the hell did they want? Jesus, their intensity. As scorching as the sun. Know what?"

"What?"

"I think they're mad?"

She laughed. "You do, do you?"

"No, really, seriously." Jonas stopped. The muggy heat hung on him, despite a breeze. He gulped down some water from his canteen, patted his brow with a kerchief. Maybe he should take her advice after all. Get a wide-brimmed hat. "Absolutely one hundred percent pure mad."

"Why?"

"You'd have to be to start a country out here."

"What do you mean?"

"Just look around, will you. Building a country in this god forsaken miserable corner of the earth? A good part of Palestine is desert and mosquito-infested swamp, know that? Around sixty percent or so. No wonder many Arabs sell their land to them. It's worthless. Those men back there, Abraham, Isaac, and that Jacob kid, they could care less. Just like they could care less fighting the Brits. I overheard them chattering away about some canon they had gotten hold off. Excited like kids opening Christmas presents."

"You mean Hanukkah."

Jonas laughed. You're right, Hanukkah. A Napoleonchik."

"A what?"

"That's what they called it. A Napoleonchik. A 65 mm relic from who knows what past war. And, get this, with the canon's aiming sight missing. To be used against a well-equipped enemy...I should say enemies. They have the hardiness of Bedouin Arabs, those guys. They all have. Not fazed one bit building a country here. I felt in awe of them. I really did."

Charly brushed away some dandruff from his shoulder. "Why should they be daunted? Look at Tel Aviv. Started from scratch. Just sixty-six of them. Day after day shoveling away sand dunes north of Jaffa in this brutal heat."

"But we're talking about an *entire* nation, Charly. With few natural resources. With few friends and a ragtag militia. With just fifty bullets per rifle. So short of canteens some use beer bottles to carry their water. A big, big difference."

"Yeah, you're right."

"With millions of enemies with professional armies on three sides. Lebanon to the north. Syria, Iraq, and Transjordan, trained by crack Brit officers, to the east. Egypt to the south. And from what I gather, no tanks, no warships, no heavy artillery. Not even one single antiaircraft gun to defend Tel Aviv." He nodded off to his left. "And with that, the Mediterranean on the fourth. You'd have to be stark raving mad to do that."

"Or tough as nails dreamers."

"Or tough as nails dreamers. Frankly, I don't see how they can pull it off."

"Fighting for their own country?"

"Yep, that. Crazy, crazy people. It'll be an absolute, total bloodbath. I heard they're collecting beds from people to use for make-shift hospitals."

Charly shot him a glance. "Really?"

"And preparing a soccer field to be a graveyard. At least according to Abdul."

"They're that desperate?"

"No, Charly, that dedicated, that willing to face overwhelming odds, to fight and die. They've been pushed around by too many countries and slaughtered too much, and they've had it, and you know, I find that fascinating," he said, turning to her and smiling. "Absolutely fascinating. Their devotion to their cause. They go to sleep under the gun. Wake up under the gun. Go through the day under the gun. Get married under the gun. Fighting against enemies, the desert, the weather, epidemics, deadly snakes. Fighting against the odds. Yet they get on with building their homeland. Amazing."

"Palestine isn't for the faint hearted, that's for sure."

He squinted from the sun's glare off the ocean, and he slipped on his own dark glasses. The beach was deserted, but for a group of bathers in the distance ahead who had gathered at the water's edge.

During his years as a New York detective, he continued, he had met loan sharks, mafia gangsters, hitmen, and drug dealers in one of the city's worst hellholes. These Bronx cons were dainty choir boys compared to the three slightly built men they had just met. Palestine was for hard men and hard women. Those three must have seen their loved ones and friends murdered in Europe. They must have escaped from Germany or Poland or Lithuania or one of the many other bloodlands. Somehow, they had made their way to the Promised Land. And here they and others intended to fight to build their sanctuary country or die trying. No matter the odds. No matter what the so-called civilized, opinionated world thought.

Charly slipped off her sandals, shook sand from them, and tucked them under an arm. She now walked bare foot in the wet sand with the breeze whipping her auburn hair around, and Jonas thought how absolutely lovely she looked and that they could be on holiday. Except as they drew closer to the crowd, he saw the illusion break. They weren't bathers, after all. They were several British soldiers and a group of Palestinians. They clustered around a near lifeless body of a man, flopped out on his back. He was gasping for air.

Chapter 28

Several yards out in the Mediterranean, an overturned rowboat tossed in the rough sea. On the beach, some military personal had stuck a metal sign in English, Arabic, and Hebrew in the wet sand: NO ONE ALLOWED BEYOND THIS POINT. But some spectators had ignored it, had stepped beyond, and an argument had broken out. One Palestinian pleaded to administer mouth-to-mouth resuscitation. A British soldier yanked him back by an arm. Another British soldier wanted to take the near-drowned victim to the Government Hospital in Jaffa. His superior, a man with a florid baby face, kept smacking his riding crop hard against his polished black jackboot. Absolutely not, he insisted, shaking his head vigorously and whacking his whip again against his boot. Absolutely not. To Acre Prison for a good interrogation and only there.

Several Palestinian women chanted "Shame, shame," and moved closer to him. He stepped back, looking scared. He withdrew his pistol and fired several warning shots into the air, wincing from the gun's force. He turned, suddenly noticing Jonas and Charly, now writing in her notebook. "I am Commander Angus Frost of the Tel Aviv sector. And you, sir, are?"

"Jonas Shaw."

"And you, Missus?"

"Charly Lawrence."

"Well now, you two, this is a security matter. As you can very well see. Put your pen away, Missus, and move along. Both of you. Now. Quickly."

Charly gestured to the gasping man on the beach. "What about him?"

"That poor guy needs help," Jonas said.

Charly dropped her notebook back into her shoulder bag. "He appears half dead."

"I'm in charge here. I decide." Commander Frost stretched his short, stumpy body for height. "We'll determine what he needs. And when. I'm ordering you two to move along."

"Security matter, him?" Jonas pointed to the gasping man. "Look at him for Christ's sake. That poor guy almost drowned." He stepped toward him, now moaning, but a tall soldier grabbed him by the shirt sleeve.

"Jonas," Charly said. "Please, honey. We better go."

"Yes, you best do that. Do what your Missus says, lad," Frost said. "Move along. This doesn't concern you."

"But what about—"

"Lad." Captain Frost whacked his riding whip hard against his jackboot sending sand flying off from the force of his anger. "Did you hear me? I said move it!" A murmur of support from the surrounding soldiers sounded. "Move your arse, Jew lover," one of them said and spit at Jonas's feet.

Jonas glared at him, then at the captain. "Bastards," he muttered under his breath.

"Lad, I'll disregard that...at least for now. For the last time I'm warning you."

"Jonas, please."

"Okay, okay, dear." He shook off the British soldier's grasp, and he followed Charly toward a café, as he did so, throwing a quick look back. "A half dead immigrant, you heartless shits. I could kill that son of a bitch Frost, Charly. Kill him and not lose one moment's sleep."

"Honestly, honey, you always pick a fight where you're outnumbered."

"I like the odds." He pulled her up to the top of a dune. "I hate bullies, you know that. And that Angus Frost is one mean son of a bitch." She didn't say anything more, and he understood. She somewhat feared his Irish temper and his New York street roughness. But still she wanted to comfort him and slipped a hand into his. They paused at a paved intersection to let a flock of sheep meander past, then headed to the seaside café with its ocean front shaded patio. "I'll tell you something," he continued. He sensed the Jews only wanted to kick the damn Brits out and defeat the Arab terrorists and soldiers, not destroy an entire people. But Arab terrorists and soldiers wanted to annihilate every single Jew. Like the Nazis.

The café looked empty, and he didn't hear the usual bustle of lively talk, laughter, and of waiters shouting out orders. He wiped away some grime, cupped both hands, and peered into a window. Tables were stacked on tables; red-and-white chairs on similar chairs. He noticed a sign tapped to an adjoining window. The Roma had that day closed for remodeling.

A man staggered suddenly toward them from across the street. Sweaty and dirty, his dark disheveled hair had fallen over his forehead, and Jonas needed a moment to realize who it was.

Asher stumbled a few more steps up to them, breathing heavily. "Someone stabbed Leah. She's dead." Then he collapsed.

Chapter 29

Crouching in his Opel, Oliver Porter saw the American couple as the young man, his face twisted with exhaustion, collapsed. Well, well, well. He had tried like buggery with what free time he had to surveille them. Except for news about that Nazi Aribert Heim, he had transmitted bugger-all of value back to Father Karl. But now, at last, finally. Something interesting across the street at that café.

He had spotted youths kidnap them on the coastal road that led north to Haifa.

He had waited in his Opel on that same road, hoping they'd eventually return. They had.

He'd driven around, wondering what in bloody blazes to do, when he spotted them walking north along that Tel Aviv beach. And now this.

That kid's tormented fatigued face...he had seen it somewhere before. At some stiff diplomatic soiree? That young man in a tuxedo? Bollocks! At some dreary chamber of commerce meeting? Double bollocks! He would have stood out among those booze-swilling fat codgers.

And then Oliver Porter, feeling a jolt of memory, smiled. Something else worthwhile to encrypt back to Father Karl. Like in the good old days sending Field Station reports from Berlin to Home Station. He sat up straight and trained his binoculars across the street to verify. Keep calm, old boy. Make Karl proud of you. Easy does it. Focus in. That's it. Easy, easy, a little more. Yes, that's it. Of course, of course. He was bloody well right! His post office visit to mail that letter to his dear ol' mum. All those big wanted posters tacked up, the high price the British Colonial Office had placed on the kid's head. A man on the run out there now in plain bloody sight and his two American helpers apparently, and he, Oliver Porter, had seen it all for Karl. Blimey!

Chapter 30

Jonas caught Asher under his sweaty armpits as his legs crumpled. He felt heavier than he looked. Jonas gripped him tighter and eased him down prone onto the pavement, cradling his head in his lap. He appeared to have slept and eaten little and seemed utterly exhausted. In his wrinkled, dirty clothes, he'd suggest to any British cop or soldier or informer a desperate man on the run. He babbled incoherently, spit on his thin lips. Something about refugees. About some arms shipment about to sail. About evading the British naval blockade. About being lucky he had overheard Jonas mention the Café Roma. Jonas put his ear closer to his dry lips. "Asher, what happened?" But he didn't hear. "Asher, look at me. Where do you live?"

"We'll take you there." Charly shooed away a cat. She squatted, lifted Asher's grizzled chin, and tipped some water from her canteen into his mouth. Then she fanned him with her wide-brimmed floppy hat.

Asher stirred slightly and choked out a pleading whisper. "No, no. Not there. Please." The question had frightened him apparently into some awareness for his dull, tired eyes eased partly open at Jonas, alarmed. "They may have discovered...they may have found my...my...address and watch there."

"You mean the Brits?" Jonas asked.

Asher mustered a weak nod, coughed, and whispered, "Them, yes."

More spit dribbled onto his chin. Charly daubed it away with a kerchief, gripped a limp hand, and stroked it. "Where do you want to go?"

A shopper carrying a string bag filled with groceries stopped and asked to help. Asher shook his head no and eyed her dully until she continued on. "A pen, please." But his hand shook, his grip loosened, and the pen dropped to his side. He gestured Jonas to lean even closer to his mouth. Then he strained whispering, "ba...ba...ba-ke-ry, Hamelekh King George Street" and its number. Jonas wrote quickly.

Chapter 31

He frantically waved down a taxi with both hands. "Our friend collapsed from the heat. Here, this address." Asher flopped an arm over Jonas's shoulder, and he eased the youth onto a rear passenger seat. As their cabbie twisted around for the piece of paper, Jonas noticed some purple numbers tattooed on his left forearm. Another death camp survivor. "His brother owns a bakery. He'll know what to do. Quickly, please."

"It's near Magen David Square." Charly lifted Asher's head and helped him sip from her canteen again. "He's fine. Just a little weak, that's all. Nothing serious."

The taxi driver glanced at Asher. A frown of recognition passed across his face, but he said nothing.

Several blocks on, they stopped at an intersection. A policeman in the center of the hectic crossroad directed pedestrians and cars. A teenager girl in a hairnet escorted across three children holding hands. Two Hasidic Jews in long dark coats and black rabbit fur hats, despite the heat, strolled past. All saved from the European slaughter, Jonas thought, because of a narrow dry piece of land.

He caught something nailed onto a bank's facade as their driver drove on. The poster's heading, THE PALESTINE POLICE FORCE. WANTED, in English. The rest in English and in Arabic and Hebrew. Two rows of grim-faced men and one grim-faced woman beneath. The hair looked darker, perhaps dyed, and there were round spectacles as a disguise, but definitely Rivka Kozibrodska. An escapee from Acre Prison. Charged with arms smuggling.

Jonas nudged Charly and indicated the sought-after sign. Rivka had a five hundred-Palestinian pound price on her head. Charly nodded while writing quickly the wanted poster's specifics as their cabbie increased speed. At the Carmel Marketplace crossroad, they headed north on King George Street crammed with stores selling secondhand clothes, eyeglasses, shoes, pretzels, books. Finally they arrived at a rundown Bauhaus building with three stories of rounded balconies and the bakery on the ground floor.

The interior resembled small, family-owned bakeries he had seen in Chicago and New York. It smelled just as delicious from the freshly baked. A glass display counter ahead showcased rows of savory, exotic delights. Lebanese bread sprinkled with sesame seeds. Stacks of fluffy pita bread. Golden fried bread from North Africa. Challah rolls. The bakery looked somewhat American except that Asher, weak as he was, had insisted for some reason they bring him here and only here.

Behind the glass counter stood a plump woman with short white hair and in a lumpy peasant dress. She counted out coins into an old cash register, when, hearing the tiny bell above the entrance tinkle, she looked up. She saw Asher supported by Jonas, absently dropped some coins to the floor, and screamed, "Dov!"

A husky, unshaven man pushed through the swinging kitchen doors behind the counter. He was wiping his white hands, covered with flour, on his apron that covered a bump of a stomach. "Mama, what's—" and he too looked at them. "Mama, no more business for the day."

She slammed the cash register shut, her urgency knocking several pencils on the counter onto the linoleum floor. Ignoring them, she rushed to the front, twisted around the CLOSED sign for public viewing, locked the door, then hurried back to them. "Get him in back quickly. In the storage room. Before any British soldiers or police come."

"Asher's weak." Jonas took a closer look at Dov's mother leading the way towards the rear. Anyone's granny with a flock of grandkids except her frumpy looks concealed a possible fierce fighter.

"From lack of food," Charly added.

"He's tougher than he looks," Dov said.

"Let's hope so." Jonas kicked aside a trolly blocking the storage room's entrance, and it went crashing against a wall

"He come to right place." Dov's mother shooed away several mangy cats that had meandered across their path.

Jonas and Dov eased Asher down by the shoulders onto a narrow part of a wooden pallet, not stacked with bags of flour, against the storage room's near wall. Mama rolled up several aprons into a pillow, gently lifted Asher's head, and pushed the improvised support underneath. "You rest, my son." She caressed away some thick, sweaty strands of dark hair that had fallen across his face. "Dov, the alley. See if it's safe."

Asher stared, tears in his eyes, at Dov's mother. "Rivka's dead."

"What? Dead? No. Rivka? *Our* Rivka?" Her eyes went big with shock, and her hands shook as she put them to her wrinkled cheeks. "Oh my God in Heaven. Our Rivka, dead? No, no. Impossible. No, no, I don't believe it. She had survived Warsaw. She had survived Majdanek. She was a rock. An inspiration to everyone."

"I'm afraid it's true, Mrs. Sharon."

"The alley's safe, Mama." Dov turned the locks, his determination for security sounding with loud, forceful clicks. He gathered three chairs for Charly, Jonas, and his mother. He placed them in front of Asher, while he remained standing. "Can you tell us what happened?"

"Dov, let the poor boy rest." Mrs. Sharon settled next to Charly and Jonas, shaking her head at them in apparent disbelief. "She had cheated death so many times."

"Mama, let Asher speak. We must know what happened."

"I can rest later." Asher inhaled deeply, fighting for breath to tell what had occurred. He propped himself against the wall. Rivka was stopped in late April at a British checkpoint near the Yarkon River. That's in the north of Tel Aviv, he said looking across to Jonas and Charly. They patted her down for smuggled weapons. They found three grenades and an Enfield revolver. She said she needed them to protect herself against roving Arab gangs. They didn't believe her. They accused her of being a terrorist. They promised to charge her with possession of illegal arms stolen from a British warehouse or police station.

They took her first to Mahane Yehuda Police Headquarters. She refused to answer any questions except to say she needed them for self-defense. Even after hours of interrogating without food, little water, and sleep, she said only that.

"Good for her. Surviving that Warsaw ghetto slaughter," Charly added, "must have given her that strength."

"Survived? They fought, that's what they did, my child, for forty-two days and forty-two nights," Mrs. Sharon said. "More than those Poles did against the Germans in '39. They held out for only twenty-six."

"Mama, please let Asher continue," Dov said.

The British authorities wanted to break her, Asher continued. They questioned her for three days with no result. They then drove her, her feet and hands shackled together, her back stretched forward in pain, in the rear of a truck to Acre Prison.

The main prison in the north of Palestine, Dov explained to Charly and Jonas. An ancient fortress. Built during the Ottoman period over the remains of a crusader fortress. Massive stone walls as you'd expect. The most heavily guarded prison in the country. A medieval cage for swindlers, rapists, and murderers. Impossible to break out of.

"Impossible to break out? Ha! Ridiculous!" Mrs. Sharon handed Asher a tin cup of water. "Not for our Rivka."

Asher gulped several sips with both hands on the cup before continuing. Rivka told him afterwards, as her guards pushed her into Acre Prison, she'd never let them try her before a military court for their made-up charge of illegal possession. Never let them drop that scarlet hood over her head before hanging. She would somehow escape.

"There, you see," Mama said, refilling his cup, "the strongest willed person I've ever met. She had had enough humiliation."

"Everyone has," Asher added. At Acre Prison she faced a tougher interrogator. A mild-mannered Britisher who had questioned Nazis during the last war in something named the London Cage. Some prisoners called him the Bloodhound. Rivka called him Dr. Himmler because he looked so much like that top Nazi with his rimless glasses, frilly little mustache, and slight build. He was also just as ruthless interrogating.

Again the same procedure as at the Mahane Yehuda Police Headquarters, only for longer periods. No food. Little water. Little sleep. Dr. Himmler, just a foot away, no longer so mild-mannered. Now shouting questions at her, while he paced. Where did she get her weapons? Where did they hide them and their radio transmitter? In the Jordan Valley? In the Jezreel Valley? Who was her commander? How did she slip into Palestine? Getting his spit on her face and enjoying it. Still Rivka refused to answer, Asher said, looking proud at her defiance. Even when threatened with prison for ten years or the gallows.

The gallows or ten years in prison for defending herself? Mrs. Sharon mumbled to herself. Those British, incredible.

From time to time, another Englishman peeked into her cell to ask about any progress. Rivka thought his last name might be Frost or LaCoste or Forrest; she wasn't sure since she was delirious at times with so much pain.

Sometimes, this visitor insisted on questioning Rivka himself. His specialty, she thought, lifting her chin with the handle end of his riding whip. When she refused to answer his questions, he crashed the crop, smiling, down on a shoulder. Still she refused to reveal anything, though she felt excruciating pain.

One day while allowed out in the prison yard, Rivka overheard a rumor from a prisoner-friend. A German met sometimes in that prison's Administrative Wing with a high-ranking British civil servant.

Some color had returned to his young face, Jonas noticed, and his voice sounded stronger. Dov was right; Asher was healthier than he looked.

"The chair, Dov. Help me up." Dov slipped an arm around Asher's shoulders, hefted him to his feet, and eased him, grimacing, slowly down onto the seat. "That's a little better. Those poor British," he continued, chuckling, "they must have thought with 8,000 soldiers guarding that fortress, they had absolute privacy. Complete securi—"

Someone rapped hard on the front door. "Hello, anyone there? Mrs. Sharon, hello?" A British accent, sharp and demanding. "Anyone there?"

Dov and Mrs. Sharon darted frightened eyes to the entrance.

The front door rattled hard again. "Hello, hello, Mrs. Sharon, anyone."

"Answer it, mama," Dov whispered.

Charly nodded. "He sounds like a regular, Mrs. Sharon. A British soldier. You better answer. If you don't, he might get suspicious."

Another hard rap rattled the front door.

"Coming." She shuffled quickly toward the front door, patting into place her gray hair.

"You are closed, Mrs. Sharon? On a Wednesday? I thought only on your Sabbath," a British soldier asked.

"We're in mourning. A death of a friend. A heart attack. Terrible."

"I'm sorry to hear that."

"So are we, Captain Robinson. It was so sudden. Only thirty years old. A real *mensch*. Who would have thought? Could you come back tomorrow? We'll be open until five."

"Fine. Tomorrow then. Again, my condolences."

"One of the good ones," she explained to Charly and Jonas settling in once more.

Bravo, Jonas felt like saying about her calm lying. But Asher appeared eager to continue.

A German in Palestine? Rivka wondered. Curious about this rumor, she asked around. Soon she got a description of the visitor. Then several days later, someone stole Rivka's prisoner-friend's mat for sleeping and his flannel shirts. He went to the Prisoner Intake Room to ask for a resupply. He passed a man in a corridor hurrying past for some reason. Maybe to leave. Maybe by a back entrance. He turned his head away as if he didn't want to be recognized. But Rivka's friend got enough of a look to see he matched that German visitor's description. As he rushed past a room, someone from inside called out his name. That upset him. A lot.

"That was his real name called out?" Mrs. Sharon settled a tray of oranges, flatbread, and hummus near Asher.

"Why else would he stop to scold that bureaucrat? Why else go into such a rage? Threaten to get the warden to fire him? The secret was no longer a secret."

"So what was it?" Charly inched her chair closer to hear better. "And spell it out, please."

"I don't know."

"You don't what?" Jonas glanced at Charly, puzzled. She looked as stunned and disappointed as he felt. "Rivka never told you? You, her close friend?"

"Maybe her closest," Charly added.

"Everyone talks, she said. Everyone. Sooner or later. We had a big argument over that. One of our few big ones in all the years I've known...that I knew her. I told her she had insulted me. I told her I would never betray our chance to be free at last. To get our own country. No matter the pain, I would never ever talk. She didn't care."

"She wouldn't budge at all?" Charly asked.

"What she heard was too important to reveal. Except at the right time."

"What do you mean?" Dov asked.

"She never said. Only that she had some plan."

"She never went beyond that?"

"No, Dov, my friend. Never. Just that she planned to blackmail the British colonial power."

"Blackmail? Her? Against a great world power like Britain? Ridiculous."

"Yes, Dov, blackmail."

"Not for her was it ridiculous, Dov," his mother said. "She had escaped the Warsaw ghetto, remember? One of the few. I don't think anything was impossible with our Rivka, may God avenge her blood. I think she was tired of being pushed around. Tired of the indignity."

"If her hunch about this man, this visitor, was right," Asher continued, "then blackmail. She pricked a finger with a sliver of wood from a bench, while waiting one day to be questioned. With her blood, she wrote tiny notes on scraps of toilet paper about her time in Acre. After she escaped, she recopied them into what she called her Special Book. Her secret weapon."

"What was so special about it?" Charly flipped to another page of her notebook.

"It was a little notepad. Very small. Easy to hide in the palm of her hand. And with an orange cover."

"Wasn't that risky?" Jonas asked. "The Brits might have hung her."

"And enjoyed it," Charly said.

"It was risky," Asher said, "if she relied on memory. She feared she might forget important details so the notes."

"How did she escape?" Charly searched in her shoulder bag for another pen.

Jewish underground factions in Acre had put aside their strong differences about how to fight the British and formed a reconnaissance team. It discovered a weak point in the prison-fortress. On the south side over a Turkish bath. They planned a breakout on a Sunday. The last one.

"You mean May 4th, Asher?" Charly asked.

"May 4th, yes. A few days ago. The organizers could find only so many safehouses, so only so many could escape. Rivka was among those chosen."

"Why her, Asher?" Charly underlined twice the date in red in her notes, then continued writing.

"She had survived the Warsaw ghetto. She was a symbol."

"Of the Jewish will to live?"

"Of the will to *fight* to live. No matter what." At the right time, Rivka changed into civilian clothes her friends had smuggled in. The TNT charges blew a huge hole in the fortress wall. She fled along with others through it and escaped in a heavy truck disguised as British military.

She avoided checkpoints and soon slipped back into Tel Aviv. To one of the pre-planned hiding holes in the Florentin quarter. But the city had become too dangerous. The British sprang surprise raids almost daily to uncover arms and to gather intelligence. She decided to smuggle herself and her special orange notepad out to a kibbitz near the Lebanese border.

Asher sipped more water and nibbled on the flatbread. "I visited when I could while she was here. In Tel Aviv. When it was safe. There was a kid there in the Florentin neighborhood. Little Moshe. He'd lost his family. All thirteen members in France during a *rafle*."

"A French police roundup of stateless Jews," Dov said.

"Little Moshe clung to us, his new family," Asher continued. "He said he noticed a man hanging around her Florentin hideout. Young. Dark Middle Eastern looks. Always pretending to be busy. But we didn't take him seriously. He said crazy things. Someone who sneezed would die. Always close the Bible so the devil couldn't enter and use its wisdom. Everyone thought he was *meshuga*."

"Crazy." Mama tapped her temple. "Not right in the head."

"Whoever he spotted must have acted quickly and murdered Rivka." Asher struggled to his feet, but still looking too tired slumped back into his chair. "I want you two to rent her apartment."

Charly frowned surprise. "Us?"

"Yes, you two. The Brits know all our faces. They have us under surveillance. Not you two. You don't make much money. You can't afford anything fancy. So why not rent her little place? That will be your story. You will search it for Rivka's special notepad."

"What about Rivka's killer?" Jonas asked.

"We'll take care of him," Dov said.

"Not the Palestinian police?"

Dov said nothing, only shrugged his massive shoulders. Still not uttering a word he headed toward the rear exit, flexing his fists in rage.

Chapter 32

Daniel walked quickly south along the ocean front. He warned himself not to glance back, praying no one followed. Since he had stabbed her, praise be to Allah, he had been lucky. No Jew policeman or Arab cop liking them had stopped him for questioning about the scratches on his face. That bitch had fought him like a pack of wild animals to the very end. Not a bit of fear in her eyes as he plunged the knife in. Only hate as she glared at him.

At a sidewalk café, he slumped down into a chair overlooking the Mediterranean waves splashing onto Andromeda's Rocks. Off to his right, an Arab in headdress rode along the beach on a donkey; his wife walked behind, balancing firewood on her head. Nearby a fat man, European looking and bare chested, trod along the dunes pocketing seashells.

He closed his eyes, fighting fear of discovery. He should have stayed at his stall in Nablus, selling tomatoes and okra. It was dull, but safe work. He could listen all day on the square's loudspeakers to the brothers on Radio Cairo speaking about *jihad* and death to the criminal Jews. No, he decided, he wouldn't make nearly what he now made from the One From Beyond. It had paid for his family's four room stone home with basement, a well, that olive grove, and those goats in Ramallah. He'd been able to buy medicine at that clinic in Hebron for his mother's heart problem and a falcon for himself. Yet all that had come at a price, the One From Beyond.

After a moment, he heard a waiter approach. He ordered a Turkish coffee. It would keep him alert for hours for any threat. He grabbed a newspaper some patron had left on a nearby table and shook it open. He'd pretend he didn't have a care in the world, while he rested.

The newspaper was an English one, the headlines in big bold type. The front-page article...Britain would keep its arms embargo against the Jews. The American president Truman might follow suit in the coming months. Good for them! he thought.

Below the article, a photo of a white-haired midget of a man smiled into the camera. Daniel laughed. That was the Jews' leader, this little Ben-Gurion guy? His brother-in-law was twice as tall. All the Jordanian soldiers were. What was he smiling about? Didn't he understand the war against them would be short, quick, with no mercy. His brother fighters would hack all prisoners to death, and the battle would be easily won. Crowds in Amman, Damascus, Gaza, Jenin, from all over the Arab world, would take to the streets cheering and firing rifles into the air over their glorious victory. Some might even make the *Hajj* spiritual journey to Mecca to thank Allah.

His coffee arrived at last. He chucked the newspaper aside, took several quick sips, felt the jolt, pushed himself up for the meeting. After a time, he reached the old port of Jaffa. He checked his wristwatch under a street lamp's glow. He was on time. The One From Beyond didn't like him being late. He had yelled at him twice when he had arrived five minutes past the agreed hour. His shouting felt like a whip cracked across his back again and again. He was a busy man, he had yelled. Many responsibilities. Don't be late again. Ever. Daniel quickened his steps.

A lone seagull swooped down onto a nearby pier ahead. It picked up a scrap of bread and flapped off, soaring into the misty dusk east toward the Clock Tower. Far out to sea he could just make out the lean silhouette of a ship cruise slowly north towards Haifa Bay. Maybe a Jew arms runner. He hoped not. If it was, he prayed the British would sink it.

He paused at the arched stone entrance to some inner courtyards and buildings. In an Ottoman style bay window protruding from the limestone wall above, a lone candle flickered. The One From Beyond had approved that Friday meeting. *Hamdullah*, he thought. Praise be to God. The One From Beyond had understood the emergency.

Daniel braced himself, silently praying, *Allahu Akbar, Allahu Akbar*. God is the greatest. He trotted up the dark stairs, through a narrow passage, dimly lit by a lone flickering overhead bulb, next a courtyard fragrant with flowers, up more steps until he reached the top and the salty ocean air. A few more steps, and he was admitted.

The One From Beyond sat at a small table ahead, head bent in concentration, writing. Besides an ink well lay a plate of hummus and a stack of pita bread that smelled freshly baked. He wasn't offered any. "*Salaam aleikum*, sir."

He merely nodded as he remained engrossed in his task. After a moment more, he flourished his message to a clerk with a toothbrush mustache and fez hat, who had come running from a nearby room. "See this is encrypted immediately and sent off. One copy to our London embassy. One to Berlin. And remember, Mustafa, burn the original. Well, come closer into the light, Daniel. I'm not going to bite your head off. Why this emergency meeting? Something about their Haganah military acting up? I wouldn't doubt it. Those Jews, always trouble." He leaned forward, squinting. "Those scratches, what happened to your face?"

"From a fight, dear sir. I...I...I—"

"For God's sake, boy, out with it. We don't have all night."

"I killed a Jewish terrorist."

"You did *what?*"

"I killed a Jewish terrorist."

"You killed a Jewish terrorist?"

"Yes, dear sir. A Jewish terrorist. A Rivka Kozibrodska. I've been hiding out since then."

"Where?"

"At the worker's hostel until I could signal you. This evening starts the Jew Sabbath. Everyone's in temple praying. I thought it safe—"

"Wait. When did you do this killing business, Daniel?"

"Two days ago. On a Wednesday."

He pushed himself up and began pacing. "Why in God's name did you do that, Daniel? Why?"

"I feared she had discovered you."

He stopped in front of Daniel and stared at him. "You feared what? How could she possibly do that? No one has discovered me, Daniel. No one. Ever. But you're telling me a Jewish terrorist did?"

"Yes sir. I killed."

He resumed pacing, head now bent in thought, working things out. "How did she do this, this, this discovery of me?"

"A notebook."

"Christ, Daniel, I'm in no mood for riddles. What does a notebook have to do with it?"

"Several days ago, dear sir, a Jewish terrorist cell kidnapped two Americans. A man and a woman. They took them to a monastery in Haifa. I was close by part of the time when they questioned them."

"Slow down. Who questioned them?"

"The Jews Abraham and Isaac; I reported on them before."

"I thought they sounded familiar. Abraham and Isaac, code names obviously. There was a third Jew, wasn't there? A young boy? An orphan from Poland?"

"Jacob. At least that's what he goes by, sir. But he didn't say much."

"Find out their real identities."

"With Allah's blessing, of course. The two Jews asked the Americans what they knew about this Rivka Kozibrodska. These Zionist lovers said they didn't know the woman. They lied and lied about not knowing her. The leader, this Abraham, didn't believe they lied. The fool Jew believed them and let them go. They were driven back to Tel Aviv. On the way, I managed to read this American woman's notebook."

He stopped in front of Daniel again. "She a reporter?"

"I think she is, yes dear sir. She talks to people. Asks them questions."

"A reporter, just great. You get her name?"

"A Charly somebody. I wasn't close enough all the time to hear everything said. But someone important, I think."

"Charly, Charly, an unusual name. Haven't heard of her. Just great, another journalist. Well, get on with it."

"On one of her pages she had written the name *Rivka Kozibrodska* and what she had said to this reporter, *Even against the few Germans who help the British*."

"And you did what?"

"I was worried. I thought I must find this Jew Rivka. I must see what she knows about you. Some of the money you paid me I paid others to help. Along with the promise of arms to fight the Jew invader."

"Good. It shows initiative. Go on."

"It took work by many brothers. Listening at cafés. Watching buildings and markets. The Jaffa port. The kiosks on Rothschild Boulevard. But Allah granted me success. A cousin of a friend, Said, he noticed a young woman. Said is a newspaper dis...dis...trib—"

"Distributor, Daniel. I think that's what you mean. Someone who helps pass out the paper."

"Yes, yes, that. On his bicycle one day, he noticed her. She had left a building a few blocks south of Rothschild Boulevard. On Mizrahi Street. In the Florentin neighborhood."

"A filthy quarter. Even for rats. Go on."

"This woman walked with a limp and looked over her shoulder sometimes."

"This Rivka woman must have feared someone followed."

"My guess, too. I thought it was worth looking into. I knocked on her door. It opened a little like she was scared, and I think I'm right that I smell a Jew. That she is the one, this Rivka. I pretended I had moved from the hills around Bethlehem to Tel Aviv. Could she recommend any kosher butcher shops in Florentin? She looked suspicious. She started to close her door, but I broke in. I tied her up. I put a knife to her throat. I asked her how she knew your name. The German, the German, tell me what you know about the German. That's what I said. Over and over again. But she wouldn't tell me. Or where she hid her notes about you."

"Notes? Why would you think she had any notes about me?"

"I just assumed—"

"Assumed? Oh for God's sake. Did she actually *say* my name? *Actually* say it, Daniel?"

"No sir. She said no name. But—"

"So what made you think she did?"

"She knew some Germans were helping the British. She knew your name. I mean, she must have. She just would not tell it. I was protecting you, dear sir, when I killed her."

"Protecting me?"

"Yes, dear sir. That."

"You idiot! You fool! Daniel, you may have stirred up a hornet's nest."

The whip cracked hard across his back. Daniel winced and swallowed. "I have, dear sir?"

"Yes, you have, *dear sir.* One hell of a lot of trouble from her friends. Killing this Jew because of your stupid assumptions. You're supposed to get information on them. Where they get their guns. What kind of ammunition. How they sneak into Palestine. From Europe? From Lebanon or Syria? The planned attacks against the British. Do you understand my English, Daniel? Is it simple enough for your little brain to understand? Not kill them. Not even one...as tempting as it is."

The whip again. "Yes, dear sir."

"That's *all* you were supposed to do. Gather intelligence. Period. Nothing more than that. That's why I picked you. Because you look Moroccan or Algerian and can blend in with them."

"But sir, my parents are Egyptian."

"Of course they are. But you *look* like a Jew from that part of the Middle East. Your Hebrew is perfect, and because of this." From his desk drawer, he withdrew several items and tossed them onto his desk. "Well?"

A surprise test, Daniel realized. He studied the items for several seconds. Then he closed his eyes, hearing the ticking of a gold pocket watch, hearing an impatient tap of a shoe.

"Time."

Daniel kept his eyes shut. "A number 2 pencil. To the right, an eraser rubbed down on its left side. Below, a ten-pound English note. Two Egyptian coins, dear sir. One with an eagle, wings spread; one with three pyramids. An Iraqi coin with three palm—"

"Okay, enough. Have I made my point about your memory? To memorize maps, faces, documents."

"Yes sir," he said, opening his eyes again.

"I did not hire you to go off and do something on your own like killing... however much you enjoy killing Jews."

The whip still again. "Yes, dear sir."

"Yes, dear sir; yes, dear sir. That's all you can say? I feel like I'm talking to myself sometimes."

"Yes sir. I mean, well, there is something else, sir."

"Well, get on with it."

"A Jew ship will dock outside Haifa. The *Sufa*. I think that means *storm*. They talked about it at the last intelligence meeting."

He paused in front of Daniel again. "Oh?"

"Yes sir. A bigger ship. Bigger than normal. With more Jews. From all over. Romania. Hungary. Poland. All over."

"From all over. Shit, that's all I need." He snatched up a packet of cigarettes on his desk, lit up, and tossed his matchbook indifferently back onto his worktable.

"Sir?" For the first time, Daniel noticed he smoked. He seemed frightened of something.

"Nothing."

Mustafa, the coding clerk, rushed into the room, looking puzzled over something. He called his boss aside in a corner for a whispered conversation, their backs turned. There was some kind of printing, Daniel noticed, on the matchbook's glossy black cover. He cocked his head to better read the engraving. Embossed in raised gold letters, a business name, phone number, and an address. A part of Tel Aviv he rarely visited.

"And don't forget, Mustafa," he said, ending his chat and returning to Daniel, "burn the original."

"Weapons, this time, too, dear sir," Danial continued, "according to what I heard. Lots of them. Mauser pistols and Schmeisser submachine guns. All packed in cement barrels and farming equipment."

"If they're lucky enough to run the British blockade, Daniel. Which I doubt. When will this ship reach Haifa?"

"I'm working on it, sir."

"I hope so. And these notes this Rivka woman might have kept."

"Sir?"

"On second thought, she might have kept some, after all. Where do you think they are?"

"I don't know, sir."

"I don't pay you for your 'I don't knows.' Where do you think they are? Your best guess."

"In her little apartment."

"I want you to search for them. They might have my name on some pages."

"Yes, dear sir."

"Are my instructions clear, Daniel? Locate this dead woman's notes. If there are any. Nothing more. Locate and bring them here. You can find out who Abraham, Isaac, and Jacob are another time. Do you have any questions? Any at all?"

"No dear sir. I understand everything at last. Everything is very clear." He gave a slight bow of departure. "May Allah give you many years of happiness."

In more ways than one was it clear, he thought as he made his way to the door. He had no desire to be a *shaheed* for the One From Beyond. He'd have to get someone else for any martyrdom. He'd pass quickly by that address on that matchbook, Daniel decided. Discover who the One From Beyond really was. Perhaps in the future, mail an anonymous note to the Jews, warn of a spy in Palestine. Sell him out for all the times he had cracked the whip. It'd serve that son of a bastard Christian infidel right.

Chapter 33

During Sunday brunch at Dov's bakery, Asher explained how a foreigner could rent an apartment in a Tel Aviv that daily filled with the newly arrived. What agency to visit. What documents, which a refugee-friend Pole could quickly forge, they'd need. What forms to fill out. Who would turn a blind eye to any suspicions. Who could be bribed. Who conducted himself strictly by the book. Under absolutely no circumstance, he had stressed, must anyone suspect their real reason for renting.

What was so damn special about Rivka's orange notepad Asher thought might be hidden in that tiny rooftop apartment? Jonas wondered. But he knew the youth, battle-tough, was tight lipped.

On the following hot Tuesday morning in May, he and Charly showed up at the drab rental agency in central Tel Aviv. Near Bialik Street, its outside was modest. A lone door for an entrance. A drainage pipe to the right to channel the rare rain from the second story. Two windows to the left shuttered against the harsh heat in the desert city. An ugly duck, he thought, among the swans of the surrounding graceful, white Bauhaus buildings.

The inside was as colorless, as no-nonsense. Ahead a long wooden counter ran nearly the length of the office. Behind it were three rows of metal desks, all manned by clerks. All bent over concentrating on their work. In front of it lay four rows of chipped metal folding chairs, all but two occupied. The air was filled with cigarette smoke from anxious-looking seekers, many with bawling kids. Mixed in with their cries was a babble of European languages of the beaten down—Polish, German, Russian—in the Middle East heat.

Jonas took a slip of paper with a number and seated himself next to Charly, who had already taken her place. Then they did what all visitors did; they fanned themselves while they waited for their turn.

And waited. And waited. After a time, Charly withdrew one of her tattered journals from her red shoulder bag and scribbled away.

Jonas peeked. *More Arab troops massed on Egyptian and Syrian borders. A car bomb, Nablus. Four dead. All children. Attacker or attackers unknown. Nazi murderer Aribert Heim reportedly spotted near Damascus. Heading to Tel Aviv? Panicky Tel Aviv mob groceries to stock up food.* "You're quite the notetaker."

"It's called survival in a brutally competitive business. There are two things I've learned from rival reporters."

"Rivals, not friends?"

"Them? You kidding? Never." She glanced at him and held her gaze. "Never, never, never, Jonas. Not a one. None of them. Not *that* Martha Gellhorn. Not *that* Virginia Cowles. Certainly not *that* high society photographer Lee Miller. None of them. We're all competitors. And fierce ones at that. Like you guys. But I've learned from them. We hate another journalist scooping us. And we hate even more being wrong. As a mentor said, 'Get it first, but get it right.' So, yes, I'm quite the notetaker. You never know what you'll need."

"Think there's any truth to that Aribert Heim sighting?"

Before she could answer, a bureaucrat in short sleeves and pants hitched up above his bulging stomach, schlepped out from behind the counter. In a voice that seemed to tax him, he called out their turn and introduced himself as Ebner.

They were looking for a small apartment in Tel Aviv, Jonas said as they made their way to his messy desk.

So vhat's new? the clerk said, gesturing vaguely for them to sit. Everyone was looking for a place those days. Tel Avis was booming. Couldn't they see that? Why a boatload of Yemenites and Turks had docked just days ago at Jaffa. Where would they put everyone?

Jonas ignored the clerk's grumpiness and held his smile. They had heard a tiny rooftop apartment in the Florentin neighborhood of Tel

Aviv was recently vacated. Why, they weren't clear, but it was now on the market, and they were interested.

The bald, middle-aged clerk with the droopy, tired eyes of an overworked cipher momentarily ignored them. He had the chalk white skin of an indoor man. He stamped some document and pitched it indifferently into a wire basket on his cluttered desk. Still taking his time, he pushed his spectacles up to the bridge of his nose shiny with sweat. He moved aside a framed photo of some relative in uniform. Next he adjusted the portable swivel fan to blow directly on him, ruffling his few gray hairs. Only then did he eye them and nod yes, it was available. Someone had recently murdered a woman, who had lived there alone. A young recluse, he had heard. No relatives, he added. Probably all killed off in some European oven. Maybe Belzec. Maybe Treblinka. Poor thing, the trauma. The police had decided burglary as the crime. They could find no culprit, ended their investigation, and moved on. Her two rooms were now open to viewing. Were they interested? Jonas, surprised the clerk hadn't heard him the first time, said they were.

The clerk stretched behind him to a cluttered smaller desk, plopped down on his larger one an album, and slowly thumped through several pages of listings. "You mean this?" he asked, as if needing reassurance of their terrible choice. He tapped a finger on an ugly four-story cement rectangular block Jonas thought resembled a World War II German blockhouse. "This one?" he again asked.

"That one," Charly replied. They realized the property was a little run down, which caused an amused smile and nod from the minor, minor bureaucrat. But she and Jonas valued their privacy for, well, she felt certain he would understand. "We'll—"

"Think about it," Jonas said, which brought a startled expression to Charly's face. "Yes, we'll think about it," he repeated, more to her than him, to stress his intention. "But we'd like to first look at it, then think it over. What about a deposit to hold it, for say, five or six days?"

The clerk gave an indifferent shrug. The tiny apartment wasn't in much demand by growing families anyway. "Five days, six. Vhat does it matter?"

There were forms to fill out. Palestinian bureaucracy probably moved like its cousins the world over, Jonas assumed,…clanking slowly and ponderously. Yet by the end of that morning, he and Charly had a pleasant surprise. They had filled them out and paid a deposit to possibly rent Rivka's rooftop hideaway south of Rothschild Boulevard in the Florentin neighborhood.

Was Asher's briefing on how to rent in the city all for nothing? Jonas wondered. Did the quickness giving tourists priority over refugees and natives owe to the clerk looking smitten with Charly? He had, after all, spoken mostly to her, Jonas noticed. Did that clerk suspect that tiny rooftop apartment had served as a safehouse for one of Britain's Palestinian command's most wanted? That it might harbor some important document? He appeared too distracted for any such thought. For he had gazed from time to time at the top of Charly's blouse, the top button of which she had conveniently unbuttoned before their appointment. Or had her flirtatious laughter at his terrible jokes sabotaged any doubts? No matter. They had the keys in hand for the fifty-eight steps, six flights of stairs, to get to Rivka's drab rooftop hideout.

"Burglary," Charly said as they left the office. "Save me. Really."

"Yeah, I know. With what few things she owned."

"What was all that we'll-think-it-over business back there about?"

"A photo on that clerk's desk showed a guy looking like him in a police uniform."

"A brother?" she asked.

"That's what I'm afraid of. Renting immediately might seem odd to that clerk. He might pass on his suspicion. So we take a look. Do a quick search. If we don't find anything, return in two or three days. If we still haven't found anything, then move in to look deeper."

Chapter 34

That blistery hot Tuesday afternoon, he stood at the threshold to the rooftop apartment, keys in hand.

"Oh my God," Charly said.

Jonas nodded. "Oh my God is right." He hadn't understood how tiny the apartment really was until then. There had been little room for Rivka to stretch. There had been little room to do anything really, except sleep and pray for safety. The dirty walls pressing in made him feel claustrophobic. How could she have possibly hidden out there? Unless she had been desperate. Unless she had a hefty price on her head for a false charge. Unless a murderous authority had hunted her like all-powerful governments had hounded her, her family and friends throughout Europe.

He and Charly had rented some crap holes in Rome, Paris, and Berlin, he had to admit. But the hotels and pensions had always had some brightness...a chandelier in the dining room; threadbare red carpeting on the stairs; some art, however questionable, hung. Yet never anything as primitive, as basic as this. A simple wooden table against the wall ahead. To the right, across from it, a tiny kitchen. Straight ahead through another doorway, the living room that doubled as a bedroom. A wardrobe closet stood against the right wall. Only one wall outlet spotted. And somewhere in that barely furnished safehouse may lay hidden something that might have cost Rivka her life.

He peeked through the grimy slats of the Venetian blinds to the narrow, dusty street below. No armed personal carrier lay in wait with British soldiers primed to storm. No dubious characters hung around. No adults anywhere. Only a group of laughing school children skipping along on the opposite sidewalk.

If he and Charly were lucky, he thought. If Rivka's killer hadn't wanted to attract attention after murdering her. If he had fled immediately afterwards. Which meant her dangerous notes, whatever they were, could still be somewhere there. He looked around. Where to begin? Under the buckling floorboards? Tapping the dreary walls with its peeling paint for some cavity? Checking in the little kitchen among the pots and pans? Where to begin?

Chapter 35

"Just a minute! You there! Stop!" the British soldier in the red beret near the Café Grand Paris demanded. "You, I said stop! Are you deaf? You must open that package. Those are our orders. You know that. No exceptions! Open it. Come on, quickly, and let me see your identity card."

"But these are just socks I darned. For my grandchildren. I made—"

The young, lean soldier snatched the identity card from the gray old woman. He studied it before tossing it back into her wrinkled face, then grabbed her bundle. "That makes no difference. You've seen our warning posters everywhere. Everyone, and I mean everyone, is subject to search." He ripped away the blue and white ribbons savagely.

Oliver Porter took a step toward him, opened his mouth to object to the treatment, then stopped. Father Karl had insisted keep aloof from all British colonial matters. Always. Stay the harmless, object-of-ridicule businessman.

"There you see?" she said. "No ticking bomb. No what-do-you-call-it, grenade? Pretty socks, that's all, pretty socks. For my grandchildren. And a cute little bathing suit. I bought it on Bograshov Street. From a peddler."

The soldier thrust the mess of a package at her. "Go on, get out of here, granny." He flicked an imperious finger at Oliver Porter. "You, next."

Oliver Porter shuffled up to him and braced for his own grilling and search. But all the soldier asked was, "Where are you off to, mate?"

"The Café Grand Paris just ahead. For a nice cold drink. To cool off on this hot Wednesday."

The soldier's weary face brightened hearing a bit of home in his accent, Oliver Porter noticed. A kid really. He looked like he just wanted to finish his tour and return to London, Liverpool, Glasgow, or wherever his parents lived.

"In this weather, mate, who can blame you? Four blocks from the beach, and I've already changed uniforms twice today I've been so sweaty. Righto, on your way then, old man."

Oliver Porter paused at the entrance to the café. In a reserved booth along the left wall sat the rangy reporter for the *Chicago Press Observer*. He probably still used the Grand Paris as his mailing address. He read *Le Monde, h*is round glasses perched above his pale eyebrows, his apple strudel forgotten. No trace of grief over his son's brain cancer showed on his unlined Mid-Western face. He would later hold court for other foreign correspondents covering Palestine. They'd swap news, rumors, and gossip about their respective beats.

Several waiters against the far wall next to the bar stopped chatting and looked his way, Oliver Porter saw. But only one, as he had insisted during their planning, approached. He offered up the smile given to all customers, acting as if they were strangers who had never met.

"You wish a table inside or outside, monsieur?"

"Inside, please. Away from this terrible heat. For just me."

"This way, please, monsieur."

No small talk from Chaim as he led the way, Oliver Porter was pleased to see. No indication they had recently scripted everything out. No knowing, conspiratorial smile. No too long eye contact from a fellow plotter exchanged. Nothing that'd reveal the simple scheme. Chaim acting like he was just another customer who needed rest from the heat. Luckily, as the waiter had said, all the servers wore white gloves there. So nothing to cause any suspicion. Only some class from the City of Light in the desert outpost of Tel Aviv. Like in the old days for Chaim. Before he and his family had fled. Before their murders.

As the waiter had promised, his table was near where the man would settle in, but not too close to draw uneasy attention. Close enough to eavesdrop and observe.

An old *Time Magazine* with Princes Elizabeth on its cover lay on the little marble-topped table. Oliver Porter flipped it open and pretended to read, his mind elsewhere. That Lebanese arms dealer had failed to come through. So had that Greek antiquities robber and that camel thief. None had provided any intelligence or even a whisper of a rumor on Asher. Where had that wanted man gone after entering Dov's Bakery? What did Karl expect? He was a one-man surveillance squad; he could do just so much. Asher's trail had gone stone cold. Which left only one other lead about that stomach-churning rumor Father Karl had overheard. Chaim the waiter and a suspicion he swore made the hairs on his neck stand up.

A boisterous "hello, *shalom*" boomed out in the café.

Oliver Porter glanced across to the entrance. Just as quickly he forced himself to stare at the magazine's black print. His heart beat faster now. His man had entered. The man gave a carefree wave to two bearded Jews playing backgammon before he strolled over to his usual round marble-topped table. Just as Chaim had predicted. Reserved only for him. With cash slipped on the side to assure that. At the very back. With a clear view of everyone. And maybe armed for a quick escape, if needed.

Oliver Porter watched as Chaim straightened his black bow tie and smoothed down his buttoned black vest. Readying himself, it seemed, for the performance of his tragic life. He approached the man, then suddenly clutched a hand to his chest. Oh my God no. A heart attack for sure. From the stress serving that man and the memories that had returned. Shocked at this, Oliver Porter accidentally bumped a spoon off his own table. But no, he realized, bending to pick it up. The waiter had only caught a pen that had slipped from his shirt pocket.

"You're usual, monsieur?" Chaim asked.

Oliver Porter marveled the waiter asked without any tremor of fear in his voice. Where had he gotten that strength to force that politeness? Perhaps if you had survived Auschwitz and God knows how many other killing camps with most humans not caring, you developed an inner reserve. And used it when most needed.

"The usual, Chaim, if you don't mind."

That too surprised Oliver Porter as he casually flipped to another page of his magazine. He had expected the answer in Hebrew or Yiddish. That made for good cover, after all. But the reply came in English with only a slight accent. And a further surprise, he didn't detect any loathing of Chaim in the man's voice. Years of possibly being on the run must have buried that to elude those few authorities who still cared.

The man reached behind and took a newspaper from the rack of them, mostly European editions. It was a *Jerusalem Post,* Oliver Porter noticed. Another nice touch of cover...if Chaim was right.

The man sat for a time reading the *Post* until Chaim approached him, and Oliver Porter held his breath. In their discussion days earlier, he had insisted Chaim serve with his right hand. Doing otherwise might alert their man to an avenger. He might do, as he might have done before, flee. But Chaim had argued no. He must show he had survived and that he remembered. That was the least he could do for the twenty-three members of his family slaughtered. So Chaim took the man's coffee and chocolate pastry from the tray with his left hand and with his left hand placed both and the cutlery in front of the man. And, of all the bloody things, smiled into the man's face!

Oliver Porter, violating all security procedures, forgetting his magazine, watched transfixed at Chaim's performance. In serving, he had exposed a series of numbers inked on his upper left arm. Never had he, Oliver Porter, thought he'd hate numbers so much. They were a sort of shorthand history of the murderous and barbarous century. Of joyful indifference by the great and the ordinary to the wholesale slaughter of so many helpless innocents.

Yet from the man, nothing. No glance up at Chaim. No show of the slightest emotion. No words of sympathy uttered. He simply returned to studying the *Post*. Studying, not reading, yes, that's what the man was doing, Oliver Porter decided. Studying for something. Every single item, it seemed, from the first to the last page. A full hour sitting there, Oliver Porter noticed, checking his wristwatch. Without taking even a minute's break. Scrutinizing for what?

Something in that piddly four-page gossip sheet he now turned to? It featured only street news about clan wars between Arab families, factional fights between Jews when they weren't fighting the British colonial power and Arabs.

Next the *New York Times*. Once again reading every single page. Then all the other newspapers. All thirty-one of them. English, Italian, French, German, Russian, Yiddish, and Arabic ones. Two-page affairs put together by just-off-the-boat poor immigrants on mimeographs, multi-section offerings cranked out on expensive, well-oiled machines by wealthy American and British corporations. Oliver Porter couldn't recall knowing someone show such interest in the news. Except for Father Karl and his own private voluminous war library.

He was wrong about the customer, he decided. He had assumed the man a Francophile. That he regularly visited the Café Grand Paris because he loved French culture and food. Then he had decided the man yearned for a taste of Europe when slipping back to his own home might be far, far too dangerous. Even fatal. Now he understood the real reason. The Café Grand Paris offered the largest number of Palestinian and international newspapers in Tel Aviv. Racks of them hung head-level to the granite floor right across the long wall. His own intelligence center maybe, in a way, the Café Grand Paris. Right out in the open. And no one suspected. What cocky arrogance! What chutzpah!

After a time, Oliver Porter heard a bistro chair scrape back. He knew, without looking up, his man headed elsewhere. He knew, without looking up, Chaim collected the knife, the fork, the dainty cup, saucer and plate doing so, as instructed, with his waiter's gloved hands. He waited another few minutes to not arouse suspicion among any possible informer or reporter before he too left.

The Opel, fully tanked up, lay parked where he had left it hours ago. Next to a modest family-run pottery shop near Ben-Yehuda Street. He felt around under the driver's seat. It was there, where faithful Chaim had tucked it, the cardboard box containing the fork, the knife, the dainty cup, the saucer and plate.

He drove south out of Tel Aviv and soon reached Holon. That dreary suburb was the first of three British checkpoints he knew existed on that coastal road. But he was familiar to the guards, an amateur archeologist into Old Testament sights. Harmless. Quirky. Looking a little like a vaudeville slapstick comedian in his baggy pants. A flick of their eyes into the back with its camping gear and battered book on ancient digs, and they waved him on with an indifferent salute without searching further.

He checked his wristwatch and hit the pedal, next passing the ancient port village of Ashdod. A deadline to reach his rendezvous deep within the forbidding Negev wasteland with its canyons, wadis, and dusty mountains. Arriving well before dawn. Far from any curious British. Hopefully. Far also from Palestinian eyes, Jew or Arab, civilian or spy. Hopefully.

And somewhere in that vast desert, his needle in the haystack. He swung inland, passing a tiny kibbutz and the silhouette of its water tower. A little over an hour later, just north of the settlement town of Be'er Sheva, he pulled off the deserted narrow camel track of road. A howling, whistling wind buffeted the little car. He feared it might be a *khamsin*, the deadly wind-of-God sandstorm. Terrifying enough to keep even the hardiest of Bedouins hunkered down in tents. He saw the little trainer crate spiraling from the sky into a dune, exploding, and burning any proof positive of complicity.

Gnats buzzed around his head; with only an occasional swat, he mostly ignored them. He couldn't ignore the powdery dust that seeped into his Opel that rocked from the searing wind. It made him cough and gag. He knotted his handkerchief over his face to keep out the dust.

He shone a flashlight on the British Mandate ordinance map of the Negev Desert. The Scottish soldier well worth the bribe, he realized, for smuggling it out for its exacting detail. Frightfully vulnerable tiny kibbutzim here and there. Numerous Arab villages surrounding them. A solitary monastery in the vast wilderness. Several Bedouin camps. The biblical fortress of Masada and the elliptical Dead Sea to the east. Gaza miles to the west. That port of Eilat on the Gulf of Aqaba. The Jewish settlement of Revivim. Where the blood hell was—There. He tapped a much-chewed nail on the spot. He had found it. His needle in a haystack, a mere smudge of a short brown line. Thirty-five kilometers west of Transjordan; thirty kilometers southeast of biblical Be'er Sheva.

He pressed on, swerving once to avoid a gazelle that bounded across the make-shift road. An hour later, he found the dusty airstrip the British had abandoned at the end of the Second World War. A flimsy-looking single engine Auster idled in the desert dusk. Luckily the wind had died down, and he suffered only from some grit, thrown up by the propeller, getting into his tired eyes.

He made the hand-off to a trusted in civilian clothes, his dusty flight goggles pushed back, no identifying patches anywhere on him. He'd see it through to Malta. From there he'd safeguard it on a studier four-prop for the long-haul to its last destination. No incriminating forms signed that might alert some unsympathetic MI5 agent, who might pass them onto an even more critical MI6 one. No evidence of any transfer of the cardboard box that would end up at Croydon Airport outside London. From there a Karl-sanctioned motorcycle dispatch rider would hustle its contents, all carefully wrapped, to an anonymous Bayswater flat in London.

There, Father Karl would eagerly await the knife, fork, the dainty cup, the saucer and plate. He must surely have private copies of identifying markers of notorious Nazis on file. If he did, he'd know what to do, without leaving the slightest self-incriminating trace.

Chapter 36

As the sun rose higher scorching again Tel Aviv, Daniel could feel the rays burn his hair. He ignored the heat and waited.

He waited while he strolled to the end of the block, hands in his pockets, as if he hadn't any cares.

He waited while he bought a single orange from a street vendor, who had parked his stand across from the ugly cement tenement block.

He waited while he slowly peeled it, then slowly ate the fruit, glancing occasionally at the entrance.

He waited while further on, he stooped and scraped off some dog mess from the sole of a worn leather sandal.

He waited as long as he thought safe, waving away the swarms of flies, ignoring the skeletal cats nudging his legs for food. And still nothing. Still no opportunity spotted at that ugly cement tenement block the other side of the narrow street. Twice he had caught himself fingering imaginary worry beads and scolded himself to stop. He had glanced at his wristwatch. That American couple had been in the tiny rooftop shack an awfully long time. Were they just looking it over? Or going to move in? That cardboard vacancy sign—in Arabic, English, and Hebrew—still hung from that building's front door. They must be checking it out to maybe rent.

He had noticed them an hour earlier climb the stairs. If she were alone, he could handle her, should she catch him inside searching. But with her boyfriend or husband or whoever that guy was? With his husky build? Daniel knew he couldn't. Just looking at him made him nervous. The guy looked like some aging heavy weight boxer or bodyguard he'd seen sweating it out in a Ramallah gym. And another problem. How often could he himself walk past unnoticed? Even with pedestrians, he risked discovery. He must ask his fellow brothers to help watch.

Days ago, after he had killed that Jew woman, he had made it as far as her rooftop apartment. He had even been able to peek through the front unshaded window. That had told him everything. Tiny for her hideaway and with all her money! All that gold stored somewhere. A few pieces of furniture. A few articles of clothing scattered around. A quick in-and-out search for any notes with tools the One From Beyond had given. He was set to jimmy open the rickety front door when that fat old bag neighbor had struggled up the last stairs to the roof and demanded to know who he was!

Demanding to know who he was! Her nerve! He had almost killed her. Right then and there. Like he had done to that Jewish terrorist woman. A knife to her filthy fat gut except her grandson had appeared behind him, lugging up another basket of laundry. Probably a member of some Jewish bandit group. He certainly appeared old and fit enough.

Did she think she was Queen Nefertiti? Did she believe she owned the rooftop to that building and could do as she pleased? Lugging out still more laundry. Did she do dirty clothes for everyone in Tel Aviv?

She certainly took her time hanging out her laundry, chatting away with her grandson. About this. About that. Didn't that fat old bag have anything better to do? And just when she had left and he thought he could sneak into the little apartment, the old bag had brought out the rest of her grandchildren to escape their hot apartment.

He reached the end of the street, wiped sweat away from his forehead, and swatted away more flies. He headed back to his worker's hostel. He must pray for another chance to break in. He must somehow get into that Jew bandit's hideaway. But first he must spy on the fat old bag. Note her schedule. Then break in when it was safe.

Chapter 37

Jonas awoke with a start. Someone shouted and tried kicking their Berliner room door in. No, he realized, his head clearing of sleep, someone beat in panicky pounding bursts on their door. "Mr. Shaw, Miss Lawrence, we have an emergency. Open up, please. An emergency." Then more thunderous thumping. "Mr. Shaw, Miss Lawrence. Please, an emergency."

"What the?" Jonas mumbled to himself, then yelled, "Alright, enough! Keep your shirt on. I heard you the first time."

"What is it, honey?"

"I have no idea. I said, hold on, dammit. I'm coming." He stumbled to the door, fumbling with the cord to his bathrobe, rubbing sleep from his eyes, muttering curses at the ungodly hour. He unfastened the chain and peeked out to see a familiar, desert-browned face except it looked panic-stricken. "What's wrong, Abdul?" Up and down the carpeted long corridor a team of other clerks, in fractured English, French, and Italian, hammered on the doors of more guests.

Abdul examined a list he held in his trembling hand. "Just the two of you in Room 425, Mr. Shaw? You and your Miss Lawrence? No one else?"

"Only the two of us." Jonas caught the *New York Times* photographer next door stick his head out, his flabby cheeks lathered in soap. "Why? What's the matter?"

"Jonas, what's going on?" Charly peered over his shoulder at Abdul as she knotted her own bathrobe.

"Get dressed quickly, please. Both of you," Abdul said. In the room across from them, the Vatican correspondent had poked his head out, an electric razor in his hand. "*Signore, signore, c'e un problema?*"

Jonas suppressed a yawn. "Abdul, can you tell us what the hell is going on?"

"Someone just telephoned our switchboard. They've threatened to blow up our hotel in fifteen minutes. Oh and here, for you, Miss Lawrence," Abdul said before rushing off, "a letter from Jerusalem."

The Berliner employees and guests huddled several streets away. Abdul and his assistants had done a good job evacuating, Jonas noticed standing at the back.

Charly said the post was from the CID headquarters in the Russian Compound, Jerusalem. A captain what's-his-face offered apologies for the belated response to her questions about the Johnny Radcliffe death. They were understaffed and overworked. Murders happened almost daily in the British Mandate of Palestine. They faced a backlog of unsolved cases. But rest assured they took every case seriously. "Blah-blah-blah-blah, Jonas. In other words, you bullshitter captain so-and-so, no comment." She wadded up the letter and tossed it into her shoulder bag. "We plow on, dear. We plow on."

"Amen to that." Off to the side ahead, Jonas noticed two well-dressed, official-looking visitors. They both stood stiffly, formally, chatting only to each other and in low voices, and they kept patting their faces with their handkerchiefs. They seemed unused to the Middle East heat. They must have checked in while he and Charly were out. Each had set his bulging briefcase tucked closely between his trousered legs, as if guarding valuable papers. He could spot nothing revealing on their valises other than the leather was tarnished, much used in travel. No decals or labels of any kind boasted of exotic voyages. No embossed initials. Both cases blank. Like the two men.

Nearby stood the callow newspaper stringer from Rome, who Charly had slapped for propositioning her. He studiously avoided her, losing himself in some journal.

Steps away, that *Life Magazine* photographer, who had breezed in days ago from Cairo after finishing an assignment. He had covered the Germans defeating the Brits at Tobruk, the Brit victory over them at El-Alamein. He now looked for another big story to top his work in the last war. You've come to the right place, son, Jonas thought. There's gonna be one hell of a bloody blow-up here.

The haunted Jewish ballerina was there, too, he noticed. She had hidden out in Hitler's hellish Berlin in a cold, damp cellar for years. How she held out for so long, Jonas still couldn't understand. She now wanted to start her own dance studio.

He caught the taller of the two men ahead pull out a folder from his briefcase and thumb through several pages before withdrawing one and studying it. "How's your eyesight, Charly?"

"Why?"

"Those two men over there. By that kosher butcher shop. The taller one withdrew a paper or document or something from his valise. Can you make out what it is?"

Charly strained discreetly forward. "It looks like, I'm not sure, maybe a map?"

"A map?"

"Yes, dear, that, a map. It's got grids on it. On the left-hand bottom, an index of some kind." She turned to him. "Of streets it looks like? Why? Is something wrong?"

"Ten years working New York boroughs is nagging me about...I don't know. Maybe nothing, maybe something. That Aribert Heim Nazi fellow."

"You think he's slipped into Tel Aviv?"

"Possibly." A young man with tattoos on muscled arms trotted belatedly up to the front of the group, drawing his attention. The latecomer, an ex-U. S. Marine, clutched his suitcase, despite warnings not to return to the Berliner. The feisty novelist from New York, who hoped to write a best seller about the impending Palestinian war, must have rescued his manuscript.

They were all there now as far as he could tell, Jonas noticed, counting carefully twice. Forty-four of them now. The same number Charly, beside him, had noted. Forty-four total with one strangely missing. An important one. The Berliner's owner, Hans Peters. He had vanished.

Chapter 38

After a time and no explosion, the hotel guests became restless. Several Tel Aviv police ran down the street past the Berliner and motioned them to stay back.

But shortly after one that Thursday morning, a guest rushed toward the hotel's gated entrance, yelling he had left his passport in his room safe. A brawny British cop hustled him back into the sidewalk. He shouted through a megaphone the crowd must be patient. His Majesty's Government had shipped back several Royal Engineer Bomb Disposal Units to Britain, drawing down its Palestinian forces. But a squad from Jerusalem would arrive shortly. They were the only ones trained to defuse bombs.

The cop was right, Jonas realized. The Brits were slowly packing it in. Too many attempted assassinations. Too many successful ones. The morale of thousands of Sixth Airborne troops sagged. Many refused any longer to push persecuted families and orphans behind barbed wire.

A wiry man on crutches hobbled up to within a foot of the beefy cop. "Enough, you hear? Enough! You Brits freed us from Dachau death camp. But you kill us here."

"Go home. Everyone one of you fuckin' limey bastards," a slight man in beltless pants and undershirt heckled from a nearby street. "Go home, limey. We want our own country, limey."

"Yeah, our own country," a pack of ragtag teenagers shouted, taunting. "Our own country. Our own. Our own. Even if we have to die fighting for it." They hurled a volley of rocks at him, then scattered into the hot night.

Abdul scurried from guest to guest during the next few hours offering aid. Glasses of water, blankets, pillows, his sincerest apologies for this disruption. In the few minutes when not so occupied, he arranged with the Hotel Joseph for temporary sleeping arrangements.

The Joseph lay several blocks to the west of the Berliner and opposite an Ottoman Bank branch and Fatima Khalidi's Art Gallery. It sported a Florentine red dome three stories above its ceramic entrance of a camel caravan. But the Berliners' guests seemed too tired, Jonas noticed, to appreciate the eclectic Moroccan architecture. The Vatican correspondent bedded down on part of a plump U-shaped couch overlooking the arched main doorway. The ex-U. S. marine and best seller hopeful roughed it on blankets on the cold kitchen tiles. Others risked the aggravation of insects. They stretched out on one of the many wicker chairs in the courtyard butterfly garden.

Jonas relaxed on a sofa facing Reception. Charly curled up resting her head in his lap, smiling as he stroked her hair. Moments later Abdul collapsed next to him. Yawning, the Berliner's *de facto* second-in-charge eased off one leather sandal with a toe, then the other before closing his eyes.

"Another hot one," Jonas said.

Abdul merely nodded, looking too tired from helping guests to answer.

"I'm surprised Mr. Peters isn't here to help."

Eyes still shut, Abdul shrugged indifference. He and the hotel proprietor didn't socialize after hours, he muttered. At work, Mr. Peters talked only about hotel matters and appeared a very private man. Abdul confessed he didn't really know much about him. Only that he, like others in Tel Aviv, had fled Europe at the war's end.

Mr. Rashid Mansour, the previous owner, had shown up unexpectedly early at the hotel one rainy wintery morning. He feared a coming war between Jews and Arabs and was fleeing to the far-off safety of his beloved Cairo. He had transferred ownership to a Hans Peters, a recently arrived German emigre.

That very same day, Mr. Fadi Wahab, the assistant hotel manager, decided he missed his home city of Beirut and left for Lebanon without clearing out his office.

Other personnel also left that day, leaving him, Abdul, as the most senior employee left. The next morning, Hans Peters strode in, chatting all business from then until the present. He suspected Mr. Peters may have lost family in the vicious Berlin fighting with the Russians and didn't want to discuss that traumatic period. Abdul mustered enough energy to briefly glance at Jonas. Refugees survived, he said, by not looking back. Ever.

"What kind of boss is he?" Jonas asked.

Abdul yawned again. "He has his good days and bad. Like everyone else," he added, sounding like Hans Peters had never once yelled at him.

Mr. Peters could be anywhere now, he guessed. Maybe the German hospice in Jerusalem had called him away. He did, after all, sit on its board. Maybe he visited a good friend, as he seemed to do from time to time in the early hours. Maybe the edgy British held him up at some checkpoint. Maybe the edgy Arabs did. Or the edgy Jews. Abdul shrugged more indifference and added another yawn.

Or maybe his car had hit a land mine. All good reasons for his absence, Jonas thought. But still...

Hours later with Abdul's help, the Joseph and other hotels settled the stranded guests of the Berliner.

The explosion, when it blew, disrupted a rare Tel Aviv peaceful Friday morning, Jonas read in a newspaper in their latest hotel room. Its owner had rushed out a thin special edition in Arabic, Hebrew, and English. The journalist noted a short-staffed Bomb Disposal Unit had arrived belatedly to disarm it. A faulty fuse or faulty wire or faulty switch or faulty something had caused the minimal damage. Some casement windows blown out. A few twin silk curtains burned. Three ornate stainless-steel dining chairs singed. The fountain near Reception littered with mosaic tiles and other debris in the dirty water. But all in all, the Hotel Berliner would rise from the ashes and rather quickly, he concluded.

At breakfast, Jonas handed the special edition to one of the two suited, recently arrived guests, who had asked for it. Dark wavy hair. Average height. A quick, easy smile. But his eyes, two dark screens. He introduced himself as Ben Anderson from the States. A nice solid American name, Jonas thought. He picked up a Midwest twang, but that was it. Mr. Ben Anderson offered no more of himself. He wandered back to his companion at another table, who Jonas thought looked faintly British and well bred, and showed the extra to him. The two glanced at Jonas for some reason before Ben Anderson gestured at the special edition, leaving Jonas to his thoughts. Why was the Berliner targeted? Why not the Warshawsky or the San Remo or some other Tel Aviv lodging? And one other troubling question. Through all the night's turmoil, why hadn't Hans Peters, the hotel's prideful owner, never showed up once to check on his guests' welfare?

Chapter 39

The man who called himself Ben Anderson looked at his wristwatch, hurriedly snubbed out his cigar, and muttered something to his friend. They grabbed their bulging briefcases on the carpet, pushed back their chairs, and headed for the hotel's front entrance, Ben Anderson giving Jonas a perfunctory smile as he left.

Charly finished applying some lipstick and tossed the tube into her shoulder bag. "You're frowning. What's wrong?"

The Hotel Berliner bombing. Hans Peters missing. The two strangers just arrived, both in suits. Their inappropriate dress of knee-length coats in weather like this. Reports of Nazi fugitive Aribert Heim being in the Middle East. Something wasn't right. Jonas bunched his fists in anger with himself. He should have asked Ben Anderson some innocuous questions when he had had the chance. He might have found out more about him and his colleague. Discovered what the dickens they were up to in Tel Aviv. The damned Middle East heat had sapped him of his usual vigilance. He checked his canteen. It was filled with water.

"Jonas, I asked you a question. What's wrong?"

"I don't know. Something. That Nazi-on-the-run Aribert Heim. Or maybe nothing. We'll see." He pocketed two oranges from the breakfast buffet for the energy and kissed her on the cheek.

"Where are you going?"

"Out for a walk."

"Wait. I'll come with you."

"No! Stay here. Two might be noticed."

"For what?"

"Just stay here, Charly."

"Jonas, don't talk to me in that tone."

He walked off with only a quick glance back for a comment. The command in his voice had settled her back in her chair with a puzzled, upset look on her lovely face. He didn't want to waste time explaining his nagging interest.

The two hotel guests crossed Rothschild Boulevard. Did they have bodyguards? Were they setting up to entrap? Jonas pushed aside his worries as he saw them increase their pace. They headed east away from the beaches and towards a grim warren of crowded streets packed with old concrete and peeling plaster buildings. Charly might have been right after all, he thought, regretting his sharp tone of doubt with her. The man who called himself Ben Anderson might have really consulted a map.

The two strolled down a side road at times single file on the narrow, cracked pavement, chatting little. They focused ahead, ignoring a bakery and its delicious smells, not even glancing right out of curiosity at the trays of rolls and cakes displayed in the window. They sidestepped an arguing couple on the walkway, and Jonas was surprised when they didn't stop to even help an elderly man, whose skullcap had fallen to the pavement. And the thought flashed through his mind as he crossed still another street, the two might stay in Tel Aviv only shortly. Which might explain their overcoats. They might have flown in unprepared for the blistering heat, as though called upon suddenly for some important reason.

In their haste, they nearly bumped into a little girl, eyes closed, twirling round and round in some self-absorbed game. They must surely be sweating by now as he was. Yet they hurried on, despite any discomfort, hell bent on something, showing no indication whatsoever he followed.

Except, just past a hole-in-the wall falafel restaurant, at the next hectic narrow intersection. Ben Anderson stopped so suddenly a soldier in British military fatigue behind collided with him. And that, Jonas realized, saved him. For as the fighter apologized, he had time to duck into a store selling religious books before Ben Anderson gazed around. Did he sense a tail? Was he getting his bearings, like he would, in an exotic city with street signs not always in English? Jonas couldn't tell.

Further on, bunched around a transistor radio on an outdoor café table, a crowd listened to the latest on the impending war. The news in English was broadcast from the American colony in Jerusalem. The two paused to listen, but only momentarily. The Ben Anderson fellow checked his wristwatch, and they both continued on, now picking up their stride as though running behind schedule until they reached a crossroad. There they headed right onto a quiet side street with no cars, but one as far as Jonas could tell. He could smell its smoky exhaust and heard its rackety muffler as it idled.

He took a quick gulp of water from his canteen, counted to ten, then risked a peek around the corner before retreating to a doorway. He caught enough to be stunned, and he briefly wondered if the heat had affected what he had seen. The Ben Anderson fellow easing into the rear passenger seat. His colleague slouching into the front passenger seat. The introductions made. The unmistakable dusty rear British Mandate license plate. The unmistakable silhouette of the driver. Some kind of document passed to him. No, not a document, Jonas realized. A small camera, small enough for someone to conceal while taking secret snapshots for some reason. And what he had caught was real enough, he understood, to find himself muttering, "I'll be a New York son of a bitch."

He remained in shock over what he had seen all the way back to the Hotel Joseph. There, he found Charly lounging in the reception area, absorbed in a tattered *Great Gatsby*. Reception had crowded with arriving tourists, so he crouched down and whispered what he had to tell required absolute, total privacy.

Once inside their hotel room, he turned on their shortwave radio, dialing up to an unsuspicious level. He then drew her close to the window to let the road noise below, the cars, the street vendors' cries, further mask what he had to report. "Charly, you're not going to believe what I saw earlier." And then he told her.

Chapter 40

Angus Frost smelled the sharp snap of eucalyptus, felt cool night air on his face, and looked up from reading the ministerial circular. "Good heavens, Stefan, what are you doing here? I told you never *ever* come here to Sarona. Only in an absolute crisis. I couldn't have been clearer."

"It's exactly that. Are you alone?"

"Yes, yes. Quite. Margaret tripped over some dead camel hiking in Wadi Amud. The fool sprained her ankle badly and is in hospital. Now what is this about? And let me have the apartment key for God's sake; you won't return again to this neighborhood. Ever."

"For another *Treffen*, where then? Not Latrun, please. Those flies kept getting into my nose and ears last time."

"No, not at that Crusader castle. We'll think of something. Maybe the Romanian church."

"In Jerusalem?"

Angus Frost pocketed the key pitched across. "Yes, there, that one. Near St. George Street. It's more secure. By far. Well, don't just stand there. Come into my study."

"Have you heard?"

"Heard what? I've been up to my neck on Colonial Office matters. And close the damn back door. Want the neighbors to see? Hard, Stefan, push it hard. It's a heavy door. Bullet-proof. Against those loathsome Jews. Damnable race." Frost poked open the shutters a little with his riding crop and peered out from the thick drapes. He heard only the usual rumble of cars on Kaplan Street just to the north, but saw nothing threatening. But still... "You look a frightful mess. Now what is this all about?" He snapped on his shortwave radio on his bookcase; some syrupy Arabic music came on, a female wailed about a lost love. "Just in case."

"In case what?"

Frost realized he was jumpy over Stefan unexpectedly showing. The dwellers in the downstairs apartment had gone camping in the Judean Desert. "Nothing. Forget it." He snapped it off and motioned with his riding crop. "Have a seat. Now what happened?"

Stefan grasped a chess set on the upholstered seat of the chair opposite Frost's desk. He pushed aside Frost's family Bible on a side table, placed the board game next to it. But a trembling hand knocked several pawns onto the rug. He collapsed into the chair and wiped his hands over his sweaty face.

"You're shaking like a leaf, Stefan. Leave it. I'll pick them up later."

"You have anything to drink... except that foul-tasting Arak?"

"What do you want?"

"Anything to settle my nerves. Any Bombay Sapphire left?"

"Only what you didn't drink last time."

"Don't make such a face, Angus. What I drink, I more than make up for with my views on Soviet intentions."

"On its way. Here. Now get on with it; what is this about?"

Stefan threw back the gin in one gulp letting out an "aah" of satisfaction. "Someone bombed the Hotel Berliner?"

"What?"

Stefan stretched across for a refill. "This last Friday, I had gone out earlier to run some errands. On my way back from Jerusalem, I heard on the radio the hotel had been hit."

"Badly?"

"Bad enough to scare me."

"Anyone hurt?"

"Only an old Arab man. One of the waiters there. No one important. Some chandeliers destroyed. Some curtains burned and windows blown out. But it could have been worse."

"Any idea who did it?"

"You have to ask? Probably the same terrorists who bombed your secretariat offices at the King David Hotel a while back. And, let me add, your MI5 and MI6 stations there as well."

"Aren't you jumping to a conclusion?"

"Am I? They were ruthless enough to bomb the very heart of British administrative and military rule in the Holy Land, Angus. Why not?"

"All that infighting among those Jews. God knows they have their share of hot heads. Could be any number of factions."

"Well, whatever. A source at the Tel Aviv CID said the bombing showed the same *modus operandi* as at the King David. A woman calling the Berliner's switchboard earlier to evacuate. Terrorists dressed as Arab workmen wearing the traditional keffiyeh. Smuggling in bombs in milk churns. Placing the explosives against support columns. Someone anyway has found me out."

Captain Frost's telephone rang. Stefan jumped. Frost suppressed a smirk, snatched up the receiver before it rang again. "Yes?" He listened a moment longer, his eyes steady on Stefan. "This is the first I've heard about it. When did this happen?...I agree. Sounds like those Jews are up to their old tricks again. Keep me informed of developments." He cradled the phone. "An informer. He believes the bombs—there were two—were set near your office. An investigator found traces of TNT. Maybe taken from armor-piercing shells."

"There you see? I was right. Someone has found me out."

"So, what are your plans?"

"What do you think? Get out of Palestine. Go somewhere else."

"In time, yes. Of course. You know that. We'll make arrangements. London views your experience on Soviet spying as capital. We don't want to lose you."

"Make arrangements? What are you talking about? You've had months, years to prepare for this."

"Stefan, my dear—"

"Angus, look, I've run out of patience. Let's cut out this childish Stefan crap. Enough is enough. You know I don't like that middle name. Not one bit."

Angus Frost held in another smirk of amusement. His spy was cracking under the stress of being tracked down. "All right then, *Klaus.* How's that? Klaus, my dear fellow, I juggle two very important balls. Commander of the British Army Tel Aviv-Jaffa district and a loyal servant of MI6. So as you must surely understand, I have my hands full. As—"

"I—"

"My dear fellow, you will let me finish. You're not the only Palestinian agent on our books. But we'll work something out."

"Time is something I no longer have, Angus. Don't you understand?"

"I understand perfectly well, my good man."

"I don't think you do, Angus. I'm a hunted man."

"Klaus, you've been hunted for years. Even before the last war ended. These days, people claim you've been sighted in Finland, Saudi Arabia. Everywhere."

"This time is different. Several days ago, two war crimes investigators checked into the Berliner. An American and a Brit."

"How do you know?"

"How do you think?"

"Ah yes. The famous Klaus Kappler intuition."

"Don't laugh. It's kept me alive all these years."

"That it has. Always one jump ahead."

"There's something else. My own source tells me the Jews are sending a large ship here. With many more European refugees. The largest shipload in fact. All it takes is one of those filthy people to recognize me."

"Tel Aviv is crawling with them, but that hasn't happened."

"Not happened ye*t*. Tel Aviv isn't Berlin."

"You're right. It's harder to disappear here. You could hide out in some kibbutz."

"There is no laughing matter, Angus. For either of us. You should know that. That fake hospital death certificate. My funeral...that casket closed to public viewing in case you need reminding. My obituary in the *Times,* dying from bronchopneumonia. Burning my files. You and your MI6 are in as deep as me."

"All right, all right. Enough." Frost suddenly shifted his eyes to the rear door behind Klaus. Klaus glanced in that direction, looking worried. Frost uttered a soft "Shhh." He pushed himself up, right hand on his drawn Webley revolver. At the back door now, he jerked it quickly open and laughed.

"What's so funny?"

"It's just Moochie. A feral cat who visits us." He scooped up the mangy tabby and stroked it as he made his way back to his desk. "Now where we?"

"My escape."

"Oh yes, that. I'll see about speeding up your departure."

"Chile, Brazil, President Juan Peron's Argentina too is fine. I've heard Eichmann's there. Syria might work. Walter Rauff is helping its president with intelligence work against the peasants and students. But I'm through hiding out here in Palestine."

"Understood."

"How will you explain my disappearance?"

"To your hotel staff?"

"Them. The public at large. Everyone."

"This is Palestine, Klaus, a violent land. You've been here long enough to know that. Grudges are held. People die. Accidents happen. So do assassinations and car bombs. We'll think of something."

"Better think of something for Daniel, too."

"That Arab boy with the good memory?"

"That one. He knows way too much."

"Like I said, Palestine is a violent land. Any country preference?"

"Preference? Are you kidding? I'm on the run. Do you know what that means? Do you want me to put it in writing? Do what you can. I don't give a shit. Just get me out. And soon. I can inform your Secret Intelligence Service about Soviet spying in Europe as easily in South America as here."

Frost handed across a thick envelope from his wall safe. "This should tide you over for now."

"What's this? Palestinian pounds?"

"Calm down, Klaus! Don't be so jumpy. Of course not. American dollars. Good anywhere. Including South America, so don't worry. Go *immediately,* understand, *immediately* to our safehouse in Jaffa."

"In the Manshiya quarter?"

"Yes, there, Al-Manshiya. Only blocks from the train station. It's not much to look at, I'm afraid. But there's food for several days. Clothes, too, including a keffiyeh headdress in the closet. The fourth drawer down. That should cover most of your face when you eventually leave. Look over the passports and visas...there are all kinds of travel documents doctored with every conceivable kind of bureaucratic ink and stamp used. Our forger—first class, by the way— has vetted all of them. Oh, almost forgot. If you want to catch up on news of the fatherland, we have an old *Volksempfänger* people's receiver. It's in the fifth drawer. Just remember, use the headphones. No need to alert the neighbors."

"You've thought of everything."

"We do our best, Klaus."

"I can see that." Klaus again fingered the thick envelope.

"You can trust us. We remember our friends. Stay there. Absolutely stay there until I get word to you. From Jaffa, we'll get you to Jerusalem somehow. And from there, to Cairo. On the express. You can meet up with other *Kameraden* there. Relive the good old days." He held his smile. "Don't worry. Everything will surely sort itself out."

Angus pressed an ear against the rear door. Klaus hurried, sounding panic stricken, down the private back entrance stairs. Angus waited another ten minutes, pacing, worried, to ensure Klaus didn't return. He shouted the cat off his desk and reached for his telephone. Best get rid of the embarrassment as soon as possible. Even if violently. The scandal back in London, if word got out, after the war sacrifices. What a royal cock-up that'd be. Issues from the Conservative opposition raised during the prime minister's question time. Especially from that pesky old drunk and Jew lover Churchill. Backbenchers trying to make names for themselves. A parliamentary investigation for sure. The tabloids would have a field day. The BBC would devote God only knows how many hours to it. There would be calls and editorials for sackings and stiff prison time.

He picked up his phone and paused. Something this catastrophic, best not call MI6's Jerusalem station head. Best alert C immediately in London. He should still be at 54 Broadway.

Angus retrieved a phone number written on a slip of paper, secured within a fireproof envelope, from his wall safe. MI6's chief would appreciate the warning.

i

Chapter 41

Daniel, unable to contain his anger, kicked a stray mutt out of his way. It yelped in pain as it limped off to the shade of an alley. More rotten luck! Just when that fat old bag had squeezed into that taxi to visit family up north. His moment at last. Hopes high. Victory within reach. But now this, that American couple had returned. Was spying for the One From Beyond worth all the fear and trouble?

Over the last several days, he had lingered around that ugly cement housing block and picked up gossipy bits and pieces. The fat nosey busy body's wish to visit relatives in Netanya north of Tel Aviv. Her plan to leave on Tuesday in late May and stay at that seaside resort for a week. That tiny rooftop apartment unguarded at last. Except that old couple had moved in! Rich Americans by their looks. Each carrying a nice-looking suitcase. Jews, obviously. Now he'd have to learn *their* schedule before he could break in! More work. And at a time when the One From Beyond paced nervously, now smoking, and demanding results, as if he feared something. The notebook, the notebook, where is any notebook. Always angry about a little notebook. But that was his problem, whatever it was. That man could hang for all he cared.

He tossed down his cigarette on the sidewalk and twisted it out hard again and again and again. The One From Beyond would deserve it.

Chapter 42

Searching the tiny rooftop apartment had defeated them twice, Jonas had discovered. Their effort had yielded nothing except frustration and doubt about Rivka's damning notes possibly hidden there. The usual suspect hidey-holes he had searched as a New York detective—a wall clock, an air vent, a telephone's hollowed-out bottom—weren't in that bare-bones apartment. Charly had even wondered aloud if Rivka had buried her secret in some snake-infested cave in the vast badlands of the Negev Desert. Let's hope not, he had said, shrugging; they had to keep trying.

An hour later, they paused in their search to cool off. Not a fan in sight, Jonas noticed. Not a window fan. Not a ceiling one. Not even a little table one. Rivka must have wanted absolute protective silence. She must have been terrified of British capture. She must have preferred baking in the heat, dripping smelly sweat, rather than comfort that might reveal her presence.

Charly rested her back against a wall as she sat on the lone bed, her sandaled feet dangling over its edge. Jonas made himself comfortable sliding down to the buckling wooden floor and passed her his canteen. "There's some left. Have you recovered or still reeling?"

"You mean, your suspicions about Mr. Two Faced?"

"About him and Oliver Porter."

Charly tossed her head back and let the water trickle into her mouth. "I never realized how delicious water tasted till we came here. Still reeling, babe."

"Like a sailor on a week-long bender?"

"Like a sailor on a bender. You shouldn't have told me what you saw."

"That bad?"

"In spades. That bad. I suspected something about Oliver Porter. He was almost too clownish. Too gabby. I left it at that. I didn't take it further, think it might be cover for some government work. But Hans Peters? Never in a million years."

"You were distracted by your assignment. Working yourself nearly to the point of exhaustion sometimes. Skipping meals, too."

"Maybe."

"No maybe about it, kiddo. You were. You can pay a price for being too driven, know that? Anyway, don't worry. Hans Peters, if I'm right about him, has fooled plenty of others. Everyone makes mistakes. Even top-notch journalists."

"I certainly made a big one, taking Mr. Duplicity at face value."

"You're full of nicknames for him."

"I've got a bunch for him. I feel dirty, betrayed."

"You're too harsh on yourself, Charly."

"That's what others say. But I believe in critical self-examination."

"Just don't get too self-critical."

"I'm too harsh on myself when I screw up, they say," she continued, as though she hadn't heard him. "My standards are too high. I'm trying to compensate too much for not measuring up to dear father. Well, hon, it was a big, big blow to my big ego. Stupid me thought I was a shrewd judge of people. Stupid me took Mr. Import/Export Man and Mr. Backstabber as is. Not even close, Charly, you fool, you fool. Here, I'm done, babe." She passed back his canteen. "What I really need, Jonas, isn't water. I need one of your Johnnie Walker Red Label whiskey straights to help forget how way off I was."

"You're chuckling."

"A twenty-watt bulb just dimmed on in little Charly's head. Another moniker for Herr Peters. One way more appropriate. Mr. Sub Rosa. Well, shall we?"

So the third time now searching and at his suggestion, a different approach. They switched rooms. Charly took the room furthest from the entrance; Jonas, the one closer to the front door that led to the roof.

He heard Charly in the next room—her hard knocks on the walls searching for a cavity—showing the search skill of a professional. He entered the shoulder-width WC to the right of the entrance. He tapped on its three walls, starting at the moldy base and working his way up as high as he could reach on tiptoes. Nothing.

Next the toilet itself. He lifted its cracked porcelain cover, noted nothing taped to its underside, then checked the toilet tank. But no canister holding something valuable floated in the water.

"Anything?" Charly asked from her room.

"You'd think someone on the run would carry a revolver, a knife. Something for protection." Jonas entered the little kitchen that abutted the WC. "I haven't found anything. What about you?"

"The same here. Zero, nothing. Sorry."

A scratchy noise. Jonas jumped to the entrance, left hand inches from his shoulder holster. He peeked through the slates of the dusty blinds. Only some stray cat pawing through a pile of trash on the roof. Back to the kitchen and its cabinet underneath the sink. Two wooden shelves heavy with household odds and ends. On hands and knees, he tossed aside the contents. Several boxes of matches. A bottle of bleach. Chipped plates. Dish water soap. A dirty cleaning pad. Empty cracked jars. But nothing to implicate a supposed Jewish terrorist.

Finally, the cabinet lay empty. He ducked his head inside and knuckle-rapped on the sides and bottom. Again, a depressing solid sound. As he pushed himself up, he remembered the interruptions. That busy body Mrs. Goldstein hammering on their front door hollering out she had prepared a feast of chicken soup with matzo balls for everyone. Not wanting to arouse suspicion, they had paused in their search and accepted her invitation. Then the air raid siren had started wailing, and everyone in the building had hurried across the street to that bomb shelter. And by the time that self-appointed air raid warden had told everyone they could return home, he and Charly, too tired to continue the search, had collapsed into bed.

But now the inside of the cabinet. The upper panel of wood beneath the sink moved easily aside. And there it was, falling into his hand with its dusty orange palm-size cover. "Bingo, Charly. Found it."

Charly was at the threshold, wiping her hands off. "You found it?"

"What all the fuss has been about." Jonas held up the booklet. He flipped slowly through the pages studying Rivka's neat, deliberate penmanship. But after a time he shook his head, disappointed; it was as he had feared.

"Well? Don't keep me in suspense."

Jonas handed across the tattered little notepad. "Be my guest." She would quickly discover the reason why Asher hadn't warned them not to peek at Rivka's notes. Because he didn't care if they did. Because he knew even the best cryptologist would struggle. Maybe even fail. Because not one single word of Rivka's prison notes was in English. Not even one single name. Because everything was coded. All of it. Whatever she had found out at Acre Prison, page after page of it, a mishmash of Polish, German, Russian, and Yiddish words jumbled together. With Asher one of the few, maybe the only one, who could decipher.

Charly handed it back after only a brief look. "I see what you mean. So what do we do?"

"Come on." Jonas slipped the tattered little notepad into his waistband. Then changed his mind. The notes could easily slip down, be lost forever. Or fall into the wrong hands.

He stripped off his shirt. Then he asked Charly to encircle his chest with tape, the tattered little notepad pressed hard against his front. He couldn't risk any chance of loss. The security of a new nation, of the last hope of a tragic, but proud people, might very well depend on what secrets that little orange-covered notepad held.

Chapter 43

They walked as casually as they could to a café on Shabazi Street in southwest Tel Aviv. There, he dialed the emergency number Asher had given. In moments, a little girl answered, as if she stood watch by the telephone booth for messages. In the background a jazz quartet played *Bei Mir Bist Du Shon* loudly, and he raised his voice as discreetly as he could to be heard. Without any questions, she took his curt coded message for a nighttime pickup, a young soldier already worldly bright and brave. She'd rush the message to another café. Its owner would telephone an unassuming dingy building on HaYarton Street in a working-class quarter near the beach. British eavesdroppers, Jonas felt sure, would have to be damn lucky to intercept any message or understand it.

A perfect setup. Unless something went wrong, he thought, spotting no tail as they left. And in British controlled Palestine with informers and warring factions everywhere, that could easily happen.

They whiled away the next hours, café-hopping, checking for surveillance, until near sunset. They then reached an alley further south of still another café where a car idled. No child soldiers this time like those who had kidnapped them on Allenby Street for an interrogation. This time two full-fledged adults with strong faces of the battle hardened. One of them was the burly Big Mikki. Big Mikki, in the front passenger seat, said this was their lucky night. No British curfew. He demanded Jonas hand over Rivka's notes. Jonas said he had taped them to his chest. Not wanting to waste time, Big Mikki responded with a glare and ordered their driver to get moving.

No blindfolds this time either, Jonas noticed. They must have proven themselves, shown themselves understanding their huge underdog plight, and willing to help. They drove north through the hot night, fog rolling in from the Mediterranean, on a long stretch of coastal road leading out of Tel Aviv. Occasionally they passed a truck headed south, and once Jonas spotted in the fleeting glare of the headlights a Jewish soldier hitchhiking. But the road was mostly abandoned, as if everyone hunkered down against some impending storm.

After a time, they reached a checkpoint. Jonas worried their night expedition, whatever it was, might be cut short by their being hauled out and imprisoned.

A solitary British sentry noticed them, but he seemed to Jonas in no hurry to execute his surveillance. The Brit took another puff, snubbed out his cigarette on his machine gun's barrel again and again, picked some bits of tobacco from his tongue, and finally pitched his smoke aside. He stepped out from a sandbagged enclosure and ducked his head level with the driver with a curt greeting, "Evening, mate. A bit nasty out tonight." The driver said, "Evening to you, mate," which brought a youthful chuckle from the road guard. They muttered an exchange of words. Jonas caught something passed, driver to soldier. Sympathetic to their cause or to a bribe, he waved them on without even a security-check glance toward the back seat.

If they continued north, they'd soon reach the dangerous Lebanese border. According to rumor an army of heavily armed thousands massed for invasion there. They might link up with Syrians and Iraqis to attack the coastal town of Haifa further south.

Yet they soon pulled off the highway and headed east, bumping along a dirt trail little wider than a goat path. That shortly gave way to a gravel avenue of palm trees. Jonas caught a wooden sign nailed lopsided to a post that indicated the direction to the Sea of Galilee. He picked up the musty smell of hay and the heavy scent of a eucalyptus grove beyond. Then spotted a hoe and garden watering can next to a building's stone walkway. A kibbutz, he thought.

Big Mikki got out, ordered everyone to stay in the car, and explained he'd return shortly. Minutes later, he came running back slightly out of breath, looking worried in the pale moonlight.

"Everything's set," he said shouting to his driver some deception plan. "Quickly," he yelled, and four decoy cars against any British surveillance sprayed out of the dark ahead in different directions. "Before it starts."

Somewhere a hand-cranked siren wailed screeching full-throated higher and higher. Within seconds, Jonas discovered what Big Mikki's *it* was. The steep, rocky hills behind the kibbutz lit up again and again. Like lightening flashing. Only it wasn't, he immediately understood. Jordanian or Syrian soldiers fired heavy guns from the heights of some plateau down on the little communal farm.

A pot clanged down on the hood and bounced off. Their driver veered right, just missing a palm and a shell crater beyond. Clumps of rocks and dirt thunked down on the car's roof. Jonas gripped the door handle as their car shook under the trembling earth.

The night boomed again. Fiery splinters from something alight showered down. "There, there. Try there, Davide," Big Mikki shouted, coughing from the dust. Their driver sped through a pall of dense black smoke, knocking down a flaming fence post. "Keep going," Big Mikki, the hardened fighter, ordered. "We're almost there, Davide. At that crossroad."

"My eyes, my eyes, something's in my eyes," the driver yelled. "I can't see." Big Mikki grabbed the steering wheel. "Keep your foot on the gas, Davide."

Another explosion rumbled, this one booming closer. A water tower to their right collapsed straight down; its roof ballooned into a huge fire ball. Windows from a shed below blasted outward spewing glass shards. A shell howled overhead. This is it, Jonas thought and clutched Charly's hand. She shouted something at him as she tightened her grip, but he didn't understand. The blast wave had temporarily deafened him. Cold sweat trickled down his forehead into his eyes, stinging them. He could feel the heat from the blast. Another shock wave rocked them as they fled through the dangerous Palestinian night.

Chapter 44

Somehow, despite the fear and explosions they made it through. Jonas recalled the feeble pop-pop-pop response of the little kibbutz's response to the artillery attack. He remembered Davide's skilled, brave driving through the shelling. He remembered Big Mikki's cool-headed directions shouted at Davide. But mostly their escape stayed blurred. How had they had made it through? Maybe, he thought as they neared the northern outskirts of Tel Aviv, there might exist a benign God after all.

After a time, they reached a gritty building in an industrial area in the southern part of the city near the coast. Security was tight and layered, he noticed getting out, his legs still wobbly from almost dying. Charly also still looked shaken.

Something, maybe the barrel of a rifle or machine gun, flashed momentarily metallic on the rooftop from the rising sun. One sentry then. Maybe more. Two guards, their chests cross-hatched with ammo bandoliers, at the bullet-holed doorway. Three at the top of the dirty stairs leading to a room. Six that he could see in the room itself. Some looked frightfully young, but muscled as if they had once spent hours farming. Others were well into middle age with fat on their arms. Most clutched Stens and Brens and other World War II-era cast-offs. To his shocked surprise, he spotted in the corner a long barrel rifle that resembled something from the American colonial era. Everyone grimly serious. Ready for the worst. A fight to the death, if necessary, to protect whatever it was he and Charly had brought.

Asher sat at a table reading a Bible. He ignored a cat that rubbed against his leg. The clanking sound and acidic smell from a mimeograph machine came from a room ahead of him. He turned another page without glancing up. "What took you guys so long?"

"Syrian tankers shelled the kibbutz from the Golan Heights," Big Mikki said. "From over 3,000 feet. We were sitting ducks. We had to detour. Take some backroads."

"They were softening it up for a ground assault," Davide said.

"Schmuck. Arabs aren't night fighters," Big Mikki said. "Read Orde Wingate's notes Moshe Dayan gave us."

"I figured three hours each way." Asher turned another page, sounding not interested in their difficulty.

"Your guests are here," Big Mikki said, acting like he didn't want to get into a further argument.

Seeing Charly and Jonas Asher jumped up, hand extended, but not in greeting. He snapped his fingers for Rivka's notes, looking eager to decipher them. Jonas stripped the tape off his chest, but before he could hand the tattered little notepad over, Asher snatched it from him.

He sat alone with it and his thoughts, his Bible pushed off to the side, still ignoring the cat that brushed against his leg. The mimeograph machine clanked to a stop. "Eight hundred copies!" a man shouted. "My God, can you believe that. Eight hundred! To announce our freedom from those Bits. A record!" The six others smiled. "It can't come quickly enough," one of them said, and everyone applauded. Asher didn't lift his head to join in. He stayed focused only on the pages before him, decoding them.

After a while, he called one of his men over. He was young with tousled reddish hair and had a lean body with muscled arms as though he had once worked the land before enlisting in the underground. Now he seemed to Jonas a high-level subordinate. He bent head level, Asher pointed to something in Rivka's notes and whispered into his ear. He looked overcome with emotion and his subordinate patted him on his back, comforting him.

The subordinate yelled out an order in Hebrew. Five men checked to ensure they had loaded their weapons. There was a sudden rush towards the stairs and the apartment's front door. Six armed men, a paper map of some kind in the hand of their leader. Moments later, a car roared off.

"What's going on?" Jonas asked.

"For now, Miss Lawrence and you, Mr. Shaw, you are our prisoners."

"What are you talking about?"

"We are here to execute Rivka Kozibrodska's last will and testament. That's what," was Asher's only comment. A black crayon in his hand, he disappeared into the room ahead as he called out, "Tamar, quit babying your typewriter. Over here. You have guard duty."

A hefty blonde, gripping a sporting rifle, stepped past Asher toward the top of the stairs, and Jonas thought she looked vaguely, oddly familiar. The same color hair. The same build. Almost the same height. The same war-aged look. She reached the stairs leading to the street and glared back at him and Charly, blocking any flight. He felt certain she would shoot them, if needed, to prevent escape.

Chapter 45

He awoke from an uneasy captive's sleep to manly shouts and laughter at pleas for mercy. He lifted his head from his folded jacket on the dirty cement floor and stared across the room to the stairs, unsure over what he saw. The same six feet height, yes. Same trim weight, yes. But the polish was gone. Now his golden blond hair looked disheveled and wet with sweat. A beaten-up bloody mess. At least from the neck down to his silk underwear patches of bluish bruises showed. From the neck up, oddly untouched. But still, could it be? He felt his gut flare in hate, his suspicion confirmed. He shook awake Charly, sleeping next to him, and indicated the far side. She too stared in that direction, her mouth gaped open, believing yet not believing.

They pushed him further into the room, his hands tied in front of him. "We have him," a stocky man with shoulders rounded like boulders said. "But you better work quickly, Asher. There was a gun fight, and we took out Frost. His men will tear up Tel Aviv looking for their precious boy." He kicked their prisoner from behind. He stumbled forward and fell to his knees.

And there was something else, Jonas noticed getting to his feet. There was fear now in the German blue eyes making him look like a man found out. His true self revealed. Hans Peters or whoever he really was, naked before his accusers.

Asher entered from the adjoining room, clapping his hands. "Quickly, quickly then, everyone. We must work quickly."

Two of his men lurched their captive to his feet, his legs wobbly. They threw him hard against the near wall, untied his hands, and held him, arms pinned to his sides. "Wait!" Asher shouted like some director of a play or movie dissatisfied with some detail. The lighting or the makeup.

"His face, they must recognize his face beyond doubt. Otherwise, everything will be meaningless." Asher shook out a handkerchief from a back pocket and roughly daubed away some specks of blood that had landed on a cheek from a beating. "Remember Sarah, three shots."

No, don't, Jonas thought, but then realized he had overreacted. There would be no shooting. A petite redhead, looking in her early twenties, entered behind Asher. She clutched an old Kodak with a flash attachment. "One front," he instructed. "One profile, left side. One from the right side. Eleven sets."

"Stand up straight," someone in back of the small crowd yelled. Asher shoved a sign at him. "Here. Hold this under your chin and look directly into the camera." Their captive hesitated. "Directly!" Asher gripped his bristly chin and roughly jerked the man's head straight ahead. "Like this. Into the camera."

He stiffened and scrunched up his face in distaste over the order.

"Do we beat you more, or do you do as I said?"

He glared at Asher. But finally he held the sign in black crayon under his unshaved chin while staring glumly ahead. Charly showed shock on her face. Jonas imagined he looked the same. Charly, stunned at the sign, dropped her pen to the floor. Jonas forced himself to look away from the message as he handed the pen back to her, their eyes meeting as he mouthed, *Can you believe that?* Charly simply shook her head yes.

An explosion of light. Jonas glanced away as a flash bulb from the camera went off. The prisoner blinked, recoiling from the intensity. Another flash. More blinking. Then several more flashes. Eleven sets of photos in all taken, he counted. For what purpose?

Sarah hurried into the back to a rigged-up darkroom, Jonas noticed. But they were far from finished with their prisoner. One of Asher's men brought in another wooden chair, which he placed next to his leader. A file half as thick as a New York City telephone directory lay tucked under his other arm. This, he dropped onto the table, then stepped back looking expectant for something important to happen.

"Miss Lawrence, forgive me, but I am not familiar with your *London Daily News.* It is a big paper?"

"One of the biggest in Britain, Asher."

"You are proud of it?"

"Very much so."

"It is read only during the weekdays?"

"There's a Sunday edition, too, Asher."

"Only in London does it come out?"

"There, Manchester, Paris, other big cities as well."

"Berlin?"

"Yes, they've opened a bureau there. Why?"

"And the American capital, your Washington D. C.?"

"There as well, Asher. Why do you ask?"

"You are famous or not?"

"Well, I wouldn't say famous."

"She's much too modest," Jonas said. "She's more than earned her stripes in a difficult profession for women."

"She has won prizes then, Mr. Shaw?"

"Oh yes, Asher. And how."

"Many?"

"Several."

"And is followed widely?"

"Absolutely."

"In your United States and elsewhere, Mr. Shaw?"

"All over really."

"Good." Asher turned to a man, whose thick chest was crosshatched with bandoliers. "Davide, bring in two chairs for our guests. You, Miss Lawrence, you will write. You have everything? Your pens? Enough paper? Good. You see that empty British ammunition box in your corner? You can use that as your desk." He jabbed a finger at their prisoner. "You, you stand." As he seated himself, he flipped open the dossier and momentarily studied the first page. The hefty blonde who had earlier stood guard seated herself next to him. In front of her, an ancient, bulky typewriter and a pile of fresh paper. Asher once more looked over his shoulder. "Miss Lawrence, we can begin?" When she said yes, he turned to the second page of the file.

Chapter 46

He looked up from his file and at the hefty blonde seated next to him, who would memorialize the event. "Tamar, type at the top of each page today's date, May 21, 1947, and the Jewish calendar year 5707. On each page."

Charly withdrew a thick hardback, *The History of Roman Palestine*, from her shoulder bag and quickly ran a finger down a dogeared table. It was a Gregorian- to-Hebrew calendar, Jonas noticed seated next to her, along with commentary. *Ancient*, she mouthed to him as she showed the table to him.

Jonas nodded as he shot his eyebrows up, amazed. Good God, he thought. Ancient is right. Over 3,000 years old, these people. Way, way before the U. S. started. Way before much of European civilization started, as well. Surviving pogrom massacres, the mass slaughter of millions in ovens, doors for a better life slammed in their face time and again. Yet there they were, still around, now fighting tooth and nail to return to their biblical homeland. "Your name?" he heard Asher ask and jerked his head toward Rivka's confidant once more.

"*Mein Name ist—*"

"English, English," Asher shouted as he knuckled-rapped hard on the table. "You will speak only English for your answers. Only that. Your name?"

"You already know it. Ask your toughs. They shouted it when they kidnapped me from Jaffa in that gun fight."

"For the record, your name. First and last. And in English."

"Ask your guys."

"Your life depends on how well you cooperate. For the last time, for the record, your true birth name."

"Since you put it that way, Hans Peters."

"Not Klaus Kappler?"

"I'm sorry. Who?"

"Klaus Kappler. That is your real name."

"My real name is Hans Peters. I insist you call me that. Hans Peters."

"For the record here, KIaus Stefan Kappler."

"Again, I must insist you call me Hans Peters."

"You can insist all you want. But we will call you Klaus Kappler. Your place of birth."

"Berlin. As Hans Peters."

"Where exactly? The district."

"Mitte. As Hans Peters."

A court of judgement? Jonas wondered. No, not really, he realized, seeing Charly seated off in the corner next to him. For her benefit as a journalist, Asher spoke English and insisted their prisoner do the same so she could clearly understand whatever he said.

"You age."

"Thirty-eight."

"Speak up! Your age, Herr Kappler!"

"I said thirty-eight. Is that loud enough? And again I'm Hans Peters. You kidnapped the wrong man from Jaffa. I was visiting a—"

"Enough of that! Married or single?"

"Single."

"Tamar, put down married. Their ceremony in a Catholic church in Hamburg. Wife's name, Ilse. They have three children, two sons and one daughter. Before the war, Herr Kappler, you did what, please?"

"I worked as a furniture salesman."

"In Munich. Until the owner fired you for stealing."

Kappler shrugged; it was a small matter.

Months of unemployment followed, until he joined the Nazi Party, Asher continued. He hurried through Kappler's early years as a Nazi storm trooper, his street fights, the number of Leftists he supposedly killed, the number of Party commendations for being a confirmed anti-Communist. Asher seemed to provide the information, Jonas noticed, solely for Charly's benefit. Purely as background for something more important. He took a sip of water, then looked over his shoulder. "Miss Lawrence, you are fine? Plenty of paper?"

"Two notebooks at the ready, Asher," Charly said, not glancing up, only flipping to another page, and continuing to write quickly.

"I am going too fast?"

"No, no, no. Not at all, Asher. Word for word. Everything."

"Word for word, good. Let us hope so." Asher thumbed through several pages. Now mentioning Kappler switching to the even more feared SS, eventually rising to the rank of SS *Sturmbannführer.* "A major in the SS," he explained over his shoulder to Charly, and he looked surprised by her nodding understanding. "*Sprechen Sie Deutsch,* Miss Lawrence?"

Charly bobbed her head yes, still not glancing at him, too busy taking notes. "*Ein bisschen Deutsch.* A little. Jonas and I were in Berlin last year."

"She covered the post-war scene there," Jonas said.

"For my newspaper. So we picked up some *Deutsch* here and there."

"Then you might know the word, *Referent?*"

"In this context, Asher, Desk Chief?"

"*Sehr gut.* Bravo. You picked up more than a little. Yes, that. An important bureaucrat. In that role of SS major," Asher continued, staring once more at Kappler, "you were responsible for catching Soviet agents who parachuted into Europe. But your main work was elsewhere: taking apart the Rote Kapelle. The Red Orchestra," he again explained shifting around to Charly. "A loose network, Miss Lawrence, of anti-Nazi resisters in Europe." But she seemed to already understand. For she merely nodded as she flipped a page and continued writing.

"Their network in Germany, destroyed," Asher said. "Thanks to you, Herr Kappler. Their network in France, destroyed. Thanks to you, Herr Kappler. The network in Belgium, yes, that too destroyed. Again, thanks to you, Herr Kappler. Over six hundred resisters killed, surviving records at Gestapo headquarters on Prinz Albrecht Strasse, Berlin, and elsewhere show. Not counting their families, babies and grandparents included, who also were shot. Some in the back of the head. Or hanged. Or gassed. Or injected with poison. All with absolutely no trial whatsoever. Your killing was here too, wasn't it, Herr Kappler?"

"In Palestine? I don't know what you talk about. I own a hotel. Or did until some terrorists bombed it."

"With little damage," Asher insisted. "In Tel Aviv, here, too, your killing happened," he continued. "Didn't it, Herr Kappler."

"My older sister." The hefty blonde next to Asher paused typing and stared across for a long moment, her hate for him evident. "My older sister, Rivka Kozibrodska."

Of course, Rivka's sister, the resemblance was clear, and another Warsaw ghetto survivor? Jonas whispered his question to Charly, but she just shrugged, too engrossed in writing to reply.

Klaus Kapper turned pale. His admission of guilt over his killing on his stunned, tired face. Or at least knowing about the murder.

"A week before her murder, she visited your hotel," the typist said. "As a guest. She had to see for herself. Rivka was like that. Always curious. Even as a child. A Talmudist scholar. A family joke. Always questioning. Maybe you *were* like others here. A refugee from Hitler's Europe as others said. Starting over by buying a hotel. Maybe not. Maybe something else. Others wanted to put that past behind. Start again. Not her. Two nights before her death, she told me she suspected something else. Your Berlin accent. Your charm. The eagerness to please. Something wasn't kosher. What, she didn't quite know. But something 'smelled.' That was the word my sister, may her name be blessed, used. 'Smelled.'"

"You bastard," Jonas muttered to himself, then louder. "You kill Johnny Radcliffe, too?"

"Johnny who?" Kappler shifted his eyes to Jonas.

"Radcliffe. Johnny Radcliffe. A newspaper friend of Charly's publisher. Killed maybe because he had stumbled onto your true past."

Asher turned around and glared at Jonas. This wasn't his show, he seemed to say. But Jonas felt certain Kappler had something to do with that journalist's death.

"Some at Gestapo headquarters," Asher continued, "gave you a nickname for your killing work, didn't they?" Asher asked.

"You seem to know the answer," their captive said regaining his composure. "Why ask me?"

"What is your answer, Herr Kappler?"

Kappler turned silent.

"Your nickname, what was it?"

"You are fools. All of you, fools. I refuse to be a party to this extra-judicial proceeding."

Asher knuckled-rapped hard on the table. "Your nickname, what was your nickname? Answer my question."

Their prisoner stood up straight, staring ahead into the safe distance, ignoring Asher, ignoring everyone.

"I'll tell you what it was, Herr Kappler. The Memory Man. Why? Because you could recall hundreds of Communist agents, their addresses, their relatives, how they fit into the Red Orchestra network in Europe. Things stuck to your memory. Like a fly to flypaper. Or like questions a hotel guest asked that might mean something bad. At least for you. Isn't that right, Herr Kappler?"

"Once again I must protest and do so as Hans Peters."

He would remain Hans Peters until his dying day, Jonas decided. Which might not be far off.

Rivka's sister paused typing and pointed emphatically to a word near the bottom of a page. "Tamar is right," Asher said. "I have overlooked something. You, Herr Kappler, knew so much of Soviet agents, a fellow worker said your mind was, and I hope I say the word properly, 'en-cy-clo-pea-dic.'"

Charly looked up from writing. "Encyclo*pedic*, Asher." Then nudged Jonas and showed what she'd written, *Kappler, a gold mine of info on Sovs.*

"Thank you, Miss Lawrence. Encyclopedic. The war ends," Asher continued. "You fled Berlin. On or around the night of late April 1945, we think. You briefly thought of escaping to Rome, didn't you?"

Kappler nodded yes. "As a civilian whose hotel the Nazis had taken over."

"Wrong!" Asher shouted so strongly he momentarily rose out of his seat. "Not as a civilian! You briefly thought of escaping to Bolzano as a Nazi who had served his Fuehrer Adolf Hitler. To link up with other *Kameraden* there. But Italy was too far away. So what did you do? You changed from your SS uniform into civilian clothes. You got hold of false ID papers. Maybe off some dead man. And you fled north. That's what you did. You Nazis didn't destroy all records. See how much we know about you? But you were captured. Where?"

"I fled the Soviets. It was no secret they hated us Germans, soldiers *and* civilians. It made no difference to them. We were all the same. All killers."

"Answer my question, Herr Kappler. Where were you captured?"

"As a frightened citizen. In the Baltic port of Rostock."

"Yes, in the Baltic port of Rostock. May, 1945. At a hotel near the docks. While waiting to slip abroad a ship. Captured by...?"

Herr Kappler turned silent.

"In the Baltic port of Rostock captured by...?" Asher repeated.

"Alright. By the British military police."

"Yes. By. The. British," Asher said accenting each word. "Why they suspected you, we couldn't find out. But you were taken into custody by them. By the British." And then he, who until then had been very talkative and feisty and seemed to relish bashing Kappler, said nothing. For a long dramatic moment, he let Kappler's answer hang in the silence broken only by the clattering of the blonde typist memorializing the interrogation. Then he slowly, theatrically turned to Charly as though to ensure she heard every word. "Yes. By. The. Brit-ish."

Finally. At last, Jonas suspected. Asher had probably arrived at the main point of the questioning. An indictment. And not against evil Germans, but apparently against the virtuous English.

"So the British. To"—Asher turned a dossier page—"to one of their many internment camps in Germany. There, MI5 and MI6 counter-intelligence people with much experience in these matters questioned you for many, many weeks."

"That's in my records," Kappler said. "So what?"

"So what, Herr Kappler? So this. These agents after so many weeks questioning and questioning understood something important; they had on their hands a prize. That is so what. And what a prize it was."

Tamar held up a finger; she needed to change ribbons. Asher slumped back in his chair, sighing, clearly disappointed she had interrupted his fierce pace of questioning. Jonas nudged Charly; she continued writing a moment longer before she looked over. Jonas mouthed, *What the hell is he getting at*? She only shrugged, then returned to her notes.

"An expert spy catcher of Communists," Asher continued. "One who could help them, I mean the British, help them afterwards. In the new war against the Soviets. Even if you were a Nazi. Even if a mass murderer. A killer of hundreds. Maybe many, many hundreds. Including children and the old. Character meant nothing. What you had done meant nothing. Only ability to help. Except"—Asher turned to another dossier page—"except British and American war crimes detectives were after you. So MI6 had you die. With a death certificate given to prove you had died. How nice of those British."

"From bronchopneumonia."

"Tamar is right. From bronchopneumonia."

One of the men, looking agitated, broke from the crowd and shouted at Kappler as he approached. "I say we kill him. Now! To hell with your plans, Asher."

"No, Mordecai. My plan is the best revenge. For a rebirth of our people." Asher grabbed him by the arm, pulled him aside, and whispered in his ear.

The room was momentarily quiet. All Jonas heard was his heart beating wildly from shock and disgust. For as long as he lived, he thought. For as long as he lived, he'd remember that day and that hour of confession.

Charly, too, looked stunned into silence. All she could do was mouth, *What the fuck did we fight World War II for?*

His thoughts exactly, Jonas thought. What was it all about? Their worlds turned upside down. Asher's captive staring glumly into the camera, fearing his fate, while holding his sign in black crayon letters. KLAUS KAPPLER. NAZI WAR CRIMINAL. FUGITIVE FROM JUSTICE. TOP SPY FOR BRITISH FOREIGN INTELLIGENCE, MI6.

Chapter 47

A boy in patched shorts and looking no older than fifteen to Jonas burst into the room, panting. Asher crouched beside him. "Yossi, you're supposed to be on lookout across the street."

Yossi gestured excitedly toward an east-facing window. But not too quickly for Jonas to miss the purple tattoo on his fleshy little arm, another Nazi death camp survivor. Maybe an orphan. The British, the British, the child said. They're coming. They're coming.

Asher told him to slow down. Despite his age, the teenager sounded street-wise to Jonas as he rattled off his alarm. Radio detection vans to pick up any secret transmissions. Armored personnel carriers. Tanks. Apartment-to-apartment searches. A military man in a Jeep speaking from a bull horn, which they could hear booming off buildings several blocks away. "Attention! Attention! This is the British Military Authority of Palestine. Anyone helping or harboring Jewish terrorists will be severely punished by His Majesty's forces. Attention! Attention!"

"Asher," Tamar said, "they're acting quicker than we thought after that gunfight."

Kappler darted his eyes out towards the street, hoping for rescue.

Asher glanced at his wristwatch. Still hours of daylight left. Too dangerous for a mass break. He peeked out the east-facing window, spent a long moment studying the street below. Others checked their weapons.

"Attention! Attention! This is the Palestinian British Military Authority. Harboring Jewish terrorists is a severely punishable offence by his Majesty's forces. Attention! Attention! They are wanted for kidnapping a Hans Peters and for assassinating Captain Angus Frost. Commander of British forces, Tel Aviv and Jaffa. Attention! Attention!"

"We warned him, Asher," Mordecai said. "Warned him twice. We'd fire back if he shot at us."

Charly leaned over and whispered to Jonas. "That horrible man on the beach, remember?"

He nodded. Now the British military maybe only two or three blocks away, he guessed. They'd swarm their neighborhood soon.

Asher scribbled something on a scrap of paper, then clapped a hand on Yossi's bony little shoulder, big brother to little. Yossi should hop on the back of his cousin's motorbike, find the British forces, toss them the note, then flee.

Charly eyed Jonas. Jonas shrugged; her guess was as good as his. Maybe Asher wrote a false lead little Yossi would throw. Maybe Asher had threatened to kill the prize of Hans Kappler, if British soldiers approached.

"We go now?" Mordecai asked.

"No," Asher said. "We wait."

"What if he's late?"

"I said we wait."

And so they did.

Until a heavy-footed man huffed and stumbled his way up the stairs. Dov staggered up the last step into the room, carrying a bulky bag over his broad sweaty shoulders. Through its opening poked several sticks of bread. "Here, Asher. What you wanted. This is all we could find." He dropped his bag heavily onto the table, yanked it open, then plopped down in Asher's chair, still breathing heavily.

"Dov, quit eating your own baked goods." Asher withdrew one long baguette, cracked it open, and smiled as he withdrew a gun from the hollow. "Were you stopped by any British?"

"By one. Near Allenby Street. I told him this bread was for a Bar Mitzvah."

"And he believed you?"

"He said he was hurt he wasn't invited, gave me a wink, and let me pass."

"Now we go." Asher said.

"Attention! Attention!" The booming warning faded from the densely housed neighborhood of tumble-down apartment blocks. The clanking rumble of tanks on asphalt grew fainter. So did the sound of armored cars and the tramp of boots as the massive British search party shifted towards the west and the beaches, away from their hideout.

Everyone looked tense on their tanned young features. Their fates on their faces if caught. A brief trial, if a trial at all. Then hanging or a firing squad.

Asher approached Charly and stood directly in front of her. Everyone in the room turned their intense eyes to watch. Asher no longer appeared the gracious host. Now looming over her, he looked threatening.

Which was what Klaus Kappler seemed to wait for, Jonas saw. A distraction of seconds. For he had whipped out a tiny gun hidden in the lining of his underwear, and he aimed it at the back of Asher's head. "Gun," Jonas shouted. "Gun!"

Chapter 48

At the same time, he flung the empty ammo box across the room at Klaus. Klaus, surprised at being discovered ready to shoot, instinctively ducked. The ammo box crashed against the wall, missing its target by a foot. Yet his effort, Jonas saw, threw off Klaus's shot by inches at Asher.

"Alive, alive," Asher who had dropped to his knees shouted. "We must have him alive. Wound. Only wound."

From somewhere in the crowd, Jonas heard a shot fired. Who had pulled the trigger, he couldn't tell in the confusion. But Klaus Kappler now clutched his lower left leg, moaning. A mini gun, a little over two inches long and looking like one he had seen in Switzerland, lay nearby. Some bloody streaks covered its stainless-steel grip. Asher's men evidently hadn't thoroughly searched him.

Big Mikki jerked up Klaus by the neck and appeared to delight in the pain caused. He jammed their German captive's hands behind him, bound them with rope, and finished off his treatment by pushing Klaus's forehead against the wall and holding it there with one of his huge hands.

Asher nodded thanks to Jonas and added a slight smile. But that was the extent of his gratitude. He seemed preoccupied with more important matters. "We are finished with Herr Kappler," he said. "At least for now. Now then, your notes, Charly Lawrence, you will sign your notes with your title."

"Title? I don't really have a title as such, Asher. I'm just a journalist."

"*Just* a journalist? No, no, Miss Lawrence, I do not think so. Not at all. I've asked around. I have heard things about you. Good things. You must have a title for what you've done. You must. Something important. Journalist-in-Chief. Foreign Affairs Contributor or Correspondent. Something like that."

"Asher, Charly is first and foremost a reporter," Jonas said, trying to keep irritation out of his voice. "She cares only about the story. Getting the interview. Getting the facts. Checking and rechecking them. That's all the matters."

"Jonas is right," Charly said. "I don't really care if someone calls me a journalist, a reporter, or whatever. It's the story that matters. Nothing else... oh, all right. Look, if it's that important, then journalist. There, okay? Journalist."

"Then sign your name as that. As journalist. To your article, Miss Lawrence. First page and last."

"There is no article, Asher. At least not yet. These are rough notes. Nothing more than that. Nothing is finished."

"We understand. They will do."

"I'll go back to my hotel, organize them, make an outline. Type them up into a series of articles with my byline. Polish them. Then—"

"Polish? What is this polish business nonsense?"

"I tighten the articles up. Take out unnecessary words. Check for spelling, etc. Then wire—"

"Enough of this polish business talk, Miss Lawrence. We don't care about your pretty articles. Only your notes."

"But I can't—"

"Miss Lawrence, we don't have time to argue."

"What does time have to do with it?"

"Everything. Now sign. And sign as *Charly Lawrence, foreign correspondent for the London Daily News.* Exactly like that. That is what I've decided. On the first page of each of your two notebooks. Not *journalist.* Not *reporter.* But *foreign correspondent!*"

"We can make life here very uncomfortable," Tamar said. "For both of you."

Charly's shoulders sagged in seeming resignation. Considering what Tamar and others had been through, she appeared not to doubt their ruthless will to act. She signed the first page of each of her two notebooks quickly as if she wanted to get their silly demand over with. "Done. I hope your happy now."

Asher snatched her notebooks from her. "These are all your notes on Herr Kappler? All of them?" Not waiting for her answer, he searched through her shoulder bag.

"Hey, what are you doing? Those are mine."

Jonas jumped to his feet and faced Asher. "You heard her. They're hers, Asher."

"Not for now."

Not for now? What the damn hell did that mean? Jonas watched Asher casually walk into the adjoining room. He flipped through the pages, studying them as though what he had stolen belonged rightfully to him all along.

Chapter 49

Charly looked too wide-eyed shocked over the brazen theft to say anything. Jonas mumbled some curses, but he understood arguing with Asher was pointless. The remaining Jewish fighters blocked any pursuit of their leader.

Two husky guards gagged, tied, and blindfolded Kappler. Then they bundled him, squirming, down the stairs to some unknown, unpleasant fate.

Asher returned. He gripped a Sten submachine gun in one hand; in the other, what looked like, with columns for the date and time and height, an ocean tide table. "As for you two, you are leaving."

"Leaving?" Charly glanced, puzzled, at Jonas.

Asher angled up the Sten and jabbed it at her to stress his point. "Yes, that, leaving. You can seek your fame and fortune elsewhere. We will escort you both to your hotel. You will pack. Tomorrow, early, we escort you to Lydda Airport. A nice handsome Wellington bomber with some important people on it will be there. It will take you back to London."

"Back there, to London?" Charly glanced with a questioning look from Asher to Jonas.

Jonas shrugged. Her guess about why Asher was kicking them out was as good as his. But he had a feeling they had been unwilling players in some scheme, whatever it was.

"You are done here," Asher continued. "Finished. Here in Tel Aviv. In Palestine, too. Both of you. Finished for good. You have served your purpose." But what that purpose was, Asher didn't say. He only gave them an enigmatic thin smile as he escorted them down the stairs.

An old dusty Studebaker, spewing out dirty exhaust, idled at the hideout's entrance. Charly had slumped into a depressing silence. Jonas knew he couldn't budge her out it.

The news from the car radio filled the quiet, and it was all bad. Arab armies massed at the Palestinian borders. The British had rounded up European refugees who had landed on some beach near Haifa and herded them onto a ship bound for Cypress. The British had also uncovered an arms cache of three pistols on some kibbitz near the Jordan Valley.

Reaching the Hotel Joseph, a kid, looking no older than eighteen or nineteen to Jonas, trailed them into the lobby. A glint from a grip flashed from a gun tucked into the waistband of his patched pants. Just enough of a sight, he thought, to promise violence should they try to flee.

He excused himself past some robbed priests checking in and headed to the stairs to pack. But Charly yanked him into the smoky, noisy El Arish Bar off to their right. "We're going to have a parting drink," she said, glaring over her shoulder at their pimply chaperone, daring him to stop them.

The youth shrugged indifference. Whiskey, a martini, Arak, whatever, a parting drink was fine, he seemed to say. But he settled at a nearby table with a view of their sweaty hunched backs at the bar. His message was clear. They were prisoners, allowed only up to their room after a final toast to whatever.

A radio on a shelf beside a row of liquors blared an approaching Jewish bloodbath. But Charly, Jonas knew, had something else on her mind. She ordered a whiskey neat. After tossing it back, she ordered another. She was preparing herself, he could tell, for the call. The call to break the bad news about the two stolen notebooks, the call that might very well end her illustrious career.

She stared ahead in near catatonic silence, occasionally sighing. The struggle for a Jewish homeland, one of the century's biggest stories, along with the two world wars and the dropping of the atomic bombs. A reporter's dream to cover. A publisher's, too. But no notebooks meant no series with her byline. And no exclusive for Maurice Rumbold's struggling *London Daily News.*

An hour later, she made the call from their hotel room. The result was what he had feared. Charly winced at Maurice Rumbold's booming unforgiving rage over the staticky line. A tycoon, whose flagship newspaper's slogan was "Never Give In" didn't care to hear about failure. He didn't appear to grasp their danger. How could she and Jonas possibly go up against a gang of armed captors led by an equally armed, determined leader? No way could she get her notebooks back, she pleaded. "Mr. Rumbold, I—. Mr. Rumbold, please sir, if I may finish." But Maurice Rumbold refused to pay a single shilling more for her failed assignment. Pack up. Fly home. Then he slammed down the phone, loudly ending maybe her career.

Chapter 50

Nigel met them at Croydon Airport in their repaired Rolls-Royce. Their chauffeur stooped to take their meager two pieces of luggage. But Jonas, hating as ever class distinctions, snatched up their baggage. Picking them up on time after their long, exhausting flight was enough, he said.

They rode back to their Cotswold manor in sullen silence. As if trying to cheer them up, Nigel reported some good news. There were no more death threats on any household personnel since the failed try on their drive to the airport some time back. That elicited from Jonas merely a nod he had heard. It also didn't lessen his anxiety of an attack for he glanced out their rear car window from time to time.

Charly ignored their household's welcome home chocolate truffles from Fortnum & Mason by her side. Instead, she gazed out her left rear window, far way in thought, brooding; Jonas, in his own black Irish mood, glanced at an invitation for a fox hunt, beside the latest edition of the *Financial Times* on the plush leather seat. Without opening it, he tossed it out his window. He stuffed the newspaper, also unopened, into Charly's red shoulder bag. The weather—drizzly, chilly, an English gray overcast— matched his mood. He clutched her hand and squeezed. Through thick or thin, no matter the disappointment he'd be there. And what a disappointment it was. All that time in Palestine, and for what? Charly had run up expenses, the hotels, meals, taxis, the occasional bribe. She had risked her life. His, too. And all for bloody hell nothing. Nigel seemed to know better than to chat further when his masters looked in full boil.

Within days Jones returned to his failed endeavor, becoming British. He grabbed his golf clubs, a present from some ex-Churchill minister that mostly had collected dust in one of his manor's many closets. He marched off to the nearby green, grimly determined to master the nerve-wracking sport. But after finishing three over par on each of three holes, he feared another eighty-five-over-par game. He threw down his 3-iron onto the lawn and stalked off to the association's bar to drink off his frustration.

Days later, squeezed into a Triumph, he drove with a neighbor who insisted he try the fascinating sport of fly fishing. But casting out his line, Jonas somehow snagged a very sharp hook on his backside. He snapped his fly rod over a wet thigh, tossed it downstream, waded ashore, once more stalked off.

He was restless. Charly suspected his spying on the Continent for Churchill during the last war as the cause. His long months on the run from Nazis, little sleep and food, always on guard, had traumatize him, according to the family doctor.

Jonas retreated to his mansion-office. There he forced himself to sit as he struggled with possible titles for his writing project. *My Years with Churchill? Churchill as I Knew Him? Churchill, Man and Myth?* He'd write something, he decided, just to get his blasted London publisher off his back.

At times entrenched at his desk when no words came, he thought back to those left behind. Why Abraham, Isaac, and Jacob wanted Rivka's little booklet of damning secrets was anyone's guess. Maybe they wanted the power and prestige among their own cell for putting the screws to their British colonial masters.

For all the other dispossessed in Palestine, their stubborn, prideful refusal to abide by the norms of others caused awe in him. They had a fanatical insistence they had as much right to live as others and they would die, if needed, so that others of their own could live as equals. He could not recall seeing such almost mythic courage against such staggering odds that'd defeat others.

And Charly during this period? She holed up in her adjacent cluttered mansion-office day and night. But he heard not a sound from her old Royal typewriter. Even when he pressed an ear hard against the wall. Nothing. Not even the snap of one solitary key smacking the virgin white rolled-in paper. Only mutterings about that "that rotten son of a bitch thief Asher" and "I could slit that bastard's throat for what he did."

He could hear her pacing, talking to herself, trying to boost her spirits, readying herself to appeal once more to Maurice Rumbold. Maybe if he, with all his contacts, could contact Asher? She knew she had one hell of a story. In theory anyway. A rare Warsaw ghetto survivor tracked down, interviewed, then discovered murdered. A Nazi war criminal disguised as a respected hotelier hiding out in Palestine where many Jews lived. That criminal, Klaus Kappler, possibly responsible for murdering that rare Warsaw ghetto survivor. Or at least knowing about it. Maybe even killing the friend of Charly's publisher. The respected, glamorous MI6 acting despicably. Morally blind, it hid that Nazi fugitive from British and American wartime investigators, while paying him to inform on Communists.

But, but, but she sputtered, frustrated that she lacked the critical notes, thanks to that "thief Asher." "Details," she cried out one rare morning when she emerged for a very English breakfast Jonas had prepared. "I need details that are beyond doubt. Truth that's ironclad. I've tried and tried, but I can't remember all the goddamn bastards. The dates. Who said what and when and where. The tension. The fiercely determined looks on their warrior faces. All taken down in on-the-record interviews, in off-the-record chats for background, in profiles meant for sidebar articles. All, all lost, Jonas. Just crappy bits and pieces tumbling around in my hazy memory."

Going up against the dangerous, wily, well-connected MI6 required solid evidence of their treachery. Without it, what reader would believe her? How would she defend herself in any libel suit? Would Mr. Rumbold even publish the expose? Memory wasn't good enough. It was faulty. She needed the precise written word. The notes written as events had occurred.

Maud, their cook and trusted errand runner, appeared from time to time at his own office door. She'd knocked timidly, her charm bracelet of trinkets on her fleshy arm signaling her presence. She'd nervously clear her throat, whisper her question until Jonas would shout she must speak up, dammit! Which she did. Did they need anything on her semi-weekly shopping trips into the village? Just the usual, he replied, and off she'd go, trundling as best she could to escape, leaving him to his creative struggle.

On a shelf, a hefty short wave radio squealed away next to a dictionary and thesaurus. The BBC news was on, and a report the commentator had noted caught his attention. Was something afoot in Palestine, and could Asher be in the thick of it? The reception faded in and out, and he was momentarily tempted to thump the wooden box in frustration. Instead, he put down his pen and dialed up the volume. Good heavens, he thought, had he heard correctly? He turned up the volume even more and realized he had.

Unnamed Czech friends of the Jewish underground in Palestine had come to their aid. Smugglers had somehow slipped several ships past the British blockade. They had somehow offloaded several tons of weapons on a long stretch of beach north of Tel Aviv. Millions of rounds of World War II ammunition and huge quantities of MG-34 machine guns, flame throwers, tanks, piat anti-tank guns, deadly accurate Brens. And ironically, the journalist noted, a delivery of two beaten up Spitfires that had made it out of their old nemesis, Great Britain. The Jews, Jonas realized, kicked around for centuries from country to country, maybe now had a fighting chance. For the first time ever, they might be able to return to their biblical home. For the first time, they might have their own country.

All this had happened with not a single sailor of the Royal Navy in view to arrest the embargo runners. No British cops or soldiers on the beach either. And the offloading, which reportedly took several hours, within sight of two mighty destroyers anchored nearby. An unprecedented feat, the announcer added.

Asher must have played his ace, bless his scheming heart, Jonas thought. He must have used Rivka's little notepad as she had planned, against the British. He must have shown them photos of Klaus Kappler in captivity and Charly's notes. He must have threatened blackmail, exposing a murderous Nazi on MI6's payroll, unless the Royal Navy eased its arms blockade against the Jews. The panic within the not-so-secret, not-so-bright Secret Intelligence Service over that threat. The high government officials awakened in the dead of night over possible scandal!

The news, he discovered, didn't lift Charly's spirits beyond a weak smile and a few mumbled words acknowledging the event. She appeared beyond reach. It was best, he decided, to let her come out of her depression in her own time.

Chapter 51

Several days later, reliable Maud again tapped at the office door and meekly called out. Jonas sat hunched over his desk, still debating titles. *My Years With Churchill? Churchill as I Knew Him? Churchill, Man and Myth?* "Well, what the hell is it?" he groused, not glancing over his shoulder, crunching up still another fruitless attempt, and tossing it indifferently into the corner. Maud responded and hurried away. He pushed back his chair, trudged to his office door, bent down, and stared. Then hollered. Then he was hammering on her office door. "Charly! Charly! For God's sake, woman, open the goddamn door!"

Had the sender gotten too busy with life-and-death issues and only recently remembered what he possessed? Did someone higher up, overburdened on some battle front, need to make the decision? Could cultural differences explain the delay, how bureaucratic clerks in that part of the world handled things? Maybe they had had to scrounge around for someone to translate the nuances of American English into Hebrew. Or maybe even Charly's sometimes hard-to-read writing when in the throes of note taking were to blame. Who knew? The Middle East, Jonas knew, was way too mysterious for an outsider like himself to understand. But there they were, in his hands that trembled with excitement. "Charly, for God's—" The door finally creaked open an inch or so. A very tired, depressed Charly in bathrobe peeked through the opening. "Here, dear," he said, thrusting.

Charly's notes in full, both notebooks. All 277 pages. And attached an invitation: *Shalom, To use as you want. Asher.*

Chapter 52

That was the end of the matter. Charly had her notebooks at last. Many in the Jewish underground were amply armed. The desert sand and heat, the ever-present danger of death in Palestine in the past. Or so he thought. A week later he heard another timorous knock on his office door, while at his desk. He ignored the interruption and stared smiling at what he had just written. *Winston Churchill. The Man Behind the Mask.* He leaned back in his chair, twiddling his ink-stained thumbs. That was it. Finally. After much struggle, his title. That should please his publisher. Next, the 75,000 words the old goat wanted. That would come later, thank God. But there was still that hesitant polite tap tapping on his door.

"Well, what the hell is it?" he shouted over his shoulder. In answer, he heard something dropped with a thud onto the wood floor near his door and the messenger's quick patter of flight.

"Oh hell, criminy," he muttered to himself as he made his way past the trail of wadded up false title starts. An ordinary-looking package, larger than Asher's, lay near his office's entrance. It was addressed to "Charlotte Lawrence," her *London Daily News'* byline. Maud must have dropped it at his door rather than at Charly's. She understood when Charly worked on her articles, she was even more ornery than he was at the slightest disturbance.

For a moment he just stared, brows lifted in alarm, at the suspicious delivery. Who the bloody hell blazes knew of their Cotswold hideaway? Maurice Rumbold, their trusted servants, their families back in the States, an old war French friend who wrote rarely, and that was it. Yet somehow the sender had tracked them down. Very strange. And very unsettling.

No name, no initials or return address showed. The postmark on the row of stamps of Big Ben was London. A city of millions. A useless clue. The clever bastard apparently wanted to hide his identity. Yet the detective in Jonas thought he had still revealed. A professional, he guessed. It had to be. Someone with access to privileged information to track them down, despite their best efforts to stay hidden. Someone versed in the art of secrecy. Someone insisting on anonymity to protect himself for whatever reason. Someone who kept up with the news and was familiar with Charly's cut-above-the-rest reputation as a reporter.

The typing on the label displaying her byline was sharp from a well-maintained, modern machine. Government issue maybe. Not from some ancient rickety device like the one Asher had used for his note. Again the thought, a professional.

He tore open the mail, looked at the meager two contents, and uttered an astonished, "Well, I'll be a son of a bitch." The first consisted of four candid color photos. Hans Peters in Tel Aviv, caught unaware, at the front desk examining the guests register, the vase of white orchids clearly visible. Hans Peters, in Tel Aviv caught greeting guests, the crisp black metallic signage of the Hotel Berliner clearly visible over the entrance. Hans Peters, in Tel Aviv, on a deserted side street, caught crouching down to examine, for whatever reason, the rear license plate of his dusty Ford. Hans Peters secretly photographed while he read some newspaper at some café.

Jonas's hands shook so much with excitement now he had trouble ripping open the second content, a solitary envelope. To his surprise, there were two cards under plastic overlay, and they were scotch taped at the edges on cardboard backing. Almost like what he'd seen in his New York detective days, he realized. Except this didn't involve a run-of-the-mill robbery, a murder, or involuntary manslaughter case. This was something much, much bigger. It was earth-shaking. Someone had gone digging into the recent past and somehow unearthed one hell of a giant gold nugget.

This is my coup de grâce, he thought, and dear Charly's iron clad. This is our clincher of clinchers. Briefly he felt so dizzy at what he saw, he braced a shaky hand against his door's jam. "Good Lord!" he muttered. "Lordy, Lordy." The print on the left card was smudged with age, but the vital data was still clear. MAY 7, 1945, the day Germany had surrendered. The day that saw a continuing massive flight of Germans escaping the advancing Soviets.

He shifted his attention to the type below. HEIGHT: 6'1", WEIGHT: 165 pounds, CLASSIFICATION: GERMAN REFUGEE, and most damning below that, the irrefutable proof of uniqueness with the loops and such.

How the devil had that mysterious, crafty professional unearthed this old card? Had the fleeing panicky criminal forgotten to ditch his hidden ID of Party membership with his real name on it? Or had he kept it to show fidelity to other escaping comrades he might meet up with? Had some kid soldier British MP stopped him in Rostock and inspected only his false ID? Had he, in the chaos of huge numbers of German fugitives, had him processed on that one card, let the man go, quickly moved to the next desperate, and not realized the war criminal accidentally released? Mid 1945 was anarchy in Germany, Jonas recalled. Especially, if memory served him right, in East Prussia near Rostock, where hundreds of thousands had fled west from the advancing Russian soldiers.

That scenario was certainly possible, he knew, but speculating was pointless. All that mattered was he held two cards, the one on the left from the past, the one on the right current. A professional had somehow matched the damning evidence, and he couldn't contain his excitement any longer. "Charly!" he yelled from the safe side of her office doorway.

"What, dammit?" she hollered back from deep within her office.

"Get your sweet ass over her," he yelled back.

"My sweet ass is in my chair. I'm in the throes, luv. It better be good."

"It is, luv. Quit your damn typing and open the goddamn door, will you."

She inched her office door open and peeked out, clearly upset at his intrusion. A cigarette dangled from her mouth. Dressed in her wrinkled bathrobe, she looked like she hadn't slept much. He glanced over her shoulder. Her desk looked even more cluttered against the windowless far wall. A plate with the remnant of a barely eaten meal lay on a huge stack of documents. Her nearby camp bed was unmade. She should air her office out, he thought. "Just thought I'd drop by to see if you're still alive."

"Ha ha. Very funny. What do you want, Jonas?"

He ignored her sharpness. "I haven't seen you in days."

"As you can see, Jonas dear, I'm very much alive, and I have a deadline to meet...in case that matters to you. It matters to me. A lot. It also matters to Mr. Maurice Rumbold, my boss, remember? A lot."

"Of course, it matters to me. A lot."

"Do we stand here sparing with each other? Is this social or business?"

"Both. How's the five-part series going?"

She made a hand gesture, side to side. "*Comme ci, comme ca.*"

"Why so-so? At the beginning of the week, you were upbeat."

"That was then. This is now. I've re-read Asher's interrogation in my notes. I realize now Klaus Kappler is one slick shit of a smooth-talking swine. There are enough Jew hating idiots out there, including in the government and media, to take his side. An innocent hotelier wrongly accused."

"I know, the usual garbage. This might brighten your mood. Special delivery."

"Special what?" She frowned at the package he shoved at her.

She gazed at the four candid color photos. Next the transparent plastic overlay that protected its sole two enclosures on the cardboard backing. She glanced up at him momentarily in a look of wide-eyed disbelief before again staring, open mouthed, at the mail. Once more, he thought a professional of high ability lay behind what lay on the left and right cards under the overlay.

The Party card on the left from May 7, 1945 with fingerprints of the fleeing Klaus Stefan Kappler. Right thumb. Right index. Right middle. Right ring finger. Right little finger. The same classification for the left hand.

The card on the right from 1947 with a typed note in anonymous bold letters: SOURCE, "HANS PETERS," CAFE GRAND PARIS, TEL AVIV, PALESTINE 1947. The prints below lifted from some surface, whatever it was, with clear tape. Then the tape placed on that special card on the right. Right thumb. Right index. Right middle. Right ring finger. Right little finger. The same classification for the left hand.

Thank you very much, Mr. X, whoever you are, Jonas thought. Thank you, thank you, thank you for the gorgeous two sets of matching fingerprints.

Fatigue lifted from Charly's face, and she broke into the widest grin he had ever seen. And there were tears of joy in her green eyes, too. He could tell she understood. There was no wiggle room. No way to deny. No way to explain away from even his fiercest supporters. She flung herself at him and covered his face with kisses.

They had 'em, he knew, Hans Peters hotelier AKA Klaus Stefan Kappler, Nazi Party murderer and MI6 informant. They had 'em dead to rights, finally.

The End

Don't miss out!

Visit the website below and you can sign up to receive emails whenever Steve Haberman publishes a new book. There's no charge and no obligation.

https://books2read.com/r/B-A-IVCF-PVCBD

BOOKS 2 READ

Connecting independent readers to independent writers.

Also by Steve Haberman

Jonas Shaw and Charly Lawrence
Where the Bones Lie
The Spy from Palestine

Standalone
The Killing Ploy
Murder Without Pity
Darkness and Blood
Winston Churchill's Renegade Spy

Watch for more at www.murderthrillermysteries.com.

About the Author

Steve earned a B. A. Degree from the University of Texas in Austin, majoring in political science and minoring in history. Afterwards he passed his stock broker's exam and worked for a time at a brokerage house before returning to school. Upon getting his legal assistant certification from UCLA, he worked at a law firm in Los Angeles. Successful stock market investments allowed him to retire early and to pursue two dreams, writing and foreign travel, and he has since traveled extensively and frequently to Europe. He speaks some French, a little less Italian, and four words in German and hopes to expand his fluency in all three languages.

He enjoys the cosmopolitan bustle, sidewalk cafes, the museums of Berlin, Rome, Vienna, London, Budapest, and Paris. Many of these capitals find their way into his stories of intrigue..."Murder Without Pity" (Paris), "The Killing Ploy" (London, Berlin, Paris, and Lugano) and the soon-to-be-released "Darkness and Blood" (London and Paris) and "Winston Churchill's Renegade Spy" (London and Zurich). He's also researching for a fifth novel, this one to be set in 1946 Berlin.

I
Read more at www.murderthrillermysteries.com.